Titus Maccius Plautus, Edward H. (Edward Holdsworth) Sugden

Comedies of T. Maccius Plautus

(Amphitruo, Asinaria, Aulularia, Bacchides, Captivi)

Titus Maccius Plautus, Edward H. (Edward Holdsworth) Sugden

Comedies of T. Maccius Plautus
(Amphitruo, Asinaria, Aulularia, Bacchides, Captivi)

ISBN/EAN: 9783744778442

Printed in Europe, USA, Canada, Australia, Japan

Cover: Foto ©Andreas Hilbeck / pixelio.de

More available books at **www.hansebooks.com**

COMEDIES

OF

T. MACCIUS PLAUTUS

(AMPHITRUO, ASINARIA, AULULARIA, BACCHIDES, CAPTIVI)

TRANSLATED IN THE ORIGINAL METRES

BY

EDWARD H. SUGDEN

B.A., B.SC.

MASTER OF QUEEN'S COLLEGE, UNIVERSITY OF MELBOURNE

LONDON

SWAN SONNENSCHEIN & CO

NEW YORK: MACMILLAN & CO

1893

PREFACE.

includes all the plays and fragments, but blank verse is employed throughout ; and besides, the work is out of print, and not very easily procurable.

For convenience of reference, Ritschl's numbering of the lines in the original is indicated in the margin; the division into acts and scenes, which is not Plautine but dates from the time of the Revival of Learning, is indicated in the head line of each page.

I have not troubled to discuss questions of read-

PREFACE.

I HAVE undertaken this translation with the intention of introducing Plautus to English readers in a form as nearly approaching his own as the differences of the two languages permit. To this end an attempt has been made to reproduce each scene in its original metre. Hitherto this has not been attempted, except in the case of two plays (the *Mostellaria* and the *Captivi*) by Professor Strong, late of Melbourne, now of Liverpool. Bonnell Thornton's translation (published in 1769) includes all the plays and fragments, but blank verse is employed throughout; and besides, the work is out of print, and not very easily procurable.

For convenience of reference, Ritschl's numbering of the lines in the original is indicated in the margin; the division into acts and scenes, which is not Plautine but dates from the time of the Revival of Learning, is indicated in the head line of each page.

I have not troubled to discuss questions of read-

ing, as such discussions would have no interest or
intelligibility for most English readers.   I have
had Ritschl, Ussing, and Weise always before me,
and have also consulted Fleckeisen, as well as
editions of separate plays by other scholars ; and
have followed the reading that seemed to me best.

It is obvious that Plautus must either be ex-
purgated or confined to a small class of readers.   I
have with some diffidence undertaken the former
task ; and this has involved two things : namely,
the omission or modification of some words and
phrases too gross for modern taste, and a slight
modification of the plot in almost all the plays.

With regard to this second point, it must be remembered that love, as we understand it, had
little or no connexion with marriage, either in the
Roman society of Plautus' own day, or in the
society of Greece, on which his originals were based.
Marriage was a matter of business or social neces-
sity ; love was, therefore, only to be discovered in
relations from our point of view illicit.   Almost all
the girls in the plays of Plautus are professional
courtesans, or, at all events, slaves, with whom
marriage is practically out of the question, but
whose society may be purchased for a longer or
shorter time.   But it has surprised me to find how

very little alteration has been required in order to raise the plots to the level required by our current morality. This is what I have tried to do ; how far I have succeeded, I must leave it to my readers to determine. I quite expect that I shall be condemned on the one hand for altering my author at all ; and on the other, for not altering him a great deal more. I shall offend the pedants and shock the prudes ; but between the two I hope to find some who will be glad of the chance of enjoying Plautus without having, at times, to hold their noses ; and who are nevertheless aware that mankind is divided into two sexes. After all, the obscenities in Plautus are remarkably few ; and their removal does not in the least affect the excellences of his work. An Elizabethan mansion is not desecrated by being drained.

With regard to the frequent puns and alliterations in which Plautus indulges, it is not often possible to translate them literally ; but usually some more or less equivalent play upon the words has been attempted in the English ; and I think I may claim that, however bad my puns may be, they are no worse than those in the Latin text.

I hope to be able to complete the translation of the whole of the plays of Plautus in this same form ;

and, perhaps, those of Terence also. Meanwhile, I commit this first instalment of the work to the kindly consideration of the public; I need hardly say that I shall greatly value any suggestions that may be made as to possible improvements in future volumes.

In conclusion, I desire to express my obligation to the Trustees of the Melbourne Public Library, and especially to my friend, Professor Morris, for the ready permission they have given me to make use of the editions of Plautus in their collection; to Professor A. S. Wilkins for his kindness in reading over this translation, and furnishing me with many valuable suggestions; and particularly to Professor Sonnenschein, who has most kindly read the proof-sheets for me; to his judicious criticisms and emendations, much of whatever value this work may possess is due.

EDWARD H. SUGDEN.

QUEEN'S COLLEGE,
  UNIVERSITY OF MELBOURNE.

To

AUGUSTUS SAMUEL WILKINS

M.A., LITT.D., ETC.

PROFESSOR OF LATIN IN THE OWEN'S COLLEGE

VICTORIA UNIVERSITY

WITH WHOM I FIRST READ PLAUTUS

I DEDICATE THIS TRANSLATION

WITH

UNFEIGNED RESPECT AND SINCERE GRATITUDE

CONTENTS

->>*<<-

PREFACE .

GENERAL INTRODUCTION

AMPHITRYON .   .

ASINARIA

AULULARIA .   .

BACCHIDES

CAPTIVI   .

GENERAL INTRODUCTION.

§ 1. THE author of the following plays, Titus Maccius
Plautus, was a native of Sarsina, a village in Umbria, and
was born about[1] the middle of the 3rd century before
Christ. He died during the censorship of Cato, in the
year 184 B.C. Having saved a little money in some
menial occupation connected with the stage, he embarked in foreign trade ; but he lost all his capital in his
ventures, and had to return to Rome and there earn his
living as the hired servant of a corn-miller. Whilst he
was engaged in this business, he wrote three plays, which
brought him fame and profit enough to enable him to
devote himself altogether to dramatic authorship. He
was probably about thirty years of age at this time ; so
that we may take 224 B.C. as the date of the commence-
ment of his literary activity. He continued to write
plays up till the time of his death. No less than 130
comedies were said to have come from his pen ; but of
these the critic Varro judged only 21 to be genuine,
*viz :—Amphitruo, Asinaria, Aulularia, Bacchides, Captivi,
Curculio, Casina, Cistellaria, Epidicus, Mostellaria, Menæchmi, Miles, Mercator, Pseudolus, Pœnulus, Persa, Rudens,*

---

[1] B.C. 254 is the probable date of his birth.

A

Stichus, Trinummus, Truculentus and *Vidularia*. Of these
we possess all but the last, which exists only in fragments.

§ 2. The poet's life fell in a stirring time. Rome was
taking the first of those steps which were to lead on to
the conquest of the world. The first province, Sicily,
was constituted in 241 B.C., when Plautus was a lad in
his teens. Three years later Sardinia and Corsica were
annexed. Then turning eastward, the future mistress of
the world supported the rebel Demetrius in his struggle
against Teuta, Queen of Illyria, and received Corcyra as
her share of the spoils. Her action in repressing the free-
booters of the Adriatic was gratefully recognised by the
Greeks, who were glad to be able to make out that this
vigorous young State was in some sense akin to themselves, and the Romans were invited to take part in the
Isthmian games, and received the franchise of Athens and
the right of admission to the mysteries of Eleusis. This
was in 228 B.C., whilst Plautus was wearily grinding corn
in his master's *pistrinum* at Rome, with little thought of
the way in which his own immortality was bound up with
these events across the sea. A Gallic war followed in
226 B.C. Plautus, no doubt, was one of the crowd who
thronged the Forum when the consuls buried alive there
two Gauls and two Greeks, in order to evade the force of
the old oracle that Greeks and Gauls should one day
occupy the Forum ; and he watched the triumphs of
Æmilius (225 B.C.), and Flaminius (223 B.C.), when they
returned from the conquests of formidable foes ; and
saw, what was never to be seen again at Rome, the dedi-

cation of the *spolia opima* of a Gallic chieftain, Viridomarus, by the famous Marcellus. It was probably as a part of the festival celebrations connected with these victories that his first plays were performed.

But darker days were at hand. Hannibal was already crossing the Alps, and Plautus heard from the pale and breathless fugitives the awful tidings of the successive disasters of Trasimenus (217 B.C.), and Cannæ (216 B.C.) ; and was the eyewitness of that indomitable patience, that inexhaustible resource, that most politic daring, by which Rome, with Hannibal at her gates, carried war into Sicily, Macedonia, Spain, and finally into Africa itself; and was revenged at last for Cannæ by the crowning victory of Zama (202 B.C.). Six years later, the successful issue of the Macedonian war placed all Hellas at the feet of Rome, and, at the Isthmian games of 196 B.C., Flamininus, the conqueror of Philip, was hailed by the gathered representatives of the old Greek republics as the saviour and protector of their native land. Another stride took the legions across the Archipelago into Asia Minor ; and the battle of Magnesia, in 190 B.C., compelled the great Antiochus, mightiest of the heirs of Alexander's conquests, to sue for peace on any terms that the Roman republic might grant him. Plautus, now an old man, but with intellect as keen as ever, saw the triumphal procession of L. Scipio Asiaticus pass up the Sacred Way in 189 B.C., as he had seen that of his greater brother, P. Scipio Africanus, twelve years before. When Plautus was born, Rome was the chief city of the Italian peninsula, and nothing more ;

when he died she was the mistress of the Mediterranean,
from the pillars of Hercules to the shores of Syria. Such
a period of exuberant national growth could not fail to be
a period of intellectual and literary activity; and the
names of Andronicus, Naevius, Plautus, and Ennius add
no less lustre to it than those of Fabius, Marcellus, Scipio
and Flamininus.

§ 3. The native elements of the Italian drama consist of
the Fescennine verses, the Saturæ, and the Fabulæ
Atellanæ. The Fescennine verses were recited on festival
occasions, such as marriages and triumphs, by alternate
speakers, whose banter, probably for the most part extem-
poraneous, amused the not too critical spectators, and
paved the way for the introduction of regular dialogue.
The Saturæ appear to have consisted of detached scenes
without any connected plot, something like the harlequin-
ade that concludes a modern pantomime, but were not
exclusively dramatic. The Atellanæ were comedies in
which certain conventional characters (the fool, the dotard,
the glutton, etc.), appeared in various mirth-moving situations. To these native forms of dramatic representation
Plautus may owe something of his broad fun and of his
love for bustling and uproarious situations; but he was
indebted for the form and plots of his plays to the *Attic
New Comedy*, which flourished at Athens from about
330 B.C. onwards, the leading authors being Menander,
Philemon, Philippides, Diphilus, Apollodorus of Gela, and
Apollodorus of Carystus. In it the tendency, already
discernible in the *Middle Comedy*, is completely developed.

The political comedy of Aristophanes is replaced by the *Comedy of Manners*, in which love is usually the predominant motive; and the characters are those of contemporary society. These characters are treated, however, somewhat conventionally, and a few types reappear in almost every play. The foolish old father; the fast young son, whose love affairs furnish the motive of the plot; the beautiful slave girl or courtesan, with whom the son is in love, and for whose purchase money must be secured; the unscrupulous pimp, who owns the-girl;-the clever slave, who lays the plot by which the money is obtained; the braggart soldier, who takes towns with his tongue, and whose counterclaim upon the young lady has to be disposed of by fraud or force; the hungry parasite, who will sell his soul to any buyer for a meal; these are the stock characters who appear in various combinations in almost all these comedies. Their originals are to be sought in the Athens of the early part of the 3rd century before Christ; and though Plautus has adapted rather than translated the Greek plays, and has put them into a Roman setting, the characters are, on the whole, rather Athenian than Roman.

In form, Plautus closely followed his Greek models. These differed from the old comedy mainly by the absence of the chorus; for which were substituted lyrical monologues (sometimes dialogues), in which anapæsts, bacchiacs, and cretics were chiefly employed. These were sung or rather chanted in a kind of recitative, not by the actor himself but by a singer, who occupied one corner of

the stage, whilst the actor furnished appropriate gesticula-
tion.   The accompaniment was played on the *tibia*, or
flute.   In the Latin plays these lyrical portions are called
Cantica,[1] the scenes of spoken dialogue being distinguished
as *Diverbia*.

§ 4.   The metres employed by Plautus are Greek in
origin, and closely imitated from his models, though his
rules of versification are much laxer than those which obtained in the later Latin poets, owing partly to the influence of the old national Saturnian verse; and his prosody
is dependent upon the metrical accent as well as upon the
quantity.   The chief metres employed by him are :—

I. Metres Composed of Two-Syllable Feet.

(1.) The *Iambic Senarius*, or *Iambic Trimeter Acatalectic.*

$$\smile- \mid \smile- \mid\mid \smile- \mid \smile- \mid\mid \smile- \mid \smile- \mid\mid$$

" When Phœbus lifts his head out of the winter's wave,
No sooner doth the earth her flowery bosom brave."
                              (*Drayton's Polyolbion.*)

This is the ordinary line for unimpassioned dialogue in all
the Greek and Latin dramatists ; and though, as will be
seen from the above example, it is a foot longer than our
English blank verse, I have thought it best to consider the
two as metrically equivalent for the purposes of this translation.

---

[1] With regard to the wider sense of the word *Canticum* see
Sonnenschein's " Mostellaria," Intr., p. xxiv., note.

(2.) The *Iambic Septenarius*, or *Iambic Tetrameter Catalectic.*

˘— | ˘— || ˘— | ˘— || ˘— | ˘— || ˘— | ˘ ||

" A chieftain to the Highlands bound cries, ' Boatman, do not tarry,
And I'll give thee a silver pound to row us o'er the ferry.' "
(*Scott: Lord Ullin's Daughter.*)

This metre is specially fitted for comic effect, and is, therefore, most often used in scenes of broad and lively fun.

(3.) The *Iambic Octonarius*, or *Iambic Tetrameter Acatalectic.*

˘— | ˘— || ˘— | ˘— || ˘— | ˘— || ˘— | ˘— ||

" Strong Son of God, immortal Love, whom we, that have not seen
  Thy face,
By faith and faith alone embrace, believing where we cannot prove."
(*Tennyson : In Memoriam.*)

(4.) The *Trochaic Septenarius*, or *Trochaic Tetrameter Catalectic.*

—˘ | —˘ || —˘ | —˘ || —˘ | —˘ || —˘ | — ||

" In the Spring a livelier Iris changes on the burnished dove ;
  In the Spring a young man's fancy lightly turns to thoughts of
  Love."
(*Tennyson : Locksley Hall.*)

This is the usual metre for more impassioned or excited dialogue, and in some plays is even more common than the iambic senarius. It is the "eights and sevens" of our English hymn-books.

(5.) The *Trochaic Octonarius*, or *Trochaic Tetrameter Acatalectic.*

$$-\smile \mid -\smile \parallel -\smile \mid -\smile \parallel -\smile \mid -\smile \parallel -\smile \mid -\smile \parallel$$

" Deep into that darkness peering, long I stood there, wondering, fearing,
But the silence was unbroken, and the stillness gave no token."

(Poe : The Raven.)

The iambic and trochaic octonarii are less common, especially the latter, and are confined to scenes of strong passion.

II. *Metres Composed of Three-Syllable Feet.*

The feet employed are *anapæsts* ($\smile\smile-$), *bacchiacs* ($\smile--$), *dactyls* ($-\smile\smile$), and *cretics* ($-\smile-$). The most usual line is composed of four feet, but lines of two and three feet occur not infrequently. The following English lines illustrate these metres fairly well, though the inadequacy of lines scanned by accent to represent lines scanned by quantity is more obvious here than in the case of the two-syllable feet.

(1.) *Anapæstic.*
" The Assy | rian came down | like a wolf | on the fold || ."

(Byron.)

(2.) *Bacchiac.*
" The Syrian | came down like | a wolf on | the sheepfold || ."

(3.) *Dactylic.*
" Brightest and | best of the | sons of the | morning || ."

(Heber.)

(4.) *Cretic.*
" Baby bye ! | Here's a fly ! | Let us watch, | you and I ! || "

(Nursery Rhyme.)

These metres are confined to lyric passages, though anapæsts, dactyls, and tribrachs (᷉᷉᷉) also occur as substitutes
for the regular feet in iambic and trochaic lines.

In rendering these metres into English, I have rhymed
all except the iambic senarii, as English custom
seemed to demand that concession. It need hardly be
said that there are no rhymes in Plautus. Also, I have
not thought it necessary to follow exactly the metre of
each individual line in the *Cantica*, but have been satisfied
to give something like the general effect. And, indeed,
different editors scan these lyrics so differently, that it is
often impossible to determine exactly what the poet's own
intention was as regards the division of the lines. Further,
I have often allowed myself to use the English ballad (or
common) metre for the iambic septenarian, both because
of its familiarity, and in order to save the labour of finding
double rhymes.

§ 5. The theatres in which the plays of Plautus were represented were temporary wooden structures, the first stone
theatre in Rome not having been built till 55 B.C. The
stone theatres were, however, modelled on older wooden
ones, and the accompanying plan of the theatre of Marcellus (13 B.C.), the ruins of which still exist, will sufficiently
illustrate their leading features. The stage was of great
length, as much in some cases as 180 feet ; and this must
constantly be borne in mind by the reader of these plays,
as it explains the otherwise seeming absurdity of the long
interval which often elapses between the entrance of an
actor upon the stage and his recognition of another actor

who is already there. It also afforded plenty of room for
the boisterous horse-play that occurs so frequently in the
plays of Plautus. The scene was almost invariably a

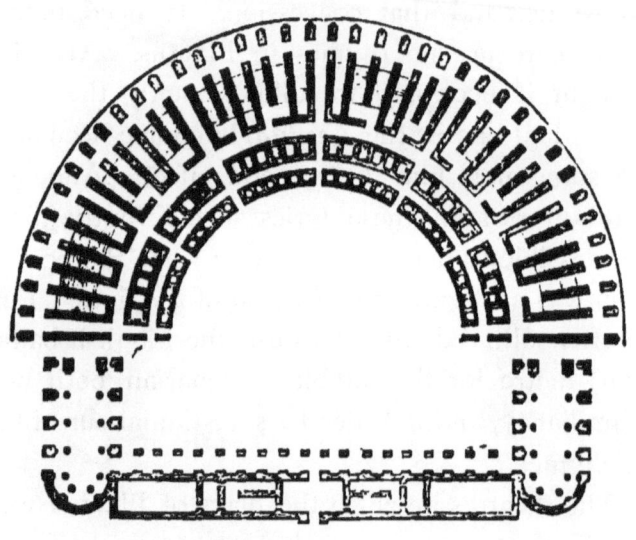

street, with (usually) two houses side by side, appropriated
to the two leading characters of the play. These houses
had doors opening outwards, according to the Greek practice, porches, small balconies over the doors, and flat roofs.
The front part of the houses could be removed so as to
disclose the room within, as *e.g.* in the last scene of the
Asinaria. The exits to the left and right of the stage (*i.e.*
of an actor standing upon the stage and facing the audience) were understood to lead respectively to the forum
or market-place, and to the country or harbour or some

outlying part of the town.[1] In the centre of the stage stood an altar of Apollo, raised, probably, upon two or three steps.

The orchestra, being no longer required as in the Greek theatres for the chorus, was appropriated to the senators and other persons of official rank, who were accommodated with seats. The rest of the spectators occupied the sloping banks of the amphitheatre known as the *cavea*, which were not yet provided with seats; those, therefore, who did not wish to stand during the whole performance, had to bring their own stools with them. Behind the stage was a covered portico, in which the audience could take refuge in case of a sudden storm of rain, the theatre itself being open to the sky.

§ 6. The dress of the actors was regulated by conven-

---

[1] Thus persons using the door to the left of the stage were understood to be inhabitants of the place ; persons using the door to the right of the stage were understood to be coming from or going to some place at a distance *(peregre)*. " This standing custom helped to make the action of the piece intelligible to the spectators, serving to some extent the purpose of the programme in the modern theatre " : Sonnenschein, Intr. to the *Rudens*, p. xv., where *Amphitruo*, 333, is quoted as evidence of the above arrangement : " Sosia arrives from the harbour ; Mercury, *who is facing the spectators*, says, *Hinc enim mihi dextrā vox auris, ut videtur, verberat ; i.e.* Sosia was on his right and on the left of the spectators " : see Translation, p. 34. In the *Rudens*, the above arrangement appears to have been modified to suit the special circumstances of the play. The reader may translate the indications given in the headings of the scenes in corresponding fashion : " From the town " means "to the left of the stage " ; " from the harbour " means " to the right of the stage."

Harbour (Country.)   Forum (Town)

tion, which the absence of play-bills rendered the more necessary. The men wore a white, sleeveless tunic *(chiton)*, and over it a cloak *(pallium)*, which varied in colour; the old men wore white, the young men purple, the slaves brown or grey, and of rougher material. Soldiers were distinguished by sword, helmet, and shield; parasites had a grey or black *pallium*, and were stuffed out and padded so as to present a ridiculous appearance; pimps wore a striped tunic with a parti-coloured scarf over it; peasants had a sheepskin cloak. Persons coming from abroad, like the ass-dealer in the *Asinaria*, wore the *chlamys*, a shorter cloak than the *pallium*. The girls were dressed in white, old women in blue or yellow; slaves naturally wearing coarser materials. The frontispiece to this volume, published by the kind permission of Dr. Leeper, Warden of Trinity College, Melbourne, will give a sufficiently correct idea of the costumes of the usual characters.

Masks were not worn as a rule; but the actors were familiar with the mysteries of false hair, and paint, and make-up, which was technically known as *galear*. The slaves usually had red wigs, the old men, of course, white ones.

§ 7. The play was usually introduced by a prologue. The present prologues are in most cases not the work of Plautus, but were of later origin, doubtless modified and brought up to date at each successive representation of a play. The prologues to the *Amphitruo, Captivi, Casina, Menæchmi*, and *Pænulus* were certainly not written till about 150 B.C.; the remaining and shorter prologues may or may not be genuine, at least in parts.

§ 8. The conventional division into acts and scenes is arbitrary and often misleading, and dates only from the 15th century A.D.; it has, however, been retained for purposes of reference. The reader must remember that the scenes are continuous with one another; the actors already upon the stage do not necessarily leave it when a new scene begins. I have indicated all the exits and entrances; it must be understood, therefore, that until it is distinctly stated *exit A* or *B*, he remains upon the stage, no matter how often the scene is changed.

§ 9. As a money transaction is an integral part of almost every play of Plautus, it may be worth while to append a table of the system of coinage employed, for which I am indebted to the Appendix to Professor Ramsay's edition of the "Mostellaria," where a full discussion will be found.

1 Talent	= 60 Minæ	= £225	0	0
1 Mina	= 100 Drachmæ	=	3	15	0
1 Drachma	= 6 Obols	=	0	0	9
1 Obol[1]		=	0	0	1½

The *didrachma*, also called *nummus*, was equivalent to two drachmæ or eighteenpence. The *philippus* was a gold coin, first minted by Philip II. of Macedon, the father of Alexander the Great; it was of the same weight as the silver didrachma, and may, therefore, be reckoned as worth

---

[1] Plautus does not use the term *obolus*.

about twenty-four shillings. But it must always be borne in mind that these values do not represent the purchasing power of ancient money, which may be taken at from eight to ten times its nominal value.

AMPHITRYON

INTRODUCTION.

THIS play stands alone amongst the comedies of Plautus. It is a burlesque rather than a comedy. The story of the birth of Herakles in consequence of the secret visits of Jupiter to Alcmena, the wife of Amphitryon, is its basis; but the particular Greek play from which it is taken is not known. The date is also uncertain; the excellence of the play points to the author's later period. The characters are firmly drawn and well sustained. Alcmena's wifely devotion, and Amphitryon's simple manly affection for her, are admirably portrayed; and the high tone of purity which characterises the play is not affected by the incident which underlies the whole story, when it is remembered that Alcmena never had the slightest suspicion that her visitor was not her husband.

The prologue, at any rate in its present form, is of later date than the rest of the play; it was probably composed during a Plautine revival about the time of the Third Punic War, 149-146 B.C.; the evidence for this is indicated in the notes (pp. 21, 22). The scene is laid at Thebes.

I have used Palmer's edition of this play with advantage.

DRAMATIS PERSONÆ.

MERCURY - - *A God.*

SOSIA - - - *Slave of Amphitryon.*

JUPITER - - - *A God.*

ALCMENA[1] - - *Wife of Amphitryon.*

AMPHITRYON[2] - - *A Theban General.*

MESSALA - - - *Maid to Alcmena.*

BLEPHARO - - *A Pilot.*

BROMIA - - - *Maid to Alcmena.*

---

[1] Spelt by Plautus Alcumena.   [2] Spelt by Plautus Amphitruo.

ARGUMENT I.

GREAT Jupiter assumes Amphitryon's shape
Whilst he is fighting with the Teleboians,
And so secures admission to Alcmena ;
Mercurius takes the form of Sosia,
An absent slave : Alcmena's thus deceived.
The true Amphitryon and Sosia come,
And both are most amazingly beguiled ;
Hence quarrels rise and strife 'twixt wife and husband,
Until with voice of thunder from the sky
Great Jupiter confesses he's the sinner.

ARGUMENT II. *(ACROSTIC.)*

A LCMENA's charms enslaving Jupiter,
M ake him assume her husband's outward form,
P oor fellow ! whilst he fights his country's foes.
H is slave is Mercury in Sosia's shape ;
I n turn he fools them both on their return.
T roubles arise between the man and wife,
R ecriminations too.   Then Blepharo
U mpire is chosen, but he can't decide
O n it.   All's cleared at last, and twins are born.

MERCURY AS PROLOGUE.

[Scene : a street in Thebes, before the palace of Amphitryon.
Mercury is disclosed, disguised as Sosia. The time is the
middle of the night.¹]

MERC. Of course you all want me to stand your friend
In buying, selling, trading, and all else,
That all your plans and schemes may turn out well
At home and abroad ; you wish that I should bless
With rich, and ample, and increasing profits
All you have done, and all you mean to do.
You wish me, too, to bring to you and yours
Good news, and always to announce to you
What's profitable for your common weal ;   10
Since you all know that it is given and granted
To me by the other gods to superintend
Both news and profit. Well, then, as you wish
These blessings from my hand, I'll do my best
To make your gains perennial ; that's provided
You'll give a quiet hearing to our play,
And all of you be fair, impartial critics.

¹ As the plays were performed in the afternoon, it is difficult to see
how the stage could be darkened. Probably Sosia's entrance with a
lighted lantern in the next scene was sufficient indication that it was
supposed to be still dark.

Now I must tell you by whose dread command
And why I'm here ; and also my own name.
Jove bade me come ; my name is Mercury.
20 My father sent me here to ask a favour ;
Though, if he'd chosen to command, he knew
You'd do it ; for, of course, he understood
The awe and reverence you feel towards Jove ;
And quite right, too ! however, it's a fact,
He ordered me to play the suppliant,
And speak to you in gentle, kindly phrase.
For the particular Jove, who sent me here,
Fears whipping just as much as any of you ;[1]
And, as his father and mother are mortals both,
You needn't be surprised that he's afraid.
30 And I too, who am Jupiter's own son,
Am sure to catch it if my father does ;
Wherefore I come in peace and bring you peace.
The favour that I'm going to ask from you
Is just and fair ; for, being just myself,
I plead for justice from the just ; for 'tis
Indecent to ask injustice from the just,
And folly from the unjust to seek for justice,
Since they nor know nor practise her behests.
Now, pray attend to what I have to say :
You ought to grant our wish ; for father and I
40 Deserve it, both of you and of your state.
I won't make a long tale, such as I've heard
Other gods tell in plays about their goodness,
Neptune, and Virtue too, and Victory,
Mars, and Bellona ; I will not, I say,

---

[1] It must be remembered that the actors were slaves, and were liable
to be flogged if they acted badly.

Remind you here of all the kindnesses
My father, king of all the gods, has shown
To men ; it never was my father's way
To throw in good folk's teeth the good he'd done 'em.
He knows that you are grateful to him for it,
And that you merit all the good you've got.
Well, first I'll tell the favour I'm to ask,   50
And then the story of our tragedy.
What are you frowning at ? because I said
'Twas going to be a tragedy? Never mind !
I am a god : I'll alter it. If you like,
I'll turn the tragedy to comedy
And never change a line. Come, which d'ye want ?—
I beg your pardon ! What a fool I am !
As if I didn't know just what you wish !
I am a god, of course ; I'm quite aware
Of all that's in your minds about it. Well,
I'll mix 'em, and make a tragi-comedy.
You see, to make it comedy all through   60
Would never do with kings and gods about :
However, as there is a slave's part too,
I'll make it tragi-comedy, as I said.
      And now about the favour which I told you
Jupiter bade me ask ; it's simply this :—
Let the detectives go from seat to seat[1]
Through all the house, and if they chance to see
A *claqueur*[2] sitting, hired by any party,
Let 'em take his coat as pledge upon the spot :

---

[1] This passage proves that the prologue was not written by Plautus ; for it was not until B.C. 155, at earliest, that fixed seats were introduced into the theatres at Rome. *See* General Introduction, page 11.

[2] Latin *fauitor*.

And be it known to all men by.these presents :— [1]
If any person have solicited
The palm [2] for any actor or for the author,
70 Whether it was by written documents,
Or in his person, or by a third party ;
Or further, if the magistrates themselves [3]
Bestow the palm aforesaid upon any
In contravention of their oath and duty,
Great Jove decrees that the same penalty
Shall be imposed on them as in the case
Of bribery and corruption in elections, [4]
In favour of oneself or of another.
He said that you were masters of the world [5]
By valour, not by bribery and cheating.
Why should the actor have a different law
From the noblest hero ?   He must win the day
By excellence and not by hired applause.
Applause enough will ever come to him
Who acts aright, whilst honour reigns in those

---

[1] I have attempted to imitate the ostentatiously legal style of this passage by a free translation.

[2] Both the actors and the author of a successful play received branches of palm from the managers of the festival.

[3] *i.e.*, the ædiles, who exhibited plays as part of their function.

[4] The Lex Cornelia Fulvia, passed B.C. 159, prescribed banishment as the penalty for bribery. This may help to fix the date of the prologue, which, on other grounds, has been supposed to date from about B.C. 150.

[5] The year 168 B.C. had seen the end of the third Macedonian War, and the magnificent triumph of L. Æmilius Paullus. The following is a list of the Roman provinces at the close of B.C. 146, with the dates of their constitutions : Sicily (241); Sardinia (238); Hither and Further Spain (285); Cisalpine Gaul (circa 191) ; Illyria (167); Africa (146) : Macedonia and Achaia (146). This would seem to indicate a date slightly later than 146 for the prologue.

Who have the judgment of his deeds in hand.   80
This, too, my father gave to me in charge,
That the detectives go amongst the actors ;
Whoso of them has hired men to clap him,
Or tried to damage any of his fellows,
His hide and jacket shall be scourged to ribbons.
I see you're wondering that Jupiter
Cares about actors ; don't you be surprised,
For Jupiter himself is going to act
This comedy.—What are you staring at ?
It's no new thing for Jove to turn an actor.   90
Only last year, upon this very stage,
When the actors called on Jove, he came and helped them.
Besides, he's often on in tragedy.
This play, I tell you, Jupiter will act in,
And I along with him.   Now pay attention
Whilst I unfold the plot o' the comedy.
  This city here is Thebes ; and in this house
Amphitryon dwells, son of an Argive, born
At Argos, whom the daughter of Electrus,
Alcmena, married.   This Amphitryon
Is now at the head of the legions, for the Thebans   100
Are hard at war against the Teleboians ;
But when he went away to join the army,
He left Alcmena hopeful of a son.
You know the kind of fellow father is,
A trifle free sometimes in certain matters,
And a hot lover when he's in the mind ;
Well, this Alcmena is his latest flame,
And he has wooed and won her, whilst her husband
Remains in blissful ignorance ; and now
She's like to make him father for his pains.
In fact, to tell the truth about the lady,   110

She'll probably be mother of twin sons,
The one her husband's, and the other Jove's.
My father now is lying in her arms,
And that is why the night's a little longer,
That he may take his fill of her sweet love,
Pretending that he is Amphitryon.

  I see you're staring at this dress of mine,
And wondering why I'm come upon the stage
In a slave's clothes. I fear the story's stale,
But never mind, I'll tell it you anew.
This is the reason of my strange attire ;
120 My father Jupiter is here inside ;
He's turned himself into Amphitryon's shape,
And all the slaves who see him, think it's he.
O, when he likes, he is so versatile !
I took the form of Sosia, his slave,
Who went to battle with Amphitryon.
I wished to humour my most amorous sire,
And stop the servants asking who I was,
When they should see me busy in the house.
Now that they think that I'm their fellow-slave,
There's none of them will ever dream of asking
130 Who I may be, or what I've come about.

  Ah well, my father's suited to a T !
He lies within the arms of his sweet love,
And tells her all that's happening at the wars ;
And she believes he is her very husband,
Whilst all the time—oh dear ! Well, now he's telling
How all the legions of the foe were routed,
And how they honoured him with heaps of gifts.
The fact is, what they gave Amphitryon
We stole ; a god, you see, does what he likes !
140   Now then, to-day, Amphitryon's coming home

From the campaign, and with him that same slave,
Whose bodily presentment I've assumed.
So, that you may distinguish which is which,
I'll wear these little feathers in my hat ;
My father too will wear a golden cord
Round his ; Amphitryon will not have that sign.
None of the household shall have power to see
These signs, but all of you, of course, will see them.
    But here comes Sosia, Amphitryon's slave,
Up from the port, a lantern in his hand.
I'll drive him from the house when he arrives.   150
    Attend ! it will be worth your while to see,
When Mercury and Jove the actors be.

SOSIA. MERCURY.

[*Enter Sosia from the harbour with a lantern—Mercury remaining concealed in the shadow.*]

    Sos. I'm sure there never was a man so brave and bold
    as I am !
I know the dangers of the night, and yet I dare defy 'em.
The roysterers may catch me or the night police may run
    me in,
And then to-morrow I shall pay the score upon my wretched
    skin.
I cannot make my own defence :[1] my noble master's not in
    sight,
And everybody else of course will say, "O serve the rascal
    right ! "
Just as if I were an anvil, will those sturdy hangmen whack,

---

[1] The evidence of a slave being inadmissible.

And give the poor stranger a public reception upon
160   his bare back.
        Master couldn't wait,
But hurried me up from the harbour to do his fool's
    errand so late :
    'Twould have done just as well in the day ;
    But there ! it is always the way
    When you've got a rich man to obey !
Night and day you're always at it, though you do your very
    best ;
Always something to be said or done, and not a moment's
    rest.
170 For your wealthy lord, who never did a single hour's work,
If you can't do all his whimsies, thinks that you are on the
    shirk.
      Oh, it's right enough, of course,
      Though you labour like a horse !
    Whether fair or unfair, doesn't matter a jot ;
    And so the poor slave has a very hard lot,
    For burdens and troubles are all that he's got !
    MERC. [*aside*].   It's time *I* lamented my wretched condi-
      tion !
    Who was free as the air yesterday,
      But now am reduced to this menial position ;
    If a born slave has so much to say !
180   Sos.   Oh, what a rascal slave I am ! 'twas all too soon I
      had intended
To thank the gods as they deserved from me, because my
    trip was ended.
By Pollux, if, as I deserve, the gods propose to show me
    grace,
They'd best commission somebody to come and slap me in
    the face.

For all my applecart of blessings I've most thanklessly upset.
  MERC. [*aside*]. He's not like most folk, for he knows
    exactly what he ought to get.
  Sos. Well, here I am at home again, although none of
    us, I'll be bound,
Expected from that dreadful war that he would get back safe
    and sound.
Our conquering hosts have thrashed the foe ; now homeward
    they return again,
For the big fight is finished and our vaunting enemies are
    slain.
The town that from their lives and homes so many Thebans 190
    sadly sundered,
Was bravely captured by our men and then most valorously
    plundered.
My mighty lord, Amphitryon, was our commander in the fray,
And made his comrades rich with spoil, and land, and corn
    that glorious day,
And set King Creon firm again on his ancestral Theban
    throne.
And now he's sent me from the port to tell his wife the deeds
    he's done,
And how he served his country as her leader, general, and
    guide ;
Now, let me think what I must say to her when I have got
    inside.
And if I have to lie a bit, ah well! that's nothing new, I doubt!
When they were busy fighting, I was very busy—clearing out!
But still I'll reckon I was there, for I have heard from one 200
    who knows ;
And now I'll think it over with myself, and see how I propose
To tell my yarn the neatest way that's possible.   Ahem !
    here goes !—

As soon as we had reached the place and touched upon the
   foeman's strand,
Straightway Amphitryon chooses out the chiefs of all his
   noble band ;
He sends them forth, he bids them tell the Teleboians all
   his mind ;
If without force and without fight they will the treacherous
   bandits bind,
And hand them over with their spoils, he'll lead the Theban
   army back,
And, leaving peace and ease behind, the dreaded Argives
   off will pack ;
But if they're otherwise disposed, and so refuse his will to do,
210 He'll storm their town with all his might, and sadly he will
   make them rue.
Amphitryon's ambassadors at once their message duly told ;
But trusting to their valorous might and strength, the Tele-
   boians bold
Dismissed those brave ambassadors of ours with insult and
   with scorn,
And said that they could well defend the town and land
   where they were born,
And quickly make our general and all his host evacuate.
When their reply is brought to him, Amphitryon, with hope
   elate,
Leads forth his army from the camp. At once the Tele-
   boians too,
With flashing arms, from forth the town, bring out in pride
   their hardy crew.
When both sides had come forth all prepared for the fray,
220   And the soldiers were stationed in battle array,
   Then we drew up our troops on the regular plan,
   And the enemy theirs, and we stood man to man,

Next from out either army the generals stalk,
And away from the throng of our ranks hold a talk.
They agree that whichever is beaten that day
Shall surrender their town, lands, and persons a prey.
When that's settled, the trumpets blare out loud and clear,
And the startled earth echoes and cheer answers cheer.
Then the generals on either side offer their vows
To great Jove, and with bold words their armies arouse. 230
Now then to it ! and each man does all that he knows,
And swords flash, lances quiver, as madly they close.
Heaven bellows with shouts, their breath rises like vapour ;
One is choked by the dust, one is pinked with a rapier ;
Till, at last, as we hoped, we have won ! we have won !
And the foe falls in heaps, and our brave boys charge on,
      Fiercely fighting !
And yet no one was found in the enemy's host,
Who would fly from his station, or give up his post.
They could die, but they wouldn't retreat from the fray, 240
And they fell, where they stood, in unbroken array.
When Amphitryon, my lord, saw this soul-stirring sight,
He commanded the horsemen to charge on the right.
They obey ; from the right they rush on with a shout—
With a lightning-like swoop their opponents they rout,
And they utterly vanquish their foemen so stout,
      Our wrongs righting.
Merc. [*aside*].   There's nothing that he's said so far that
  isn't absolutely true,
For I was present at the fight and so was Jove, my father, too.
  Sos. The enemy now take to flight ; that cheers our noble 250
  fellows' hearts,
And as the Teleboians turn their backs, they stick them full
  of darts ;
Amphitryon's own hands did of his head King Pterelas bereave.

The battle lasted all day long, from early morn to dewy
    eve;
I never shall forget it, for I got no lunch at all that day.
However, night comes down at last, and terminates the
    bloody fray.
Next day from town their chiefs came down to us in tears, a
    sad procession;
With suppliant hands they beg that we will overlook their
    late transgression;
Themselves, their temples, and their gods, their sons, their
    city, and their glebes,
They yield up to the conquering power and mighty sove-
    reignty of Thebes.
260 Then as a prize for valour, to my lord Amphitryon so bold,
Was given by the general voice the goblet, framed of solid
    gold,
From which King Pterelas was wont to drink; this must my
    lady know.
So now to carry out my lord's behest within the house I'll go.
    MERC. [*aside*].   Ohoho! he's coming hither! I'll go meet
        him on his way;
I don't mean to let the rascal get inside the house to-day;
Won't it play the dickens with him when he sees his double
    here?
But, I say, since I've adopted for my use his outward cheer,
I must ape his style and manner, imitate his native brogue,
Turn myself into a cunning, scheming, tricky, downright
    rogue;
And with his own roguish weapons drive him from his
    master's gate.
270 Stop! he's staring at the sky! I wonder what the fellow's at!
    SOS.   Well, upon my word and honour, if I haven't lost
        my head,

Sure to-night good old Nocturnus[1] has got drunk and gone
　　to bed!

Look! the Great Bear hasn't moved a single step across the
　　sky,

And the moon stays where she started, hours ago, to rise on
　　high.

See! Orion and the Pleiads, and the evening star won't set;

All the stars are stuck, and daylight shows no signs of com-
　　ing yet.

　　MERC. [*aside*]. Well done, Night! just keep it going!
　　give my good old dad a show!

Nobly for that noble god a noble work you'll do! Bravo!

　　Sos. Well, a longer night than this is I don't think I ever
　　knew,

Save that one when I was flogged, and left to hang the　280
　　whole night through;

Nay, and even that, by Pollux, wasn't really quite as long.

I suppose the Sun's asleep; I guess he mixed his drinks too
　　strong!

Gave himself a little dinner and got just a trifle tight!

　　MERC. [*aside*]. Oh, you scoundrel! that's the way you
　　talk about the gods! all right!

I'll give you a warm reception! I'll be even with you yet!

Just come here to me, you gallows, and I'll show you what
　　you'll get.

　　Sos. Well, I'll go and tell Alcmena what my master bade　290
　　me say.

　　　　　　　　[*He sees Mercury by the door.*]

Eh? Who's this at our front door? A stranger at this time
　　of day?

　　MERC. [*aside*]. Oh, he is the biggest coward!

---

[1] The god of night.

Sos.   Ah, it just occurs to me,
He's the man that wants to dust my jacket for me.   Yes, it's
    he!
MERC. [*aside*].   Ain't he frightened?   Watch me fool him!
Sos.   My poor teeth!   How they'll be missed!
As I come, he'll give me welcome with a hospitable fist.
Oh, he's kind!   I've been kept waking all night at my lord's
    behest,
So he will considerately knock me down to take a rest!
Well, my goose is cooked completely!   See how strong and
    tall he is!
300   MERC. [*aside*].   Now I'll tell a little story!   Not a syllable
    he'll miss;
And I'll scare him worse than ever, make him shiver, I'll
    engage!
[*Aloud.*]   Come, my fists, it's getting time you gave a victim
    to my rage.
Yesterday you sent to byebye four fine fellows I had robbed;
Yet to me it seems an age since.
Sos.   Mercy, how I shall be bobbed!
I shall have to change my name from Sosia to Quintus[1]
    soon.
Four he boasts he gave their requiescat but this afternoon;
I shall be the *fifth*, I take it!
    MERC. [*squaring his fists*].   Now then for it!   That's the
    way!
Sos.   Now his coat is off!   He's ready!
MERC.   Oh, he'll have sore bones to-day!
Sos.   Whom does he mean?
MERC.   Whoever comes, shall eat my fists,
    as I'm a sinner!

---

[1] *i.e.,* Fifth; a common name amongst the Romans.

Sos. O no, thanks! it's much too late! besides, you 310
know, I've had my dinner.

I'd advise you to bestow that dinner on the out-o'-works.

Merc. Um, this fist weighs pretty heavy!

Sos.   Weighty trouble therein lurks!

Merc. Say I tickled him quite gently, just until the
fellow slept?

Sos. You'd confer on me a favour! Three long nights
my watch I've kept.

Merc. [sparring out]. It's no go! My hand won't learn
in feeble fashion to be raised!

His own mother shouldn't know him, whom thou, fist of
mine, hast grazed.

Sos. Oh, I see! he'll patch me up and give me a new
face again.

Merc. Should'st thou smite his face in earnest, not a
whole bone should remain.

Sos. Yes, that's it! he means to bone me just as if I were
an eel.

Woe to him who bones his fellows! Would that I away 320
could steal!

Merc. Ha! I smell a man! he'll catch it.

Sos.   Dear me! is it possible?

Merc. He can't be so very far off; yet he *was*, I know
it well.

Sos. Oh, the fellow is a wizard![1]

Merc.   How my fists itch for a brawl!

Sos. If on me you're going to try them, practise first upon
the wall.

Merc. Ha! a voice flew to my ears!

Sos.   See there! that's just my beastly luck!

First a flying speech I utter, then forget its wings to pluck.

---

[1] His last words indicate that he knows that Sosia has been away.

MERC.   Yonder fellow wants a thrashing fetched with his beast [1] from me.

Sos.   Nay, I haven't got a beast.

MERC.   I'll load him with my fists, you'll see.

Sos.   I'm so tired with the voyage, even now I'm feeling sick ;

330 I can hardly walk unloaded ; if you load me I shall stick.

MERC.   Someone's talking !

Sos.   Saved again ! he doesn't see me ! that's the way !

He says *Someone's* talking ; now I know *my* name is *Sosia.*

MERC.   From the right it was I fancy that the voice smote on my ear.

Sos.   Ah ! because my voice *smote* on him, he will *smite* on me, I fear.

MERC.   Bravo ! here he's coming to me !

Sos.   Oh, I'm frozen stiff with dread !

Where've I got to ? Am I standing on my heels or on my head ?

Wretched me ! I cannot move a single step for very fear !

It's all over ! Sosia and his lord's commissions perish here.

Never mind, I'll up and cheek him ; that's the best thing I can see.

340 If I make him think I'm plucky, then, perhaps, he'll let me be.

MERC.   [2] Whither goest thou, who bearest Vulcan prisoned in thy lamp?

Sos.   Pray attend to your own business, you bone-smashing, bruising scamp !

MERC.   Are you slave or freeman, eh, sir?

---

[1] *i.e.* brought upon himself—due to his own action in approaching me.

[2] Up to this point the actors have not directly addressed each other.

Sos.   Just whichever I desire.
Merc.   Do you say so?
Sos.   Yes, I do, sir!
Merc.   You whipped slave!
Sos.   There you're a liar!
Merc.   Anyway, I'll try to make my words the truth.
Sos.   No need of that!
Merc.   Will you tell me where you're going, who you are,
    and what you're at?
Sos.   I'm going here, and I'm my master's servant : is
    that what you want?
Merc.   You take care or else I give your tongue a squeeze,
    sir!
Sos.   No, you can't!
She's a chaste and modest maiden!
Merc.   Stop your chattering and go!
What's your business at this house, sir?
Sos.   *Mine!* what's *yours*, I'd like to know?   350
Merc.   I'm one of King Creon's watchmen, posted here
    from night to night.
Sos.   Oh, I see! whilst we were absent, he took care o'
    the house. All right!
Now be off, my man, and tell him that the household has
    come back.
Merc.   *You* a member of the household!   See, unless
    you quickly pack,
You'll be welcomed to the household in no hospitable
    way.
Sos.   This, I tell you, is my home, where I'm a
    slave.
Merc.   Mark what I say!
I'll make you a proud man shortly, if you don't be off.
Sos.   Pray how?

MERC. You'll be borne off in a litter,[1] if I use my club,
I trow.

Sos. I'm a servant in this household; that's what you
don't seem to know.

360 MERC. Well, I know you'll get a thrashing very soon,
unless you go !

Sos. Will you shut me out from home, then, when I've
been so long away ?

MERC. *This* your home ?

Sos.   Of course it is.

MERC.   And what's your master's name,
do you say ?

Sos. Why, Amphitryon, the general of the Thebans, and
his dame

Is the fair and sweet Alcmena.

MERC.   Come now, tell me, what's your name?

Sos. Sosia the Thebans call me, good old Davus was my
sire.

MERC. Well, I never ! You'll repent it, trying this on
me, you liar !

O you brazen tower of cheek, you know you've patched up
all this story.

Sos. With a *patched-up* shirt I came, but nothing else. I
vow to glory !

MERC. There's a patent lie ! you came here with your
feet, not with your *shirt*.

Sos. Certainly.

370 MERC. Well, *certainly* for that black lie you'll soon get
hurt.

Sos. No ! I *certainly* object.

MERC.   But *certainly* that doesn't matter,

---

[1] *i.e.* on a stretcher. Of course only rich people used litters.

For it's fixed most *certainly* that I your ribs shall soundly
    batter.   [*Mercury beats Sosia.*]
  Sos.   O have mercy !
  Merc.   Do you dare to say that you are Sosia, eh ?
I am Sosia.   [*beats him again.*]
  Sos.   Murder ! murder !
  Merc.   O, there's more upon the way !
Whose slave are you *now*, sir ?
  Sos.   Yours, sir ! for your fists make good your
                 claim.
Help me, Thebans !
  Merc.   Stop your bawling and just tell me why you
                came.
  Sos.   Oh, I came for you to kill me with your fists. O
    don't ! no more !
  Merc.   *Whose* slave are you ?
  Sos.   Why, Amphitryon's Sosia, as I said before.
  Merc.   Don't I tell you *I* am Sosia ? Oh, I'll beat you 380
    black and blue !
  Sos. [*aside*]. O good lord ! I wish you were, for then *I*
    should be beating *you*.
  Merc.   What's that muttering ?
  Sos.   Nothing, nothing !
  Merc.   Who's your master ?
  Sos.   Whom you like !
  Merc.   *Now* what do you say your name is ?
  Sos.   Anything ! O please don't strike !
  Merc.   Why, just now you said you were Amphitryon's
    Sosia !
  Sos.   I was wrong.
'Twas *associate*, not *Sosia*, I intended all along.
  Merc.   Ah, I thought I was the only slave of ours that
    bore that name.

Sure, you've missed the mark entirely.

Sos.   Would your fists had done the same!

MERC. I am that same Sosia you were mentioning just
now to me.

Sos. Please make peace and let me say a word, from fear
of beating free.

MERC. No, not peace, but truce I'll grant you, if you've
anything to say.

390   Sos. Not a word till peace is made! Your fists have
such an awkward way.

MERC. Fire away! I will not hurt you!

Sos.   Can I trust you?

MERC.   Yes, you may.

Sos. What if you deceive me?

MERC.   Then may Mercury blast Sosia!

Sos. Now pray mark me! and remember I have leave to
speak out plain.

I'm Amphitryon's servant, Sosia.

MERC.   Come, I say, not that again!

Sos. Peace was made and truce concluded! It's the
truth I'm telling you.

MERC. All the same you'll get a thrashing.

Sos.   As you please, of course you'll do;

For you've got the strongest fists; but still the truth I'm
bound to say.

MERC. But you never can persuade me that I am not
Sosia.

Sos. Well, by Pollux, you sha'n't rob me of my master, all
the same;

400 None, except myself, amongst our slaves has ever borne my
name;

And I went with brave Amphitryon forth to fight the enemy.

MERC. Oh, he's mad!

Sos.   The same to you, sir !   *You* are mad, it seems
   to me.
What the mischief! am I not Amphitryon's servant, Sosia ?
Didn't our vessel come to harbour from the Persic port [1] to-
   day?
Didn't master send me here, as soon as we had reached the
   land ?
Don't I stand before our dwelling with this lantern in my
   hand?
Aint I speaking ? aint I waking ?   Didn't he beat me with
   his fists ?
Yes, by Jove, he *did !* I know it ! for I'm still all aches and
   twists.
Why then do I tarry longer ?   Come, into our house I'll go.
   MERC.   What, *your* house, you say ?
   Sos.   W'hy, surely !
   MERC.   O you villain, would you so ?   410
You're a liar ! and I tell you *I'm* Amphitryon's Sosia ;
It was *our* ship sailed to harbour from the Persic port to-day;
It was *we* who stormed the city where King Pterelas did
   reign ;
We who 'gainst the Teleboians did that famous victory gain ;
And Amphitryon beheaded Pterelas their king in fight.
   Sos. [*aside*].   Oh, it nearly makes me doubt myself to hear
      him thus recite !
Everything that happened there he tells exactly, right straight
   on—
[*Aloud.*]   Tell me, though, what gift was given to my lord
   Amphitryon ?

---

[1] Some port between the islands of the Teleboians and Thebes. It
will be noticed that Plautus assigns a harbour to Thebes ! But does not
Shakspere tell us of the sea-coast of Bohemia?

MERC. Why, the golden goblet, out of which King
Pterelas used to drink.

Sos. Right again! and where's the goblet now?

420   MERC.   Oh, in a box, I think,
Sealed with Lord Amphitryon's signet.

Sos.   What's upon the signet, pray?

MERC. It's a rising sun and chariot. Did you think you'd
caught me, eh?

Sos. [*aside*]. Ah, he beats me with his answers! I must
find another name.

How *could* he have known? However, now I'll put the
scamp to shame.

For what I did when alone (no soul beside was there that
day)

In the tent, I rather think he'll find it difficult to say.

[*Aloud.*] If you're really Sosia, tell me, when the soldiers
were at fight,

What were you at in the tent then? I'll give in, if you tell
right.

MERC. I was drawing wine, a jugfull, from a cask.

Sos. [*aside*].   He's started well!

MERC. Then I drained it. How delicious was its flavour
430   and its smell!

Sos. Yes, it's true enough; I must confess I drained that
sweet canteen.

Why, the villain must have seen me, lying in the jug un-
seen!

MERC. Now then, have I satisfied you, that you are not
Sosia?

Sos. No, by Jove, I swear I *am* he; I'm not telling lies,
I say.

MERC. Well, by Mercury I swear it, Jove will not accept
your troth;

Me on my bare word he trusts far more than you upon your
　　oath.

　　Sos. Who am I then, if not Sosia? Will you tell me
　　　　that, I pray?

　　Merc. When I do not wish to be so, you can then be
　　　　Sosia.

Now, when I *am* he, be off or you'll excite a lively storm.　　440

　　Sos. [*aside*]. True it is, when I behold him, I can recog-
　　　　nise *my* form,

Just as like me as myself when in the glass I take a peep;

Leg and foot, and hair and stature, eyes and mouth, and nose
　　and lip,

Cheeks and chin, and beard and neck, and everything! Yes,
　　I agree!

If his back is scarred with whipping, nothing could be more
　　like me.

Still though, when I come to think on't, I'm the same I've
　　always been,

Know our house and know my master; and my mind is
　　sound and keen.

No! for all this fellow's talking, I won't yield!

　　　　　　　　　　　[*He knocks at the door.*]

　　Merc. Whither away?

　　Sos.　　　Why, home!

　　Merc.　　　Look here, sir, you may run away, nay, more,

Climb up into Jove's own chariot, but you won't escape your　450
　　doom.

　　Sos. But my master sent me! Mayn't I go into my
　　　　lady's room?

　　Merc. Yes, *your* lady's, if you like, sir! but not *mine!*
　　　　Come, off you pack!

If you plague me any more, you'll take away a broken back.

Sos.   No! I'll go first!—Ye immortal gods, to you I
    humbly pray!

Am I dead? or am I changed? or have I thrown my shape
    away?

Have I left myself behind and then perchance forgotten it?

For this man's the image of me—well, it comforts me a bit,

That I've got an image *now*, for when I'm dead, I sha'n't, I
    fear.[1]

460 But I'll go and tell my master at the port what's happened
    here.

O, I say   perhaps *he* won't know me!   May Jove grant me
    such good hap!

Then this very day I'll shave my head and don the free-
    man's cap.[2]

                        [*Exit Sosia to the harbour.*]

MERCURY.

MERC.   Come, I've not done so badly here to-day.

I've driven a beastly nuisance from the door,

So that my father mightn't be disturbed.

When he gets to his lord, Amphitryon,

He'll say that he, by a slave called Sosia,

Was driven from the door.   He'll think he lies,

---

[1] The Roman practice of setting up the images of the ancestors of the
family in the house, and carrying them out at funerals is well known.
Of course, a slave like Sosia had not the *jus imaginum*, which was confined to families of official rank.

[2] Slaves when set free shaved their heads and wore a skull-cap till
their hair grew again.

And never came here, as he'd told him to.
Thus I'll fill full of madness and confusion   470
Both them and all Amphitryon's household too,
Until my father's ready to depart
And leave his lover.   Then, and not till then,
They all shall know the truth ; and Jupiter
Shall reconcile Alcmena and her spouse.
Amphitryon is sure to make a row,
And charge his wife with shame ; and then my father
Will change their trouble to tranquillity.
I should have said before about Alcmena,
That she to-day will bring forth babies twain,   480
One in the tenth month, t'other in the seventh.
One is Amphitryon's, the other Jove's.
The younger boy has got the greater father,
And *vice versâ ;* there you have it all.
But for the greater honour of Alcmena,
My father's caused one labour to suffice,
That no suspicion might be cast on her,
And that their secret meetings might be hid ;   490
Though, as I said before, Amphitryon
Will know it all at last.   But what of that ?
None will reproach Alcmena.   For a god
Would not do right to suffer that his fault
And sin should light upon a mortal's back.
But I must stop.   I hear the door [1] is opening—
The mock Amphitryon is coming forth
Along with his presumptive wife, Alcmena.

---

[1] The doors of the houses opened outwards ; hence, people knocked at
the door before coming out, in order to warn passers-by to get out of the
way.

Jupiter. Alcmena. Mercury.

[*Enter from the house, Jupiter, as Amphitryon, and Alcmena.*]

    Jup. Well, good-bye, Alcmena dearest, mind the house
    whilst I'm away!
500 Do be careful of your health, love! for you're getting near
    the day.
I must go; but welcome kindly this young stranger that's to
    come.
    Alc. Yes; but what's the business, dearest, hurries you
    away from home?
    Jup. Not, by Pollux, that I'm weary either of my home
    or you.
But the general can't be absent from his army. 'Twouldn't do!
All things would be topsy-turvy, and a pretty life they'd lead!
    Merc. [*aside*]. Isn't he a clever rascal? Very like his
    son indeed!
Watch him how he'll soothe the lady with his artful flattery!
    Alc. Nay, by Castor, is this how you prove how much
    you care for me?
    Jup. Darling, there's no other woman that I love as I
    love you!
510   Merc. [*aside*]. Don't let Juno know it or you'll put her
    in a pretty stew!
Then I warrant you would rather be Amphitryon than Jove.
    Alc. I would rather see the proof than hear you talk
    about your love.
Why, before your couch is warm, you're up and going in a
    trice!
Yesterday you came at midnight; now you're off. It isn't nice!
    Merc. [*aside*]. I must step up and accost her, back my
    father in the strife.

[*Aloud.*]   Never, madam, I protest was there a mortal loved
    his wife
With such utter desperation ; you're his one and sole delight.
    JUP.   Ha ! you villain ! don't I know you?   Just be off
      out of my sight !
What have you to do, you rascal, muttering and meddling
    here ?
Where's my walking stick ?
    ALC.   O, don't !
    JUP.   Well, not another word, d'ye hear ?   520
    MERC. [*aside*].   Hum! my first attempt to back him don't
      seem to have had much luck !
    JUP.   That's all true enough, I grieve to say, but don't be
      cross, my duck !
On the sly I left the army, stole away the news to tell,
That from me you might be first to hear I'd served my coun-
    try well.
All I've told you.   If I hadn't loved my darling very much,
I should not have done it.
    MERC. [*aside*].   Mark now, hasn't he a gentle
                           touch ?
    JUP.   Now I must get back in secret, lest the soldiers
      should relate
How I thought more of my wifey than of the affairs of state.
    ALC.   If you go you'll make me cry, love !
    JUP.   Nay, Alcmena, get along !
Don't you spoil your eyes !   I'm coming back soon.
    ALC.   Ah, your " soon " is long !   530
    JUP.   I protest I do not leave you without sorrow.
    ALC.   Yes, I know !
On the very night that you come home you leave me.
    JUP.   Let me go !
Time is passing ; I must leave the city ere the darkness flee.

See, this goblet which for valour in the fight was given to me,
From which Pterelas was wont to drink, whom with this hand
    I slew,
There, I give it you, Alcmena !
    ALC.   Darling ! that is just like you !
O how pretty ! there's a present worthy of the giver's fame.
    MERC. Nay, excuse me, rather worthy of his noble lady's
    name.
    JUP. You again ! you gallows-bird, you ! Oh, I'll
    make your shoulders ache !

540   ALC. Please, Amphitryon, don't be angry with poor Sosia,
    for my sake.
    JUP. As you please, dear !
    MERC. [*aside*].   Well, I never ! why he's wild with
                love to-day !
    JUP. Good-bye !
    ALC.   Don't forget to love me ! I am thine,
                though far away.
    MERC. Come on, master, day is dawning.
    JUP.   Sosia, go before me then,
I will follow [*exit Merc.*]. Good-bye, darling !
    ALC.   May you come back soon !
    JUP.   Amen !
I'll be here ere you expect me. Put a cheerful courage on !

                      [*Exit Alcmena into the house.*]

Now, kind night, who stayed'st my pleasure, I'll permit thee
    to be gone,
So that day may shine on mortals with its clear and glittering
    light,
And to-day shall lack the hours which were added to last
    night ;

So I'll make the whole thing straight and proper, as it ought
    to be ;
And the day shall help the night.   And now I'll after 550
    Mercury.

                [Exit Jupiter to the harbour.]

AMPHITRYON. SOSIA.

*[Enter from the harbour Amphitryon and Sosia carrying a
    small chest.]*

AMPH. Come, follow me quickly!
Sos.   I'm now at your heels, sir.
AMPH. I think you're an absolute rascal.
Sos.   Pray why ?
AMPH. Because what is not, nor has been, nor e'er will
    be,
You tell me is true.
Sos.   O dear, no, sir ! not I !
But it's like you, you never can trust your poor servants.
    AMPH. What's that ? What d'ye mean ? O you scoun-
    drel, I swear
I'll cut out your scoundrelly tongue.
    Sos.   I am yours, sir ;
Whatever it suits you to do, I must bear.
But, do what you will, you will never deter me
From telling you truly the things that I know.   560
    AMPH. You measureless rogue, do you still dare to tell
    me
That you, who are here, are at home ?
    Sos.   Yes, that's so.
    AMPH. The gods send a mischief upon you, you villain !
I'll help them !

Sos.   I'm yours, sir; and your will is law.

Amph. You dare, O you rascal, make game of your master?

You dare to affirm, what no man ever saw,

Or ever can see, that at one and the same time

The same man can be in two places at once?

Sos. The fact's as I tell you.

Amph. [*striking him*]. O Jupiter, damn you!

570   Sos. Why, how've I deserved such a blow on my sconce?

Amph. D'ye ask me, you scoundrel, and still go on mocking?

Sos. I'd deserve to be cursed, if I did such an act,

But I'm not telling lies, and it is as I tell you.

Amph. Oh, he's drunk, and that's the fact.

Sos. Wish I was!

Amph.   You *are*, I think.

Sos. I?

Amph.   Where did you get the drink?

Sos. Not a drop, sir!

Amph.   O, he's cracked!

Sos. Ten times I have told the fact.

I'm at home, I say, yet here!

Have I spoken plain and clear?

Amph. Bah! go leave me!

Sos.   What's wrong now?

Amph. You've the plague!

580   Sos.   O master, how

Can you say so? I'm all right.

Amph. Never mind! before to-night

Comes in sight,

You'll be poorly, I'll be bound,

Once I get home safe and sound.

Come on, you, who mock your master with a silly drunken
    tale.
First I give you certain orders which to execute you
    fail.
Then, to mend it, you must mock me; tell me, thinking to
    deceive,
Things that never happened, things that no one ever could
    believe.
But, before the day is done, those lies will light upon your
    back.
    Sos. Master, 'tis the keenest sorrow to an honest slave, 590
    alack !
When he tells the truth, to find that force can over truth pre-
    vail.
    Amph. How the deuce now *could* it happen (once more
    try to prove your tale)
That you should be here and yet at home? That's what I
    want to see.
    Sos. Well, I *am* both here and there too. Greater mar-
    vel couldn't be.
I am just as much bewildered at it, master, as you are.
    Amph. What's that ?
    Sos. I'm as much bewildered as yourself, I do declare.
Nor, so help me heaven, did I believe my own self, Sosia,
Till my other self, yon Sosia, forced me in the following
    way :
He related all that happened while we were away in camp;
Then he'd stolen my outward likeness and my name, the
    thieving scamp.   600
Milk is not more like to milk than yonder fellow's like to me.
For when you, ere daybreak, sent me from the harbour
    home, you see,—
    Amph. What then ?

Sos.   Long before I got there, I was standing at the door.

Amph.   O, what deucèd nonsense!   Are you in your senses?

Sos.   To be sure.

Amph.   Someone with an evil hand bewitched him, after he left me.

Sos.   I confess it!   I was pounded with his fists most horribly.

Amph.   Why, who beat you?

Sos.   I myself did, I who now am at our house.

Amph.   Tell me truly what I ask you or my temper you'll arouse.

First of all, who is that Sosia?   That is what I want to know.

Sos.   He's your slave.

610   Amph.   I've one too many of that name already, though!
Never in my life had I another Sosia but you.

Sos.   But, I tell you on my honour, now you have another too.

Yes, when you get home you'll meet him, meet that other Sosia,

Davus' son, the same as I am, just like me in every way;

Just my age.   What need of talking?   Sosia has turned a twin.

Amph.   Well, it is the strangest tale!   But did you see my wife within?

Sos.   No, he never let me go inside the house.

Amph.   Who hindered you?

Sos.   Why, that Sosia, I tell you!   he who beat me black and blue.

Amph.   Who is he?

Sos.   Myself, I say!   How often must I tell you that?

Amph.   Tell me, have you been asleep, sir?

Sos.   No I haven't, sir, that's flat. 620

AMPH.   Oh, I thought you might have dreamed about
that other Sosia.

Sos.   I don't execute your orders in a dream ; it's not my
way.

No, awake I saw him, as awake I now see you and tell.

He awake not long since battered me awake and bruised me
well.

AMPH.   Why, who was it ?

Sos.   I myself, sir ! Sosia ! Don't you understand ?

AMPH.   Who the deuce could understand the awful
nonsense you've in hand ?

Sos.   Well, you'll know directly, sir, that that slave Sosia
is me.

AMPH.   Follow me then, for this matter must be looked
to carefully.

Meanwhile go and bring my luggage, as I bade you, from
the ship.[1]

Sos.   I'm both mindful and industrious ; oh, I'll not make 630
any slip !

When you give your orders to me, I don't mix them up with
drink.

AMPH.   Well, heaven bless us ! may your story prove as
foolish as I think.

ALCMENA.   AMPHITRYON.   SOSIA.

[*Enter from the house Alcmena and her maid Thessala.*]

ALC.   How few and how poor are the pleasures
That come in the course of our life !

---

[1] This and the next three lines are of doubtful authenticity. At all
events Sosia does not go to the ship, but remains with Amphitryon
throughout the next scene.

Compared with the troubles ; for so 'tis
Ordained in this region of strife.
The gods have decreed it, that pleasure
Shall always be followed by pain ;
Nay, more inconvenience and trouble
Oft comes, when our wishes we gain.
And now that I've learnt by experience,
I find it is true in my case.
For a short time to me 'twas permitted
To gaze on my husband's dear face ;
Just one night he stayed ; then he hastened
And suddenly went ere the dawn ;
Yes, he whom I love more than all else
640   Is gone and has left me forlorn.
Less pleasure I felt at his coming
Than pain now that he is withdrawn.
Yet this makes me glad ; he has conquered the foe,
And home has returned with fresh laurels to show.
Yes, that is my comfort.   Then let him begone,
So he may return when the victory's won.
With a brave and a resolute spirit
His absence I'll bear ; then I'll see
My husband renowned as a conqueror ;
And that is sufficient for me.
For valour's the prize of all prizes the best ;
There's nothing like valour, it must be confest ;
650   Our freedom, our safety, our goods and our life,
Our home and our children it guards in the strife.
It comprehends all things, all blessings it showers,
If valour, true valour, is ours.
AMPH.   Well, I think my darling wifey will be glad to see
me home ;
She loves me and I love her ; and then in triumph I am come ;

For our foe is beaten; those, whom all supposed invincible,
Under my command and leading, at our first attack they
    fell.
Yes, I'm sure there's no one else whom she would be so glad
    to see.

Sos.   To be sure! and so my sweetheart will rejoice to
    welcome me.

ALC. [*aside*].   Here's my husband!

AMPH.   Follow me, sir!

ALC. [*aside*].   Bless me! what has brought him   660
                        back?

But just now away he hurried! Is he trying me, alack!
And attempting to discover if I miss him when he's gone?
Bless the darling! I'm not sorry that he's coming back so
    soon.

Sos.   I say, master, we had better go back to the ship.

AMPH.   What for?

Sos.   No one's going to give us breakfast as we march
    back from the war.

AMPH.   What has got into your numskull?

Sos.   Why, that we've come back too late.

AMPH.   Why?

Sos.   Alcmena's had her breakfast, and is
                        standing at the gate.

AMPH.   No, she's going to make me happy with a son.

Sos.   O, plague on that!

AMPH.   What's the matter?

Sos.   I shall have to draw the water for the brat! [1]

Just ten months' ago we left her; yes, I see your reckoning's
    true.   670

---

[1] Sosia foresees that the advent of a baby will largely increase his
work in this direction.

AMPH.   Come, take heart !.

Sos.   Take heart ?   Now mark me, with my
                      bucket what I'll do—

If I don't, I pray you'll never trust another thing I tell—

If once I begin to draw, I'll draw the heart out of that well.

AMPH.   Follow me, now.   I will find you something
        easier, never fear !

ALC. [*aside*].   I should show my duty better if I went to
        meet my dear.

AMPH.   Gladly does Amphitryon hasten to salute his
        darling wife !

She's the best and dearest woman in all Thebes, upon my
        life !

Yea, and all the Theban people spread abroad her virtue's
        fame—

Are you well ?   Did you expect me ?

Sos. [*aside*].   Like enough !   Why, what's the game ?

680   She gives him as warm a welcome, nearly, as you would a dog.

AMPH.   When I see you look so well, dear, with delight
        I'm all agog.

ALC.   Bless me ! husband, I beseech you, why do you
        make fun of me ?

And salute and greet me fondly with your mocking courtesy,

Just as if this were the first time you'd been home here since
        the war ?

Yes, and greet me just as if we hadn't met for years before !

AMPH.   Well, I haven't seen or met you for an age until
        to-day.

ALC.   Why deny it ?

AMPH.   I have learned to speak the truth.

ALC.   *That's* not the way !

You're unlearning what you learnt, sir !   I suppose you want
        to try

What my temper's like. But really, why're you back so
    hastily?
Were the omens unpropitious, or was it some tempest rude   690
Stopped your going to your army as you lately said you would?
    AMPH.   *Lately?* Pray *how lately?*
    ALC.   O, you're teasing me,—*just lately !*
                        now !
    AMPH.   *Now? just lately?* What are you saying? How
    can that be? Tell me how!
    ALC. Do you think that I should mock you? No, 'tis
    you are mocking me!
Calling this your first appearance, though you just left
    hurriedly!
    AMPH.   O what nonsense she is talking!
    SOS.   Wait a bit, for goodness' sake,
'Till she's slept it off a little!
    AMPH.   Why, she's dreaming wide awake!
    ALC. 'Pon my word, I'm wide awake, and wide awake I
    tell you, sir,
Lately, just before the daybreak, I saw him and you.
    AMPH.   Pray where?
    ALC. Here in this house where you live, dear.
    AMPH.   Never! never!
    SOS.   Say no more!   700
When we were asleep, perhaps, our good ship brought us
    from the shore.
    AMPH. What! are you too going to back her?
    SOS.   It's the only thing to do.
If you cross a frenzied mænad, nought but trouble will ensue.
If she's mad, you'll make her madder, and she'll strike you
    all the more.
If you yield, one blow contents her.
    AMPH.   I'm determined as before;

I'll upbraid her that when homeward I my eager steps
addressed,
She refused to greet me.

Sos.   You'll be stirring up a hornet's nest.

Amph.   Silence !—Now, Alcmena, I must ask you one
thing.

Alc.   What you please.

Amph.   Well then, is it pride or folly makes you play
such tricks as these ?

Alc.   What has got into your head, dear, thus to cross-
710   examine me ?

Amph.   Why, before, when I came home, you used to greet
me lovingly,
Welcome me with warm affection, as a modest woman should;
Now I come back home and find you in a very different
mood.

Alc.   Gracious me !   Why, yesterday when you came
home and stood just there,
I both welcomed you and asked you, dearest husband, how
you were ;
And I grasped your hand and kissed you; it was only yesterday.

Sos.   Yesterday you welcomed master ?

Alc.   Yes, and you too, Sosia.

Sos.   Master, I was hoping she would happily bring forth
a son ;
But it's not a son she's big with !

Amph.   What then ?

Sos.   Madness ! other none.

720   Alc.   I'm not mad !   I pray the gods for offspring after
my own heart.
You will get an ample whipping if your master does his
part.

For that omen, omen-maker, you shall get what is your due.

Sos. No, ma'am ; *amples* [1]—I mean *apples*—are the
very thing for *you*.

Then, if you are feeling sickly, you can take and have a bite.

AMPH. Yesterday you saw me here ?

ALC. That I'll affirm from morn till night.

AMPH. Did you dream it ?

ALC. No, we both were wide awake.

AMPH. Ah, woe is me !

Sos. What's the matter ?

AMPH. Why, she's mad.

Sos. O no ! it's biliousness, may be.

Nothing makes one mad so quickly as a bilious attack.

AMPH. When did you, my wife, first feel it ? It's a nasty
thing, alack !

ALC. No, I tell you I'm quite well and in my senses.

AMPH.   Yet you say   730

Yesterday you saw me, when I only got to port to-day !

There I stopped and there I rested in the ship the livelong
night.

Never have I set my foot within this house since to the fight

I set forth against our Teleboian foes and won the day.

ALC. Why, you supped and went to bed with me last
night !

AMPH.   What's that you say ?

ALC. Just the truth.

AMPH. No, not in this at all events ; that's clearly seen.

ALC. At the break of day you hurried to the army.

AMPH.   What do you mean ?

Sos. She's quite right as far as she remembers ; but it
was a dream !

---

[1] The pun in the original depends on the double meaning and pronunci-
ation of *mala*, *viz.*, " apples " and " whippings."

But, ma'am, now that you've awakened, you should offer, so
    I deem,
740 Unto Jove, who sends these portents, salted meat and frank-
    incense.

    ALC.   Hang yourself, sir !

    Sos.   Well, that's what you ought to do, if you have sense.[1]

    ALC.   There, that's twice I've been insulted, yet the rascal
    goes scot free !

    AMPH.   Silence, sir ! Now, tell me, was I here this morn-
    ing verily ?

    ALC.   Who but you told me the story how the battle went
    that day ?

    AMPH.   Ah, you know that also, do you ?

    ALC.   Yes, and you went on to say
That you stormed their city and yourself slew Pterelas fear-
    lessly.

    AMPH.   Did I say so ?

    ALC.   Yes, you did ; and Sosia here was
                       standing by.

    AMPH. [*to Sos.*]   Did you hear me tell her this to-day ?

    Sos.   Why, where could I have heard ?

    AMPH.   Nay, ask *her !*

    Sos.   It never happened in my presence, it's
                 absurd !

    ALC.   Oh, he'll never contradict you !

750   AMPH.   Sosia, come here ! look at me !

    Sos.   Well, I'm looking.

    AMPH.   Truth is what I want and not subserviency.
Did you hear me tell the story here to-day which she relates ?

    Sos.   No, indeed ! you're mad as she is to think twice of
    what she states,

---

[1] Intentionally ambiguous : either "make an offering" or "hang yourself,"

When you know this is the first time we have seen her with
  our eyes.

AMPH. Now then, madam, do you hear him ?

ALC. Yes, I do ! he's telling lies.

AMPH. Won't you then believe your husband ?

ALC. I believe myself as well,

Yes, and better, for I'm certain of the things which now I
  tell.

AMPH. Yesterday you say I came here ?

ALC. Yes, and went away to-day.

AMPH. No, I didn't ; for this is the first time I've been
  home, I say.

ALC. Go on with your contradictions ! next you'll say it 760
  isn't true

That you gave me that gold goblet which you said they'd
  given you.

AMPH. No, indeed, I never said so, neither did I give it,
  though

It was always my intention, yes, and is still, to do so.

But who told you ?

ALC. You yourself did, and I took from your own hand

That same goblet.

AMPH. Stop, I pray you !—Sosia, I can't
  understand

How she knew I'd been presented with that drinking cup of
  gold ;

Unless *you* came here before me, when I sent you up, and
  told.

Sos. No, by Pollux, I've not told her, no, nor seen her,
  save with you.

AMPH. Well, she is the strangest creature !

ALC. Shall I fetch the goblet ?

AMPH. Do!

770   ALC.   So be it !   Go in the house and fetch that goblet,
           Thessala,
       Which to-day my husband gave me.

                              [*Exit Thessala into the house.*]

           AMPH.   Here a minute, Sosia !
       It will be a most stupendous marvel, it must be confest,
       If she's got that goblet.
           SOS.   Nonsense ! why, it's shut up in this chest,
       Sealed with your own signet.
           AMPH.   Is the seal unbroken ?
           SOS.   Come and see !
           AMPH. [*examining the chest*].   Yes, it's all right, as I sealed
           it.
           SOS.   Master, be advised by me !
       Send her off to the asylum.
           AMPH.   Something must be done that way ;
       For she's certainly bewitched and that is all that I can say.

               [*Enter Thessala with the goblet.*]

           ALC.   Here's your goblet !
           AMPH.   Let me see it !
           ALC.   There, then, scan it as you please,
       You who give, and then deny it ! now your doubts shall be
           at ease !
       Pray is this the goblet which they gave you ?
780   AMPH. [*taking the goblet*].   Jove ! what do I see ?
       Yes, it is the selfsame goblet ! Sosia, that settles me !
           SOS.   Either she's the queen of witches and the very
           cleverest,
       Or the goblet must be here, sir [*pointing to the chest*].

AMPH.   Quickly, then, undo the chest.

Sos.   But it's sealed up : why undo it?   Oh, we're getting
    on to-day !

You've brought forth a twin Amphitryon, I another Sosia.

If the goblet's got another, we're all doubled, by this light !

AMPH.   I must open and inspect it.

Sos.   First see if the seal's all right,

Then you can't blame me, sir, after.

AMPH.   O come, open it, my lad !

For this woman with her fooling means to drive me raving mad.

ALC.   Now, then, where could I have got it, but from 790
    you ?   Pray tell me where ?

AMPH.   I must look into the matter.

Sos. [*opening the chest*].   Jupiter !   O Jupiter !

AMPH.   What's the matter ?

Sos.   There's no goblet in the chest !

AMPH.   What's that I hear ?

Sos.   It's a fact !

AMPH.   Well, you'll be tortured if it's not forthcoming
    here.

ALC.   Here it is though !

AMPH.   Who was he who gave it you?

ALC.   Why, you who ask.

Sos.   O you're tricking me !   You came up secretly your
    plan to mask

From the ship another road, and took away the goblet, then

Gave it her, and straight returned, and sealed the casket up
    again.

AMPH.   O confound it !   Will you help her to keep up
    this mad idea ?

[*To Alc.*]   Yesterday, you say, we came home ?

ALC.   Yes, and when you had got here,

We exchanged our salutations, and I gave you a sweet kiss.   800

Sos. Ah, this kissing doesn't suit him !

Amph.   I shall have to see to this.

Alc. Then you washed—

Amph.   And after washing ?

Alc.   Came to supper.

Sos.   Ah, bravo !
Go ahead!

Amph. Don't interrupt, sir ! All the story let us know.

Alc. Supper laid, you supped with me, and I sat down
along with you.

Amph. On the same couch ?

Alc.   Yes, the same.

Sos.   This banquet makes him look
                         quite blue !

Amph. Let her tell her story through, sir ! Well, and
after we had fed?

Alc. Then you said that you were sleepy, so we rose and
went to bed.

Amph. Where did *you* sleep ?

Alc.   In our chamber, in the bed along with you.

Amph. Oh, you've killed me !

Sos.   What's the matter ?

Amph.   Ah, her words have stabbed me
                         through !

Alc. Why, my darling—

Amph.   Speak not to me !

Sos.   What's the matter ?

S10 Amph.   I'm undone !
For my wife has lost her honour, woe is me ! whilst I was gone.

Alc. O my husband, I beseech you, do not speak such
words of shame !

Amph. I your husband ? Do not call me, false one, by
so false a name !

Sos. [*aside*]. Here's a mess, if from a husband he's got
   turned into a wife !

ALC. What's my fault, that I should hear such words
   from you, my dearest life ?

AMPH. You proclaim your deeds ; you needn't ask me to
   repeat your shame.

ALC. I'm your married wife, and, therefore, I was with
   you. Where's the blame ?

AMPH. You were with me, were you? Why, her impudence has got no end !

If you haven't any shame, I think you might at least pretend.

   ALC. By your gross insinuations you insult my family.   820

You may try, but you will never catch me in immodesty.

AMPH. By the immortal gods, I ask you, do you know
   me, Sosia ?

Sos. Rather !

AMPH. Did I sup last night, then, in our ship upon the
   bay ?   .

ALC. I too can bring witnesses to prove the truth of all
   I've said.

Sos. Well, to tell the truth, this business sadly puzzles
   my poor head.

There must be some other fellow, called, like you, Amphitryon,

Who looks after all your business and your wife when you
   are gone.

And, though I was much astonished at that other Sosia,

Yet I'm more astonished still at this Amphitryon, I must say.

   AMPH. No, some sorcerer or other has, I fear, been 830
   fooling her.

ALC. By the realm of Jove supreme and mother Juno,
   hear me swear—

Juno, whom above all others I should reverence and dread—

That no mortal man but you has ever been within my bed,
Or has sought to hurt my honour.

AMPH. Would to Heaven that it were true !

ALC. So it is, but if you won't believe me, what am I to
do ?

AMPH. You're a woman, and swear boldly !

ALC. When a woman's innocent,
It becomes her in her answers to be bold and confident.

AMPH. Bold enough !

ALC. Because I'm pure.

AMPH. In *words* you're pure as anything !

ALC. Not such dowry did I bring you as most other
women bring,

840 But a bosom free from passion and a modest heart and pure,
Fearing God, loving my parents, of my friends' affection sure,
Pliant to your will and bounteous in kind offices to you.

Sos. Well, by Pollux, she's a model of all virtues, if that's
true.

AMPH. I am certainly bewitched, for who I am I cannot
tell.

Sos. You're Amphitryon ! O take care, or *you* will lose
yourself as well ;
For since coming off our travels we are getting changed
about.

AMPH. Madam, I must have this matter definitely sifted
out.

ALC. That is my most earnest wish too.

AMPH. Tell me this, then, if you please !
Shall I bring up from the vessel your relation Naucrates ?

850 He came in the same ship with us. Now, supposing he
denies
That I did as you affirm, what should you suffer for your
lies ?

Have you any cause to show why you should not be put
 away?

Alc. None, if I'm proved guilty.

Amph.   Well, then, that's agreed.—Now, Sosia,

Take these fellows[1] in, and I will go fetch Naucrates straightway.

     [Exit Amphitryon to the harbour.]

Sos. Now, there's no one left but us, ma'am ; therefore
 tell me seriously,

Is there any other Sosia in the house who's just like me?

Alc. Get away from me, you slave, you! worthy of your
 lord!

Sos.   I'm gone !

    [Exit Sosia and slaves into the house.]

Alc. Oh, I'm lost in dire amazement ! What has set my
 husband on

Without either rhyme or reason to bring charges such as
 these?

Well, whate'er it is, I'll learn it from my kinsman Naucrates. 860

     [Exit Alcmena into the house.]

JUPITER.

[Enter from the town (?) Jupiter as Amphitryon.]

Jup. I am Amphitryon, Sosia's my slave,

The same who turns to Mercury when he likes ;

And in the upper attic is my home ;

And sometimes, when I please, I'm Jupiter.

However, just as soon as I get here,

Amphitryon I become and change my garb.

Now am I come here from regard to you,

    Baggage carriers and attendants.

             E

So as not to leave the comedy unfinished,
And at the same time to assist Alcmena,
870 Who, innocent as she is, is foully blamed.
For I should be in fault to let my sins
Fall on the shoulders of the innocent.
Now I'll pretend to be Amphitryon,
Just as before, and I will throw the household
Into the most extreme perplexity;
Then afterwards I'll make all straight again,
And bring Alcmena help in her sore need,
And cause her at one painless birth to bear
One son for me, another for her husband.
880 I've ordered Mercury to follow close,
To get me what I want. Now I'll accost her.

ALCMENA. JUPITER.

[*Enter Alcmena from the house.*]

ALC. I cannot stay in the house! To think that I
Should be accused of vileness by my husband!
What he has done he swears he never did
With noisy repetition; and maintains
That I've committed crimes that never happened,
And then expects that I shall pass it over!
By Pollux, I will not! must I endure
This false and shameful charge? No! I will leave him,
If he does not apologise and swear
890 He's sorry that he blamed my innocence.

JUP. [*aside*]. I see that I must do what she demands,
If I'm to set her loving heart at rest.
My deeds have caused annoyance to Amphitryon:
My amorous passion, through no fault of his,
Has tortured him; now, through no fault of mine,

His wrath and taunts recoil upon my head.

ALC. See! here he comes, who charged unhappy me
With shame!

JUP.   Dear wife, I want a word with you.
Why turn your back?

ALC.   It is a way I have!
I always hate to look at enemies.   900

JUP. Eh? enemies?

ALC.   Just so! I speak the truth.
But probably you'll say that *that's* a lie!

JUP. Don't be so vexed! [*laying his hand on her.*]

ALC.   Pray take away your hand!
For surely, if you're sensible and wise,
Since you declare and deem that I'm unchaste,
You'll never speak another word to me
In jest or earnest! If, indeed, you're not
The foolishest of fools!

JUP.   Well, if I said it,
That doesn't make you so, nor did I mean it;
So I've come back to clear myself to you.
I never felt so sad and sick at heart   910
As when you told me you were vexed with me.
"Why did I say it?" I'll explain to you.
I never really thought you were unchaste,
But I was curious to try your temper,
To see what you would do and how you'd take it.
All that I said just now, I said in joke,
Just for a bit of fun. Ask Sosia!

ALC. Why don't you fetch my kinsman Naucrates,
Whom you affirmed that you would fetch as witness
That you had not been here?

JUP.   That was a joke!   920
It isn't fair to take it seriously.

ALC. One thing I know, it cut me to the heart.

JUP. By thy fair hand, Alcmena, I entreat
Forgive me, pardon me, and don't be angry!

ALC. I, by my virtue, have disproved your charges;
Now, since I've kept myself from shameless deeds,
I choose to turn my back on shameless words.
Farewell! Keep your own things and give me mine.
Bid my attendants follow.

JUP. Are you mad?

ALC. If you will not, then I'll go by myself,
930 And take as my attendant Modesty.

JUP. Stay! I will swear an oath at your dictation
That I believe my wife is virtuous.
If I play false, then, supreme Jupiter,
I pray thee, ever curse Amphitryon!

ALC. Nay, rather bless him! [1]

JUP. So I trust he may!
For 'tis a true oath I have pledged to you.
Now you're no longer angry?

ALC. N-n-no!

JUP. That's right.
For in the life of men 'tis often thus;
They grasp a pleasure, then they grasp a pain.
940 Quarrels arise, then they are reconciled.
But if, perchance, quarrels like this occur,
And then again good feeling is restored,
They're twice as good friends as they were before.

ALC. You should at first have minded not to say it;
But, as you clear yourself so handsomely,
Why, I must put up with it. Let it pass!

JUP. Then bid clean vessels be prepared for me,
That I may offer up the votive gifts

---

[1] What an admirable touch this is!

I vowed in camp, should I get safely home.

    ALC.   I'll see to that.

    JUP.   Call hither Sosia.

I'll send him to invite to lunch with us   950

Good Blepharo, the pilot of our ship.

[*Aside.*] He'll lose his lunch and find himself the fool,

When I turn out Amphitryon neck and crop.

    ALC.   I wonder what he's muttering to himself.

But the door opens. Here comes Sosia.

SOSIA. JUPITER. ALCMENA.

[*Enter Sosia from the house.*]

    SOS.   Here I am, Amphitryon, ready to receive my lord's commands.

    JUP.   You are come most opportunely.

    SOS.   Tell me, have you shaken hands?

For whene'er I see you happy, I am glad and merry too;

And it's thus in my opinion that a prudent slave should do.

Let him act just like his masters, frame his face to match with 960 theirs;

Melancholy, if his lords are; merry, if they're free from cares.

But come, tell me, have you really got your little quarrel done?

    JUP.   Stop your joking! why, you know that all the time I was in fun.

    SOS.   What, in fun? Well I, for my part, thought you were in serious mood.

    JUP.   I've apologised, and there our quarrel ended.

    SOS.   Very good!

    JUP.   I'll go in and make the offering I have vowed.

    SOS.   Yes, I should so.

    JUP.   You go to the ship and there invite the pilot Blepharo,

With my kind regards, to luncheon when the sacrifice is done.
Sos. I'll be back before you think I'm there.
Jup.   Well, hurry, get back soon.

[Exit Sosia to the harbour.]

970 Alc. Do you mind if I go in and see to all the things
you need?
Jup. Do, my dear, and as you're able, get them ready
with all speed.
Alc. There'll be no delay, I warrant! When you please,
come in the house.
Jup. Well and rightly spoken, darling, as becomes a loving spouse.

[Exit Alcmena into the house.]

Now both the slave and mistress are beguiled;
They think that I'm Amphitryon, but they're wrong.
Now you, O Sosia the divine, come here!
(You hear my words although you are not present)
And drive away Amphitryon from the house,
Some way or other. See, he's coming now!
980 Beguile him for me, while I spend an hour
With my appropriated wife. See to it;
And wait on me (you know just what I want),
While I to my great self make sacrifice!

[Exit Jupiter into the house.]

MERCURY.

[Enter Mercury as Sosia from the town (?)]

Merc. Give way, make way, good people all! Come,
quickly get out of my way!
And let no man be found so bold to seek my headlong
course to stay.

For haven't I, who am a god, as good a right to say to you,
As slavelings in your comedies,[1] " Come, clear the way with-
out ado "?
They come to tell a ship is safe, or some irate old man's at
hand ;
I, in obedience to Jove, have hastened here at his command.
Therefore I have the greater right to bid you quit and clear 990
the way ;
My father summons me, I come, his word and order to obey.
As every good son ought to be, so am I to my worthy sire ;
Now he's in love, I back him up, exhort, stand by, advise,
admire !
And everything that pleases him, to me is also excellent.
He loves ; therein he's wise.   He does quite right to follow
up his bent.
And so should everybody do : that is to say, with honesty.
Well, now he wants Amphitryon fooled, so I'll perform the
trick ; you'll see !
Under your very eyes, good friends, I'll put him in a mortal
funk.
I'll set a garland on my head and then pretend I'm jolly
drunk.
Then will I climb upon the roof and there I'll valorously stand, 1000
And when he comes I'll drive him off, for I shall have the
upper hand.
Although he's *sober* as a judge, I'll swear I will not leave him
dry !
Then straightway Sosia his slave will have to pay the penalty.
He'll think that he's done all I do to-day !   But what is that
to me?
I must obey my father's whims; 'tis mine to serve him
zealously.

Cf. Capt. 791—822.

But here's Amphitryon; he comes ! he'll be deluded properly!
So kindly give your best attention now.
I'll go inside and make up like a drunkard ;
Then climb up on the house and warn him off !

[*Exit Mercury into the house.*]

AMPHITRYON.

[*Enter Amphitryon from the town.*]

AMPH.   When I went for Naucrates, I found he wasn't on
the ship.

1010 No one's seen him in the city ; sure he's given me the slip.
I've gone limping through the squares, gymnasiums, per-
fumeries,
Race course, market place, and shambles, business quarters,
where you please,
Chemists' shops and barbers' rooms, and temples where the
gods are shrined ;
I'm just tired to death with seeking ; Naucrates I nowhere
find.
Now I'm going home, determined to discover from my wife,
Who it is for whom she's ruined and disgraced herself for life.
Rather than I'd let that matter rest unsettled one more day,
I would die. [*Goes to the door and tries to open it.*] What's
this ? the door's locked ! Very pretty, I must say !
Yes ! it fits in well enough with all the rest.   I'll knock and
see.

1020 Open here !   Hallo, who's there ?   Just open this door,
somebody !

MERCURY.   AMPHITRYON.

[*Enter Mercury as Sosia on the roof, crowned with a garland.*]

MERC.   Who is there ?
AMPH.   It's I !
MERC.   O is it ?

AMPH.   So I said.

MERC.   Then Jupiter

And the gods are surely angry with you, you door-hammerer!

AMPH.   What?

MERC.   Just this, that you're about to have a very
warm half-hour!

AMPH.   Sosia!

MERC.   Yes, I'm Sosia, unless my memory's lost its
power.

What do you want?

AMPH.   You scoundrel, dare you stand and ask me what
I want?

MERC.   Yes, I dare.   You've smashed the hinges off our
door, you miscreant!

Did you think we got our doors provided by the Revenue?

What are you staring at, you idiot?   What do you want?
and who are you?

AMPH.   Villain, do you dare to ask me who I am, death-
bed of rods?

Won't my birches make your back blush for your insolence! 1030
Ye gods!

MERC.   When you were a youth, I see you must have
sent your money skipping.

AMPH.   Why?

MERC.   Because in your old age you've come to me to
beg—a whipping!

AMPH.   Oh, I'll make you suffer, housedrudge, for these
words so bold and free.

MERC.   I will offer you—

AMPH.   Pray what?

MERC.   A holocaust of misery!

[At this point a gap occurs in the MSS.   We may probably fill it up as follows.   The present scene concludes by

Mercury's emptying a vessel of dirty water over Amphitryon,
and driving him away from the house.   In the next scene
Sosia returns from the harbour, and is met by Amphitryon,
who thrashes him soundly for his supposed conduct in the
previous scene.   Alcmena comes out to see what the dis-
turbance is about, and is in turn attacked by Amphitryon.
She is convinced that he is mad, and returns into the house.
Then the confusion is brought to a climax by the entry of
Jupiter, still disguised as Amphitryon.   The altercation between the two Amphitryons is broken off by the arrival of
Blepharo, to whom they appeal to say which of them is the
true Amphitryon.   But Blepharo is completely puzzled, and
refuses to decide.   At this point the play again resumes.]

BLEPHARO.   AMPHITRYON.   JUPITER.

*[Enter from the house Blepharo, Amphitryon, and Jupiter, as
Amphitryon.]*

BLEPH.   Share yourselves among yourselves, for I must
go ; my business calls.
Never did I see such marvels as I've seen within these walls.
AMPH.   Blepharo, I beg you, stay and be my advocate !
BLEPH.   Farewell !
I'm no use as advocate, for whose to be I cannot tell.
                              [Exit Blepharo to the harbour.]
JUP.   I'm going in.   My wife's in labour.
                              [Exit Jupiter into the house.]
AMPH.   Woe is me !   I'm quite undone !
1040What am I to do when all my friends and advocates are
gone ?
Never shall that villain mock me unavenged, whoe'er he be !
I'll betake me to the King and tell him what's befallen me.
Yes, I will take vengeance on him, with his wizard's im-
pudence,

Who has turned quite topsy-turvy all my people's common
  sense.
Where is he?   He's gone inside the house! and doubtless
  to my wife!
Thebes contains no man so wretched!   What's the use of
  my poor life?
No one knows me; everybody at his will makes fun of me.
Yes!   I'll burst into the house, and every creature that I see,
Be it maid, or man, or wife, or that accursed adulterer,
Or my father, or my grandsire, I will slay him then and there! 1050
Nor shall Jove nor all the gods prevent me, wish it as they may.
I will do what I've resolved!   Now then, to burst the door
  straightway!

[*Amphitryon rushes to the door, but a sudden flash of lightning
    strikes him to the ground.*]

BROMIA.   AMPHITRYON.

[*Enter Bromia from the house; Amphitryon still lying sense-
    less on the ground.*]

BR.   Alas! my hopes and vital force and strength lie
  buried in my breast;
All my self-confidence has gone; my heart is sinking, I pro-
  test!
For everything—both earth, and sea, and sky—is evidently
  bent
On crushing and destroying me!   Poor wretched girl, how
  I am spent!
Such miracles have happened in our house!   Alas for
  wretched me!
I feel so faint!   I want a drink!   I'm wrecked and shattered
  utterly!

My head is splitting! I'm half deaf! My dazzled eyes can
  hardly see!
1060I am the wretchedest of girls; no one in sadder plight
  could be!
For when, this luckless day, my mistress in her pangs cried
  out to heaven,
With a crashing and smashing, and thundering and sundering,
  and sudden bright flashing the sky it was riven!
As everyone fell prostrate on the spot, a mighty voice we
  hear
  Blended with the crash: "Alcmena, help is coming; do
    not fear!
  Heaven's lord is come, propitious to thy children and
    to thee!"
"Arise," it says, "ye who have fallen to the ground in
  dread of me!"
  I rose! The house seemed in a blaze,
  And flashed and glowed with fiery rays.
Alcmena calls me to her side; my own concern appals me;
But duty still prevails; I run to ask her why she calls
  me.
1070And there I see that she's brought forth two lovely, lusty,
  little boys;
But none of us had noticed it, for there was neither cry nor
  noise.
[*Seeing Amphitryon.*] What is this? Who's this old man,
  Who lies before our door so wan?
  The lightning must have struck him there!
  Yes, so it has! By Jupiter,
  He lies as still as he were dead!
  Who is it that has thus been sped?
  Why, it's my lord Amphitryon!
Amphitryon!

AMPH.   I'm killed !
BR.   Get up !
AMPH.   I'm dead.
BR.   O no ! give me your hand !
AMPH.   Who's this ?
BR.   It's Bromia, your maid.
AMPH.   I'm struck by lightning ; I
                            can't stand !
I feel as if I'd been in Hell !   But tell me, why you came
    out here ?
BR.   We girls were driven out, alarmed like you, in terror
    and in fear.
For in the house in which you live, strange miracles are com-1080
    ing thick !
Ah, woe is me ! my mind is still a-wandering !
AMPH.   But tell me quick,
Am I your lord Amphitryon ?
BR.   Of course !
AMPH.   Just look again.
BR.   You are
AMPH.   Ah, she's the only slave I have who's got a head
    that's fixed on square !
BR.   O no, they all are right enough.
AMPH.   But I, alas ! am going mad !
My wife's dishonoured !
BR.   No, she's not; Amphitryon, I'll make you glad !
Proof I'll furnish you undoubted that your wife is chaste
    and pure.
In a few brief words I'll tell you signs and tokens that
    are sure.
First of all, Alcmena's brought forth twins, two boys, alive
    and well.
AMPH.   Twins, you say ?

Br.   Yes, twins !

Amph.   Heaven helps me !

Br.   Pray let me my story tell !

1090 Then you'll see how good the gods are to your wife and you
  as well.

Amph. Well, say on !

Br.   This very morning your good wife was taken ill.

As she felt her pains beginning, just as other ladies will,

She invoked the gods immortal, that their help might be
  revealed,

With pure hands and covered head ; and then straightway
  the thunder pealed

With a mighty crash ; at first we thought the house was
  tumbling down.

Then it glowed with golden glory everywhere—Why do you
  frown ?

Amph. Get this fooling done, I pray you! then perhaps
  you'll let me go.

What came next ?

Br.   While this was doing not a single cry of woe,

Or of natural lamentation from your lady we observed ;

Without pain she bore those children.

1100 Amph.   Well, however she's deserved

At my hands, I'm very glad.

Br.   O let that be and hear my tale !

Then she bade us wash the babies ; so we popped them in
  the pail.

But the youngster I was washing, O how big he was and
  strong !

All the swaddling clothes were useless ; for his limbs were
  far too long.

Amph. It's a marvellous story truly! If the facts are
  as you say,

I don't doubt my wife has had assistance from the gods
>   to-day.

>   BR.   O that's nothing to what's coming!   When we'd put
>   them in their cot,

Two great crested snakes came gliding, and into the tank[1]
>   they got;

Then they lifted up their heads—

>   AMPH.   And killed the babes?   Oh say it not!

>   BR.   Don't be frightened!   Well, the serpents look about 1110
>   on every side,

Soon as they behold the babies, straight towards the cot they
>   glide.

I, retreating, pulled and dragged it backwards, fearing for
>   their sakes,

Frightened for myself as well; but all the more those dread-
>   ful snakes

Followed after.   When that baby saw the snakes, as if in play

Quick he jumps from out his cradle and attacks them right
>   away;

Then he grasps them swiftly, deftly, seizing one in cither
>   hand.

>   AMPH.   O, it's marvellous!   it's dreadful!   more than I
>   can understand.

Nameless horror at your story all my senses overtakes!

What comes next?   Go on and tell me!

>   BR.   Why, the baby killed the snakes!

While all this is passing, someone calls your wife in accents 1120
>   clear.

>   AMPH.   Who was that?

>   BR.   The King of gods and men, most sovereign
>   Jupiter.

---

[1] The *impluvium*, a small water tank, which stood in the middle of
the atrium or hall of a Roman house.

And he said that with Alcmena he had shared the marriage
    bed,
And that baby was his offspring by whose hand the snakes
    were dead ;
But the other child, he said, was yours.
    Amph.   Ah well, I needn't care
If I'm graciously permitted my best joys with Jove to share.
Go in home and bid the servants all the requisites prepare,
That with many a victim I may seek the grace of Jupiter.
I will go consult Tiresias, that renowned and ancient seer.
1130 Ah, what's this?   How loud it thundered!   Hear my prayer,
    in mercy hear !

JUPITER.   AMPHITRYON.

[*Enter Jupiter from above.*]

    Jup.   Be of good cheer, Amphitryon, I come
To help both thee and all thy family.
Thou needst not fear !   These seers and soothsayers,
Dismiss them straight ; for I will tell thee all
That has been and that shall be, better far
Than they can do ; for I am Jupiter.
Then first I do confess I loved Alcmena,
And made her mother of a lusty son.
You'd done the same before you went away
To join the army ; both were born at once.
The one of them, begotten of my seed,
1140 Shall bring immortal glory to thy name.
Restore Alcmena to thy wonted love !
She hath not done one deed deserving blame ;
She was compelled.   Now I return to heaven !
                  [*Exit Jupiter above.*]

AMPH.   I will do just what you bid me, if you'll bring
    your words to pass,
Go within and see my wife, and send away Tiresias.
    Now, kind hearers, clap your hands,
    For it is great Jove commands.

ASINARIA;

OR,

THE ASS-DEALER.

INTRODUCTION.

THE Asinaria is, as the prologue informs us, translated from the Greek play 'Ονηγός, by Demophilus, an author of whom nothing more is known. The name means "The Comedy of the Ass-dealer." It is an admirable play, full of rollicking humour, and abounding in effective situations. Owing to the grossness of the condition on which Demænetus undertakes to find the money his son requires to purchase his sweetheart, the play is little read. I have, by a few trifling omissions and alterations, succeeded in eliminating all that is offensive to modern taste; at least, I hope so. Nothing is known as to the date of the play; but its excellence would seem to indicate it as one of our poet's later works.

DRAMATIS PERSONÆ.

LIBANUS - - - *Slave of Demænetus.*

DEMÆNETUS - - - - *An old man.*

ARGYRIPPUS - *His son, in love with Philænium.*

CLEÆRETA - - - *Mother to Philænium.*

LEONIDA - - *Fellow-servant of Libanus.*

PHILÆNIUM - *A young lady, daughter to Cleæreta.*

DIABOLUS - *A soldier, in love with Philænium.*

A PARASITE.

ARTEMONA - - - *Wife of Demænetus.*

AN ASS-DEALER.

ARGUMENT (*ACROSTIC*).

A GOOD old man, whose lady is his lord,
S eeks money for his son who's fallen in love.
I n doing it, pay is given for some asses,
N ot to the steward, but to Leonida,
A slave of his ; and so the lover gets it.
R ival affection drives Diabolus mad ;
I n wrath he tells the whole thing to the wife,
A nd she runs in and drags her husband off.

PROLOGUE.

PRAY, gentlemen and ladies, pay attention,
And may good fortune wait on me and you,
Our company, our poets, our lessees.
Come, crier, kindly make the crowd all ears!—
There, now, sit down; and mind you charge
    for that.[1]
Now why I'm on the stage, and what I want,
I'll tell you. 'Tis that you may know the name
Of this our play. The plot's extremely simple.
Now I will tell you what I said I would;
Onagos[2] is the name o' the play in Greek;   10
Demophilus[3] wrote, Maccius translated it;
He calls it Asinaria,[4] by your leave.
The comedy is full of wit and mirth.
It's sure to make you laugh; so listen kindly,
And now and always Mars be your defence!

LIBANUS. DEMÆNETUS.

[*Scene: the street in front of the houses of Demœnetus and Clœœreta, which are side by side. Enter Libanus and Demœnetus.*][5]

---

[1] The crier is to charge for being quiet as well as for exercising his function: cf. Poenulus, Prol. 15, *Age nunc reside, duplicem ut mercedem feras.*

[2] *i.e.* The ass-merchant.   [3] A poet otherwise unknown to us.

[4] The ass-comedy: *Asinaria* is an Adjective (sc. *fabula*).

[5] Demænetus has brought Libanus outside to consult him about his

87

LI.   As you would wish your only son to live
And close your eyes in health and happiness,
So I beseech you by your hoary hairs,
By her, whom most you fear, your wife, I mean ;
20 If you don't speak the truth to me to-day,
Then may your wife outlive you many a year,
And while she lives may you find speedy death.
DE.   By all the gods, I'll swear it as you wish :
I see that I must tell you what you ask.
So hard you press me, that I really daren't
Refuse to tell you anything you want ;
So speak out quickly what you fain would know,
And if I know it, you shall know it too.
LI.   Answer me seriously what I shall ask.
Don't tell me any lies !
30   DE.   What *do* you ask?
LI.   Then are you taking me where stone rubs stone? [1]
DE.   What do you say ?   Where in the world is that ?
LI.   Where sinners weep, who feed on barley-meal.
In the cudgel-thumping, fetter-clanking isles,
Where living men are set on by dead oxen. [2]
DE.   Ah, now I see, by Pollux, where it is !
Where barley-meal is ground, you mean to say.
LI.   I neither say nor want to hear it said !

---

son's love affairs. Libanus, not knowing what his master wants, fears
that he is going to be sent off to one of the farms as punishment for
some one or other of his many misdeeds.   Hence the anxiety he
displays.

[1] *i.e.* To the farm where the barley was ground; the stone is of course
the millstone.   Libanus wishes to avoid naming the *pistrinum* (a name
of evil omen to him), and therefore speaks in riddles.

[2] That is, by whips of ox-hide.

Oh, I beseech you, spit out that foul word !

De.   All right ; I'll humour you ! [*spitting*].

Li.   Come, hawk away !

De.   Will *that* do ?   [*spitting again*].

Li.   Nay, from the bottom of your throat !   40

Away !

De.   How far away ?

Li.   Even to the death !

De.   Take care, Sir !

Li.   O, your wife's, I mean, not yours !

De.   For that good jest I pardon all your faults !

Li.   The gods fulfil your wishes !

De.   Listen here !

Why should I ask you this, or threaten you,

Because you didn't tell it me before ?

Or why should I be angry with my son,

As other fathers are ?

Li. [*aside*].   Hallo, what's this ?   50

What can he mean ?   I fear what's coming next.

De.   I'm certain sure, my son has fallen in love

With that Philænium, the girl next door.

Am I right, Libanus ?

Li.   You're on the track.

The thing is so ; but he is very ill.

De.   What's his complaint ?

Li.   His gifts don't match his words.

De.   Then you are backing up my love-sick son ?

Li.   Indeed I am, and so's Leonida.

De.   You do quite right, and you sha'n't lose by it.

But, Libanus, you do not know my wife !   60

Li.   You know her best ; but we have got a notion.

De.   Believe me, she's a fearful trial to me !

Li.   Oh, I believe you, long before you speak !

DE.   All parents, Libanus, who'll be ruled by me,
Will treat their children with indulgent care,
And so they'll make their son their truest friend.
That is my aim ; I want my sons to love me.
I'll be like my own father ; for my sake
In sailor's dress he stole away the girl
70 I loved, by trickery, from her mother's house.
Old as he was, he counted it no shame
To lay the plot, and win his son by kindness.
I'm quite resolved to follow in his steps.
Well, Argyrippus, my son, asked me to-day
To let him have some money for his sweetheart ;
In this I long to gratify my son,
To indulge his passion, and so win his love.
His mother keeps him tied up and confined
As fathers often do : so will not I.
80 And since he's thought me worthy of his trust,
I ought to honour his good disposition.
As he's approached me like a dutiful son,
I want the gold for him to give the girl.

LI.   You want what I'm afraid you'll want in vain.
Your wife brought her slave, Saurea, with her dowry,
And he's more money in his hands than you.

DE.   Ah, yes, I sold my empire for that dowry !
But now I'll briefly tell you what I wish.
What my son wants just now is fifty pounds.[1]
You get it for him !
90 LI.   Where am I to get it ?

DE.   Steal it from me.

---

[1] Lit. twenty *minæ*. The mina was a pound weight of silver, and was worth about £3 15s. sterling ; but it must be remembered that money possessed something like ten times its present purchasing power ; so that £500 would be really a better equivalent.

LI.   What nonsense you do talk!
You send me to steal clothes from nakedness! [1]
Steal it from you! Yes, fly with ne'er a wing!
Steal it from you! You've nothing left to steal,
Unless you first can steal it from your wife.

DE.   Swindle myself, my wife, and Saurea
By any means you can, and get the money.
I swear you shall not suffer if you do.

LI.   Yes, bid me go a-fishing in the air,
A-hunting in the middle of the sea!   100

DE.   Well, take Leonida to be your second.
Devise some plan, contrive some clever trick,
And get the money for my son to-day
To give the girl.

LI.   Look here, Demænetus!
Supposing I should land myself in trouble,
Will you redeem me if the enemy catch me?

DE.   I will.

LI.   All right then; leave it all to me.

DE.   I'll to the market-place.

LI.   Good; off you go!

DE.   Here, stay! [2]

LI.   Well, what?

DE.   Supposing I should want you,
Where shall you be?

LI.   Exactly where I please.   110
[*Aside.*] I'll ne'er again fear any mortal man. [3]

---

[1] *Scotice*, to take the breeks from a Highlander!

[2] Libanus begins to hurry away at once, having got an idea of what
he's going to do.

[3] That is, I see my way to get the money, and no one can hinder me.
cf. Bacch. 225.

No one can hurt me, since in your discourse
You've shown me all the secrets of your soul.
At *you* I'll snap my fingers, if successful.
Now I'll be off and get my plot in train.

DE.   And please observe, you'll find me at the banker's
LI.   In the market?
DE.   If you want me.
LI.   I'll remember.

[Exit Libanus.]

DE.   No slave could be a bigger scamp than this,
Or craftier, or more difficult to dodge.
120 Yet, if you want a thing exactly done,
Tell *him :* he'll rather die a thousand deaths
Than fail to do what he has undertaken.
He'll get that money for my son, I know,
As surely as this is my walking-stick !
But I'll be off to the market, as I purposed ;
There at the banker's I'll await events.

[Exit Demænetus.]

ARGYRIPPUS.

[*Enter Argyrippus hastily from Clæreta's house, having been
turned out.*]

ARG.   Oh, has it come to this?   Kicked out of doors
    by her !
This is the prize for my gifts that she stores by her !
Foe to your friend, and a friend to your foe, you are.
130   Curse you ! I'll soon let the magistrates know you are
Swindler and thief, of young fellows the slaughterer !
Oh, I'll bring ruin on you and your daughter there !
Sea's [1] no more sea when compared with your treachery !

---

[1] The sea is continually used by Plautus as a type of treachery.

There I got gain, which I lost by your witchery.
All my kind gifts I've bestowed so effusively
Only provoke you to treat me abusively.
Now, I'll do you all the mischief in my power, and serve you
   right !
Back to poverty I'll drive you, out of decent people's sight.
Yes, by Jove, I'll make you know, 'ma'am, what you are, and
   what you were   140
In the days before I came and gave my loving heart to her.
Dry bread was a dainty to you in your rags and poverty ;
If you got e'en that, you blessed the gods above on bended
   knee.
Now, you wretch, when things are better, you forget who
   gave good cheer.
Ah, you savage beast ! with hunger will I tame you.   Never
   fear !
I've no reason to be angry with the girl ; she's not to blame ;
She's compelled to do your bidding, tyrant with a mother's
   name !
You I'll be revenged on ! *you* to utter ruin will I send !
Ah ! the wretch ! why, don't you see, she doesn't even
   condescend
Now to come and talk with me, my grace and pardon to
   implore !   150
There ! behold the witch is coming !   Here at last, outside
   the door,
I shall speak my mind.   I couldn't there, inside the house,
   before.

CLEÆRETA.   ARGYRIPPUS.

[*Enter Cleœreta from her house.*]

CLE.   Not one single word of yours should anybody buy
   of me,

Though he tried to strike a bargain with a pound [1] apiece
    for fee.

All the insults you have uttered are just so much sterling
    gold ;

For your heart is nailed and fastened here in Cupid's grip
    and hold.

Ply the oar and hoist the sail and hasten from this loved resort.

Seek the ocean as you may, the storm will drive you back to
    port !

    ARG.   Not another cent of duty to your custom-house I'll
       pay !

160 No ! I'll treat you as your actions merit from this very day,

Though you don't do so to me ! I've not deserved to be
    turned out !

    CLE.   Yes, your tongue can chatter finely, and you'll do
       it ! O, no doubt !

    ARG.   I alone have rescued you from loneliness and
       poverty ;

I alone should wed the maiden, and that's less than's due
    to me.

    CLE.   You alone shall wed her, if alone you give me what
       I ask.

Keep your presents up, and you shall always in her favour
    bask.

    ARG.   There's no limit to this giving ! You are never
       satisfied.

After all that I have given you, you want something else
    beside.

    CLE.   There's no limit to your loving ! there's no satisfying
       you !

170 You've just left her : yet you beg to have another interview.

---

[1] Lit. *Philip*, a golden coin first struck by Philip of Macedon and
very widely used throughout Europe : cf. General Introduction, p. 13.

ARG.   Well, I gave you what you bargained.

CLE.   And I let you see your dear.
You have had your money's worth; "no credit" is our
   motto here.

ARG.   You're unkind !

CLE.   How can you blame me, if I play a mother's part?
Never sculptor, painter, poet, left on record in his art
That a mother helped her daughter's lover, when he wouldn't
   pay.

ARG.   It'll pay you to be gentle ; else you'll drive me
   clean away.

CLE.   No, sir! She who spares a lover is unkind to her
   own flesh.
For a lover's like a fish ; no good at all unless he's fresh !
Then he's full of juice and tender; you can cook him
   any way ;
Stew him, fry him, take your choice ; it doesn't matter which
   you say.   180
So your lover longs to give—" Do ask for something—I'm no
   churl !"
Doesn't care how much he loses, thinks of nothing but the
   girl.
Wants to please her, wants to please me, wants to please my
   little page,
Wants to please my men and maidens, yes, extends his
   patronage,
Your fresh lover, to my lap-dog, so to be a welcome guest.
That's the truth.   And every one must look to his own
   interest.

ARG.   Yes, it's true.   I've learnt the lesson and I've had
   to pay the price.

CLE.   If you'd anything to give me, now, you'd talk as
   nice as nice.

But because you haven't, you demand with threats my
daughter's hand.

ARG.   No, I don't.

CLE.   Nor I don't either let you have her,
190   understand !

Still in pity of your youth and gentle blood, I'll offer this :—

As you've cared more for our profits than for your own
dignities—

If you'll find five hundred pounds [1] and pay it down upon the
nail,

For the great respect I bear you, you shall have her without
fail.

ARG.   If I can't ?

CLE.   Oh, I sha'n't trust you.   Someone else
shall have her then.

ARG.   Where's the money I have given you ?

CLE.   Spent : it can't be used again.

If your cash would last for ever, I'd not ask a penny more.

True, for day and night and water we've not got to pay a
score ;

But for other necessaries we are forced to pay cash down ; [2]

200 That's the custom with the bakers and the vintners in
town ;

"Pay your cash and take your purchase !" Well, it's just
the same with me.

Day and night my hands have eyes, and only trust what they
can see.

Quoth the proverb "There's no getting"[3]—you know what !—
I'll say no more.

---

[1] Two talents.   The (Attic) talent was equal to sixty *Minæ* and was
worth about £225 sterling.   This offer is of course sarcastic : cf. p. 90, note.

[2] Lit. " we have to pay on Greek credit," *i.e.* with no credit at all.

[3] *Coactio* (MSS.), very obscure. Clexreta quotes the beginning of a

Arg. Oh yes! now you've picked my pockets, you can
turn me out o' door.
This is not the way you used me, when I had the cash to
spend,
When you used to flatter me and pay me compliments no end.
Then your house was wreathed in smiles to welcome me
whene'er I came,
And you never tired of telling how you loved me still the
same.
When I'd given you a present you were like two turtle doves,
Hanging on my lips and cooing of your deep and tender loves.
How you clung to me and ran to carry out my least desire!   210
Everything that didn't suit or please me, that you shunned
like fire !
Wouldn't dare attempt to do it ; my least wish was made
your law.
Now for my desires or wishes you don't seem to care a straw.
   Cle. O my boy, there's no such fowler as a match-making
mamma !
When your fowler sets his traps, he scatters grain both near
and far,
So the birds grow tame ; thus money must be spent if
profit's sought.
True, the birds get many a meal ; but he is paid, when once
they're caught.
So it is with me, my house here is the trap, the fowler I ;   220
My sweet daughter is the bait ; her lovers are the birds so shy.

saying of which she says Argyrippus knows the conclusion ; so, doubtless,
did the audience ; but we don't. Here is a chance for the reader's ingenuity.
May it have been like our proverb—" There's no getting anything from a
hog but a grunt"? If so, Cleæreta means, " You know what I am and
must expect me to act accordingly." [Fleckeisen reads *coctio* " broker" —
nihili coctiost " a haggler (*i.e.*, haggling) is no good."]

G

They grow tame by kindly greetings, by her soft and warm
   embrace,
By her kisses and her speeches full of sportiveness and grace;
If one steals his arm around her, that just helps the
   fowler's game;
If he takes a kiss, why, let him; I shall catch him all the
   same.
Surely you have not forgotten, who have been at school so
   long!

ARG.   Well then, don't dismiss your scholar half in-
   structed! 'Twould be wrong!

CLE.   Come back bravely, when you've got the money;
   for the present, go!

ARG.   Stay! Stay! Listen! Tell me truly, for your answer
   I must know;
What's the least you'll take to give me her?

230   CLE.   Well, fifty pounds will do.
But if any other suitor brings it first, good-bye to you.

ARG.   Oh, I'll bring it. But there's one thing more
   before you go.

CLE.   Say on.

ARG.   I'm not altogether ruined; some few pounds have
   not yet gone.
I can give you what you ask me; but before I go away,
Promise me we shall be married, if I bring the cash, to-day.

CLE.   Certainly, and if you wish it, have a settlement
   prepared
Wherein all the terms of marriage may be legally declared.

240 Only bring the money with you: that's the only thing I mind.
                    [*Exit Clœreta into her house.*]

ARG.   Yes, your door is very like a custom's office, as I
   find.
If you bring the cash, it opens; if you don't, it's closed to you.

I must find that fifty pounds.   Oh, if I can't, what shall I do?
I must either lose the money or be lost myself, that's plain !
Now to the market ! there I'll see what can be done with
   might and main.
I'll entreat and supplicate my friends, whoe'er comes in my
   way :
Good and bad, I'll try them all and get some answer, yea or nay.
If no friend will lend it me, the interest I'll have to pay.

                 [*Exit Argyrippus to the market-place.*]

LIBANUS.

        [*Enter Libanus from the market-place.*]

   LIB.   Come now, Libanus, wake up and give attention to
   this case !
Hours ago you left your lord and went down to the market- 250
   place.
Did you think you could discover how to come across the
   money,
Snoring till this time of day in idleness ?   No, no, my
   sonny !
Nay, cast off this sluggishness, or you'll be in a pretty fix !
Come, awake, recall to memory some of your old clever
   tricks !
Guard your master; don't you do, as other servants often will,
Who employ, to cheat their masters, all their cunning, craft,
   and skill.
Where to get it ? whom to swindle ? whither shall I steer my
   bark ?
Ah ! the omens favour me ; the birds permit it ! pray you,
   mark !

260 Left, a crow and wood-pecker, and right, a screech-owl and
       a raven
    Give me luck ; I must succeed !   Come, Libanus, don't be a
       craven !
    Ha, the wood-pecker's a-tapping on a birch ! [1]   What does
       that mean ?
    Yes, from master wood-pecker as much as this I surely glean;
    Birch rods are in pickle for me—or for Steward Saurea !
    But what's this ? Leonida is running breathlessly this way !
    Oh, I fear he's spoilt the omens for the tricks I mean to
       play !

                    LEONIDA.   LIBANUS.

    [*Enter Leonida running; he does not at first see Libanus.*]

    LE.   Where on earth am I to find them, Libanus or my
       master's son ?
    Joyfuller than Joy herself I'll make them if this job gets
       done.
    Yes, the greatest spoil and triumph will my advent bring to
       them.
270 Since they've shared their drinks with me and joined in many
       a stratagem,
    When I get this spoil I'm after, I will share it with them too!
    LI. [*aside*].   Oh, he's been a-burgling,[2] has he?   Just the
       sort of thing he'd do !
    Well, I'm sorry for the man that kept the door ! unlucky
       cuss !

    ---

    [1] Lit. *an elm ;* the elm being the tree from which rods were made for
    punishing slaves. But the word I have used will have a more feeling
    sense for the English reader.
    [2] Cf. " When the enterprising burglar's not a-burgling," etc., Gilbert,
    Pirates of Pensance, II. ; and Murray has the word.

LE. All my life I'd be a slave if I could meet with
Libanus.

LI. [*aside*]. Oh, if it depends on me, you'll be a slave
until the close !

LE. Might I see him, from my back I'd give two hundred
swelling blows!

LI. [*aside*]. See, he offers all he has ! His treasure's all
upon his back.

Le. If he let's this chance get past him, he may follow on
its track,

Horse and chariot, but he'll never catch it, once it gets away :

In despair he'll leave his master, fill his foes with joy to-day ! 280

But if we can bravely seize the chance that now presents
itself,

We'll enrich our noble masters with illimitable pelf,

Full of endless joy and gladness both to father and to son ;

They'll be under obligation all their lives for what we've
done,

Fettered to us by our kindness.

LI. [*aside*].   He said " fettered," 'pon my troth ! [1]

I don't like it ; I'm afraid he's making mischief for us both.

LE. I'm undone if I can't find that Libanus. What *is* he
doing ?

LI. [*aside*]. Now he's seeking a companion who will go
with him to ruin !

I don't like it ; it's a bad sign first to sweat and then to
shiver !

LE. Fool I am, to tie my feet and let my tongue run on 290
for ever !

I must bind her down to silence, cutting up this precious
day !

---

[1] The objection of the Greeks and Romans to utter unlucky words is
well known.

Li. [*aside*].   O, the wretch! to bind his best protectress
  in this shameful way!
For whene'er he gets in mischief, she is perjured for his
  blunder!
Le.   I must hurry off or I shall be too late to get the
  plunder.
Li. [*aside*].   Eh? what? plunder! I'll accost him! I won't
  go without my share.
[*Aloud.*]   Hey! good morning! How d'ye do?   Come,
  don't you hear me shouting, there?
Le.   Ah, you training ground for scourges!
Li.   What are you doing, prison bird?
Le.   Good old lodging-house for fetters!
Li.   Switches' sweetheart, how've you fared?
Le.   How much do you think you weigh now, with your
  clothes off?
Li.   I don't know.
Le.   No, I rather thought you didn't; so I weighed you
300   long ago.
Bound and naked, hanging by your feet you weigh a hundred
  pounds.
Li.   How d'ye prove it?
Le.   Oh, I'll tell you on the most convincing
                        grounds.
When a hundred pounds exactly hung suspended from your
  feet,
And your hands were shackled up and fastened to the beam
  so neat,
You weighed neither less nor more, but were—the same old
  scoundrel still!
Li.   Hang you!
Le.   No! sir! Servitus [1] has left *you* that by his last will.

The god of slavery.

Li.   Come, I say, let's stop this chaffing !   Come to business speedily !

What's this matter that's turned up ?   Nay, you can safely
trust in me.

Le.   If you want to lend a hand to help our master's
amorous son,

Such a chance presents itself !   but there'll be risk before it's 310
done !

Oh, the executioners will have a regular festival !

Now for cheek and craftiness, my Libanus !   we need it
all.

I've invented such a piece of villainy that you and I

Shall have torments heaped upon us, and deserve them
thoroughly.

Li.   Ah, I wondered what my shoulder-blades were itching
for to-day :

Now I see they were foretelling trouble that was on the way.

Tell me what it is, however.

Le.   Great the risk but great the plunder.

Li.   Then let all the world together pile their tortures on,
by thunder !

I've a back, I guess, can bear 'em ; yes, I'll give 'em all the
bluff !

Le.   Only keep that courage up, my boy, and we are safe 320
enough.

Li.   Nay, if backs can pay the piper, I would rob the
Revenue ;

Then deny it, and stick to it, and be perjured through and
through.

Le.   That's true valour which, if need be, is in suffering
evils bold.

If you suffer evils bravely, you will stuff your purse with
gold.

LI.   O get on and tell me quickly ; I just long for misery.

LE.   Easy then with all your questions ; let me rest; why, don't you see

That I still am out of breath with running ?

LI.   All right, I can stay

Till you're ready ; if you like until you die.

LE.   Where's master, eh ?

LI.   At the market-place ; his son is in the house—

LE.   I've got enough !

LI.   O then, you've been made a millionaire !

330   LE.   Come, stop your silly stuff !

LI.   Right you are ! my ears are itching till your precious news you mention.

LE.   Listen then, and you shall know as much as I.

LI.   I'm all attention !

LE.   Good !   Do you remember some Arcadian asses that were sold

By our steward to a trader come from Pella ?

LI.   Yes : that's old.

LE.   Well, then, he's sent on the money to be paid to Saurea

For those asses ; and the fellow with the money's come to-day.

LI.   Where's the man ?

LE.   Why, would you eat him, if you got him in your sight ?

LI.   Wouldn't I ? but stay a bit—you mean the asses— am I right ?

340 Old and lame, whose hoofs were worn off right away up to their thighs ?

LE.   Yes; and when you wanted birches, they would bring the fresh supplies.

LI.   Ay ! and take you to the farm [1] in fetters !

---

[1] Where slaves were sent, as we have seen already, for punishment.

LE.   What a memory!
Well, as I was at the barber's, in he comes, and asks of me,
If I knew Demænetus, the son of Strato. "Yes, I have
That distinguished honour," says I, "and, in fact, I am his
    slave."
Then I showed him where our house is.
    LI.   Get on! What's the next thing, eh?
    LE.   Well, he says he's brought the money for our
      steward, Saurea,
Fifty pounds for those same asses; but he doesn't know the
    man,
Though he knows Demænetus as well as anybody can.
When he'd done his yarn—
    LI.   What then?
    LE.   Well, listen! ain't I telling you?   350
Straight I turn myself into a splendid fellow, spick-span new!
And I tell him *I'm* the steward! Then replied my country
    tyke :—
" But, by Pollux, I don't know your Saurea, nor what he's like.
" Oh, you needn't get so savage; kindly fetch your master
    here;
" I know him; and then I'll pay the money over, never
    fear!"
Well, I said I'd fetch the master, and then wait for him at
    home.
He'll be going to have a bath; and when that's over, here
    he'll come.
Now, what trick shall we be up to? Tell me quickly!
    LI.   Well, dear sonny,
We've to swindle our friend Saurea and the stranger of that
    money.
Come, we've got to rough it out! Suppose the stranger gets 360
    here first,

Bringing that same money with him, then our bubble will be
  burst.
For to-day the old man took me, drew me quietly aside ;
Threatened that both you and I should feel the birch upon
  our hide,
If we didn't get this day for Argyrippus fifty pound.
Then he gave us full permission, if we could, to get around
Both the steward and his wife ; and promised he would help
  us too.
Go now to the market-place, and tell him what we're going
  to do.
You, Leonida, are going to be the steward Saurea,
When the dealer brings the money for the asses.

LE.   As you say !

370 LI.   Meanwhile I'll just keep him quiet, if he happens to
  come here.

LE.   O, I say !

LI.   What's that ?

LE.   Supposing I should soundly box your ear
When I'm shamming to be Saurea, don't you let your temper
  rise.

LI.   See, my friend, you'd best be careful not to touch
  me, if you're wise.
You'll be sorry that you changed your name, if you begin to
  whack.

LE.   Suffer it with patience.

LI.   Nay, *you'll* suffer, when I hit you back.

LE.   But I tell you, it's his custom.

LI.   And I tell you what I'll do.

LE.   Don't refuse me !

LI.   Oh, I promise I can hit as hard as you.

LE.   Well, I'm off ! I know you'll bear it like a man.
  What's this ? Hallo !

Here he is! I'll cut and run! Meanwhile, you keep him
   here in tow.
I must tell the master of it.

   LI.   Quick! about your business go!   380

Ass Dealer. Libanus.

[Exit Leonida to the market ; enter from the other side the Ass-
Dealer, dressed in a chlamys, the Greek national dress, to
indicate that he came from abroad, and a slave.]

  Ass-D.   Unless I've been directed wrong, this is the
   house, I'm sure,
Where dwells Demænetus. Go, boy, and knock upon the
   door,
And if the steward Saurea's in, just ask him to come here.

  LI.   Who's smashing down our door like this?[1]   Hallo
   there! Do you hear?

  Ass-D. Why, no one touched it! Are you mad?

  LI.   Ah well, I thought you'd
                       knocked,
Because I saw you coming here. Indeed, I should be
   shocked
To see our door get thrashed by you; I love my fellow-slaves.

  Ass-D. Your door will ne'er be broken down, if every
   one who craves
An entrance has so short a time to wait; it can't be shorter.

  LI.   Ah, that's a way our door has got : it always calls the 390
   porter,
Whene'er it sees a fellow come who looks too vigorous
At kicking! But who is't you seek?

   Ass-D.   I want Demænetus.

---

[1] The Roman slaves seem to have been just as sensitive about undue
knocking at the door as our servants are about ringing the bell.

LI.   He's not at home or you should know.

Ass-D.   Well, is his steward in?

LI.   He's not.

Ass-D.   Where is he?

LI.   O, he's at the barber's with his chin.

Ass-D.   I met him.   Hasn't he come back?

LI.   He's not.   What is there more?

Ass-D.   If he'd been here, I had for him this fifty pounds.

LI.   What for?

Ass-D.   He sold some asses at the fair to an ass-dealer
      from Pella.

LI.   I know: ah, well, he'll not be long, or I'm no fortune-
      teller!

Ass-D.   But tell me, what's your Saurea like?   [*Aside.*]
      I'll see if it's the same.

400   LI.   He's pot-bellied, with lantern jaws, and hair as red as
      flame,

With savage eyes, of medium height, a frown upon his brow.

Ass-D.   [*aside.*]   No painter could have pictured him
      more faithfully, I vow!

LI.   By Hercules, he's coming now!   See how he shakes
      his head!

If any one should cross his rage, I guess he'll strike him dead!

Ass-D.   Well, if he comes with Hectoring [1] threats and
      eyes with fury flashing,

And lays an angry hand on me, he'll get an angry thrashing!

LEONIDA.   ASS-DEALER.   LIBANUS.

[*Enter Leonida as Saurea from the barber's.*]

LE.   There's no one pays the slightest heed to anything I
      say!

---

[1] Literally *Achillean.*

I ordered Libanus to come to the barber's shop to-day;
He never came; his legs and back shall pay the penalty!

Ass-D.   How arrogant the fellow is!

Li.   O, wretched, wretched me!

Le.   You've been set free, no doubt, to-day!   410

Li.   Have mercy, I beseech!

Le.   O you'll be feeling sorry that you've come within my
reach!

Why weren't you at the barber's as I bade?

Li.   *He* kept me here.

Le.   By Hercules, and if you said that it was Jupiter,
And he himself should plead your cause, I'd flog you, never
doubt.

You'll disobey me, will you, hound?

Li.   Kind stranger, help me out!

Ass-D.   I beg you will not punish him for my sake, Saurea!

Le.   I only wish I had a goad—

Ass-D.   O, do be quiet, pray!

Le.   To stick it in your idle ribs, too tough to feel a blow.
Depart and let me flog this wretch, who irritates me so!   420
An order only given once he swears he never heard;
So you must yell a hundred times, until, upon my word,
I really haven't strength enough to scold and objurgate.
I bade you, villain, shift away that filth from our front gate;
I bade you clear the spiders' webs that clothe these pillars o'er;
I bade you polish, till it shone, the handle of the door.
It's all no use; I might be lame, I have to walk with sticks.[1]
Because three days I've been from home, and trying hard to
fix
On some one who would take a loan, you slumber like a
bear,
And so I find when I come back a pigstye, I declare!   430

_____

[1] *i.e.* for beating slaves.

Take that ! [*striking him*].

LI.   Kind stranger, help me, do !

Ass-D.   Good Saurea, I pray,
For my sake please to let him off.

LE.   Did anybody pay
The carriage of that oil ?

LI.   O yes !

LE.   To whom ?

LI.   Your deputy
Good Stichus.

LE.   Bah, you're flattering ! [1] my deputy is he,
Nor have I got in all the house a more trustworthy slave.
But what about the wine that I let Exærambus have ?
Has he paid Stichus ?

LI.   So I think ; on this my faith I anchor ;
I saw that Exærambus coming hither with his banker.

LE.   That's right ; last time I trusted him he took a year
          to pay ;
440   He's frightened now ; so brings him [2] home and writes the
          cheque straightway.
Has Dromo [3] brought his wages in ?

LI.   But half of it, he said.

LE.   What of the rest ?

LI.   He'll pay it you, as soon as he gets paid.
They're keeping it until he's done the job that was agreed.

LE.   The cups lent Philodamus, has he brought them
          back, d'ye heed ?

LI.   No.

LE.   Better give a thing away than lend it to a
          friend !

---

[1] By mentioning that I have a deputy or under-slave.   [2] *i.e.* the banker.
[3] A slave of Demænetus, who has been let out on hire.

Ass-D.   O hang his temper! I'll be off!

Li. [*aside to Le.*]   Come, bring this to an end.
D'ye hear him?

Le. [*aside to Li.*]   Yes; I'll hold my tongue!

Ass-D. [*aside.*]   At last he's ceased his jangle!
I'd better speak to him before he starts again to wrangle.
[*aloud.*]   How soon can you attend to me?

Le.   Have you been waiting long?
By Hercules, I didn't see you; pray don't take it wrong!   450
My anger so obstructs my sight.

Ass-D.   I've not the slightest doubt!
I've called to see Demænetus.

Le.   And does he [1] say he's out?
Well, never mind; that money you can pay *me* just the same;
I'll give you a receipt in full in my good master's name.

Ass-D.   I think I'd rather pay you when Demænetus is
    by.

Li. [*to Ass-D.*]   My master trusts him!

Ass-D.   Him I'll pay, but not upon the sly.

Li.   O give it him; I'll take the risk: I'll make the thing
    all square.
For if the old man finds you would not trust his steward there,
He *will* be mad; he trusts to him all things to regulate.

Le.   He needn't pay unless he likes; 'gad, let the fellow 460
    wait!

Li.   Pay it, I say; or else I fear he'll think that I have said
Something to make you doubt his word; come, pay, don't be
    afraid,
It's right enough.

Ass-D.   I think it is, as long as I stick to it;
I don't know Saurea.

---

[1] *i.e.* Libanus.

Li.   This is he; I thought, of course, you knew it.

Ass-D.   He may or mayn't be; *I* can't tell; if he is, it
must be so.

But I sha'n't pay the money to a man I do not know.

Le.   May all the gods confound him then!   [*To Lib.*]
And don't you say a word!

The rascal's proud because he's got my fifty pounds!   Absurd!
[*To Ass-D.*]   Come, get away! be off from here! don't vex me
more, you pup!

470   Ass-D).   O what a temper! for a slave you're rather too
stuck up!

Le.   [*to Lib.*]   By Hercules, I'll flog you if you don't
abuse him too!

Li.   You filthy villain!   [*aside to Ass-D.*]   Don't you see
he's angry?

Le.   [*aside to Lib.*]   That will do.

Li.   You cat o' nine tails!   [*aside to Ass-D.*]   Pay him, do!
or you'll get such a slanging!

Ass-D.   O, you'll be sorry for all this!

Le.   [*to Lib.*]   I'll give your legs a banging
If you don't curse that shameless rogue!

Li.   Alas!   You shameless villain,
You wretch!   [*aside to Ass-D.*]   to help poor wretched me, I
pray you will be willing!

Le.   You dare entreat that scoundrel's help?

Ass-D.   What's that? you slave, you dare
Speak of a gentleman like that!

Le.   Be thrashed!

Ass-D.   No, you'll be there;
If once I see Demænetus, you'll not have one sound member.
[I'll summons you! [1]

---

[1] The bracketed passage is doubtful on many accounts.

Le.   I'll not appear.

Ass-D.   You'll not appear?—Remember!   480

Le.   All right.

Ass-D.   I'll see I get revenged upon your back.

Le.   Be hanged!

Don't think, you hangman, that by you we're going to be banged.

    Ass-D.   Ah, well, for all you. slanderous words the pen-
    alty you'll pay.]

    Le.   What, you whipped cur!

Ass-D.   Well, gallows-bird!

Le.   Don't think I'll run away!

Go to my master, whom you call and want so much to see.

    Ass-D.   At last! But you will never get the money out
    of me

Until Demænetus commands.

    Le.   All right; come, walk away.

If you insult your fellow man, you must expect rough play.

I'm just as good a man as you.

    Ass-D.   Quite so.

Le.   Then follow me.   490

Without offence I now may say there's no one that would be

So bold as to impugn my faith; there's not another man

In Athens whom they trust so much.

    Ass-D.   Maybe! but nothing can

Persuade me to transfer the cash to you whom I don't
    know.

A man you don't know is a wolf; the proverb tells us so.

    Le.   Ah, now you're coming round a bit; I knew you'd
    make amends

For all the wrong you've done to me. Although my dress
    offends,

For all that I'm a careful man, my savings can't be counted.

    Ass-D.   Maybe!

H

Le.   Periphanes brought from Rhodes a sum that
just amounted

500 To good two hundred pounds; although my master was away,
He counted it and paid it, nor did I his trust betray.

Ass-D. Maybe!

Le.   And if you'd only made inquiry on the quiet,
You would have trusted me with all you've got.

Ass-D.   I don't deny it.

[*Exeunt Libanus, Leonida, and Ass-Dealer to the market-place.*]

CLEÆRETA.   PHILÆNIUM.

[*Enter Cleæreta and Philænium from Cleæreta's house.*]

Cl. Can I never hinder you from doing things that I
forbid?

If you had your way, you minx, you'd soon be of your
mother rid.

Is it right to disobey me? Come, what have you got to say?[1]

Ph. How could I do right, dear mother, if I acted in the
way

You prescribe, and tried to please you, doing as you order me?

Cl. Right, indeed! D'you call it right to sneer at my
authority?

510   Ph. Mothers who do right I blame not, love them not
when wrong they do.

Cl. You can chatter well enough, miss!

Ph.   Mother, 'tis my nature to!
What I think I'm bound to utter, when I've opportunity.

Cl. Why, I brought you here to scold *you*; don't begin
to lecture me!

---

[1] I venture to transpose this line from its position two lines later.

Ph.   Lecture you?   I couldn't, mother! for I shouldn't
think it right—
Only I lament the fate which keeps my sweetheart from my
sight.
Cl.   Won't you let me have a chance of speaking all this
live-long day?
Ph.   Take my share and yours as well; dear mother,
gladly I give way.
You shall give me sailing orders, you shall urge me on or check;
Though if I laid down my oar and fell asleep upon the deck,
All the ship would stop, I fancy, you and all your household 520
too!
Cl.   Listen! you're the sauciest girl with whom I ever
had to do.
How much oftener must I tell you, you're to let that fellow go,
Argyrippus, son of old Demænetus; O yes! you know!
What's he given us?   What's he sent us?   Oh, his love
is growing cold.
You think witty words are presents, tender speeches good as
gold.
So you love him and pursue him and invite him to the house;
Mock your generous suitors, dote on one who's impecunious.
For we can't afford to wait, although it's true he promises
He will make you roll in riches, when his good old mother dies.
Can't you see that all our household is with deadly peril cursed? 530
While we're waiting for her death, we'll die ourselves of
hunger first.
If he doesn't bring that fifty pounds I told him of before,
Never shall your lavish giver of his tears come in this door.
For the last time I have listened to his plea of poverty.
Ph.   Mother, stint me of my food and I will bear it patiently.
Cl.   Love the men that give you presents that they may
be loved by you.

Pʜ. But I've lost my heart! O, mother, tell me what I
    ought to do.

Cʟ. Look at my grey hairs, my dear, and think of your
    own interest.

540 Pʜ. Many a shepherd, who is feeding others' sheep,
    himself is blessed

With just one ewe lamb, the earnest of the flock he hopes
    to own ;

Let me love my Argyrippus, darling of my heart alone !

Cʟ. Get you in ! I've heard enough of your impertinence
    to-day.

Pʜ. Mother, you have trained me well, and so to hear is
    to obey.

                [*Exeunt into Clecæreta's house.*]

LIBANUS. LEONIDA.

[*Enter Libanus and Leonida from the market-place.*]

Lɪ. Great laud and praise we ought to pay to thee, great
    god of swindling,

For certainly our knavishness has shown no signs of dwindling.

Despising all the birch rod's might, and trusting to our shoulders,

We've bravely stood against hot-plates and crosses and shin-
    holders,

550 And stocks and chains and prison-cells, and shackles, bonds,
    and fetters,

And those infernal dogs who live by scourging of their betters.

(Alas, they know our backs too well by many an ancient scarring.)

Now all their regiments and troops and soldiers armed for
    warring,

By force of fight and lying hard, we've put to dreadful
    slaughter.

All this was done by my address, and this my brave supporter.

I'll suffer stripes with any man, although it's true they hurt you.

Le.   By Pollux, I can tell you this, you cannot praise
   your virtue
As well as I your villainies, though I should not have said it;
In countless numbers they abound, and greatly to your credit. 560
You've cheated those who trusted you, you've used your
   master badly,
And with a fabricated tale you've perjured yourself gladly.
You've broken into houses, you've been often caught in thieving,
And hanging by your feet maintained your cause past all believing
Against eight strong and sturdy men, who plied their rods upon
   you.
Li.   I must confess, Leonida, that all you say is quite true.
But yours are just as plentiful.   O yes, I will be just too
And tell them all: you always prove a rogue to those who
   trust you ;
You've been discovered in a theft, red-handed, and got beaten ;
You've sworn to lies, you've robbed a shrine, your words
   you've often eaten ;   570
You've always proved a loss, disgrace, and nuisance to your
   masters ;
If anybody trusted you, you collared the piastres !
Your mistress you have always more than any friend befriended;
And often by your toughness you've successfully contended
With strongest lictors' birches till their vigour was expended.
And now I think we're even, so your praises shall be ended.
Le.   Your catalogue adds lustre to our well-known ingenuity.
Li.   Come, drop it now and tell me this.
Le.   Ask on with perspicuity.
Li.   Well, have you got that fifty pounds ?
Le.   You have the right afflatus !
How nobly did Demænetus his best to vindicate us !   580
How cleverly the old man shammed I was his faithful factor!
I almost burst out laughing, as he ranted like an actor,

Because the stranger wouldn't trust me with that precious
    money.
To hear him call me, "Saurea, my steward!" O 'twas funny!
    LI.   Hold on !
    LE.   What's up ?
    LI.   Why, isn't that Philænium appearing
And Argyrippus?
    LE.   Hold your tongue; let's give attentive
               hearing.
    LI.   They're crying, and she's grasping at his cloak! What
    can it be now ?
Be still ! let's listen !
    LE.   Out alas ! it just occurs to me, how
I wish to heaven I had a stick !
    LI.   What for?
    LE.   Why, just to knock it
590 About those asses,[1] if they start to bray inside my pocket !

      ARGYRIPPUS. PHILÆNIUM. LIBANUS. LEONIDA.
    [*Enter from Clœreta's house Argyrippus and Philœnium.*]
    ARG.   Why do you hold me back ?
    PH.   Because I'm sad when you're away.
    ARG.   Farewell !
    PH.   I'd *fare* much *better*, love, if only you would stay.
    ARG.   Good-bye !
    PH.   When you are gone, no *good* remains, but
    bitter woe.
    ARG.   Your mother's sung my funeral dirge and ordered
    me to go.
    PH.   Her daughter she may bury next, if she sends you
    away.
    LI. [*apart to Le.*] By Jove he's been turned out !

---

[1] *i.e.*, The money paid for them. The *as* is a Latin coin.

LE. [*apart to Li.*]   He has !

ARG.   Come, let me go, I pray !

PH.   Where are you going ?   Why not stop ?

ARG.   I'll come again to-night.

LI. [*apart to Le.*]   The evening's all that he can spare !
  Oh isn't he polite ?

Of course, he's busy all the day, a second Solon he !

A-making laws to regulate the people's manners.   See ?   600

If he had power to make the laws, and folks had to obey,

They'd squander all their property, and drink both night and
    day.

LE. [*apart*].   By Jove he'd never move a step, if he had
  any choice.

In spite of all his hurry and his threats, he don't rejoice.

LI. [*apart*].   O stop your talking ; it is *his* I want to hear.
                                            Now then !

ARG.   Farewell !

PH.   Where goest thou ?

ARG.   Fare thee well !   In heaven we'll meet again.

For as for me I am resolved from this vile life to fly !

PH.   Ah, why should you condemn me thus, an innocent,
  to die ?

ARG.   Condemn you ? I ? Why, if I thought that you were
  dying, love,

I'd give my life instead of yours my faithfulness to prove.   610

PH.   Then don't you threaten any more to die by suicide.

For what d'you think that I should do, supposing you had
    died ?

I'm quite resolved that I should do the same as you had done.

ARG.   O sweeter than sweet honey !

PH.   O my life, my darling one !

Embrace me, love !

ARG.   Ay, that I will. [*They fall into one another's arms.*]

PH.   O that we so might die !

LE. [*apart to Li.*] O Libanus, how wretched is a man in
love !

LI. [*apart to Le.*]   Ay, ay !

But one who's flogged is wretcheder.

LE. [*apart to Li.*]   I know it, for I've tried.

Come, let's accost them ; I on this and you on t'other side.

LI. Hail, master !   Is this woman smoke that in your
arms is lying ?

ARG. What's that ?

620 LI.   I see she's got into your eyes and set them crying.

ARG. You've lost a man who would have been your
patron and no bad one.

LI. O no, I haven't lost him, sir—because I never had one.

LE. Philænium, hail !

PH.   May heaven grant you all your heart is craving !

LE. I'll have a cask of wine and kiss from you, if wish-
ing's having.

ARG. You scoundrel, take care what you say !

LE.   My wishes were for *you*, sir !

ARG. O well, say what you like.

LE.   Then let me beat him [1] black and blue, sir.

LI. What, *you* flog *me*, you foolish fop, you scented
Sybarite !

Why flogging suits your back as well as food your appetite !

ARG. Ah, Libanus, though you're a slave, you're better
off than I.

Before this evening's shadows fall, I shall be dead.

630 LI.   Pray why ?

ARG. Why, I love her and she loves me ; I've nothing left
to give ;

---

[1] *i.e.* Libanus,

And as her mother's turned me out, why should I longer
  live?
Yes, I am driven to my death by that curs'd fifty pound,
Which young Diabolus has sworn to give to bring her round,
That she may give her daughter's hand to him this very
  night.
To think that fifty pounds should have such wondrous power
  and might!
He who can spend them saves himself, whilst I am lost who
  can't.

Li.   But has he paid the cash?
Arg.   Not yet.
Li.   Cheer up then! fear, avaunt!
Le.   Here, Libanus, a word with you.
Li.   All right. [*They converse apart.*]
Arg.   Look here, I say,
You might as well embrace outright;[1] it's much the nicer 640
  way.
Li.   Tastes differ, sir; and what suits you may not so
  well suit me.
You lovers like embracing well enough, as we can see.
I wouldn't mind embracing *her*, but she's too coy and nice;
So go ahead yourself, dear sir, and take your own advice.
Arg.   Ay, that I will, and gladly too; you two withdraw
  meanwhile.
Le. [*apart*].   Well, shall we make a fool of him?
Li.   We will, boy! that's the style!
Le.   Suppose I make Philænium kiss me before his eyes?
Li.   The very thing!
Le.   Then come along! [*They return to Arg. and Phil.*]
Arg.   Now what is your device?

---

[1] The two slaves are whispering with their heads together.

LE.   Come listen and attend to me ; devour the words I
      say !
650 Well, first of all, we don't deny that we're your slaves this day.
    But if we find you fifty pounds to take to that old matron's,
    By what name would you call us then?
    ARG.   O, freed-men !
    LE.   Why not patrons ?
    ARG.   O certainly !
    LE.   Well, in this bag I have just fifty pound ;
    And if you like I'll give it you.
    ARG.   May heaven's best gifts abound
    To you, your master's saviour, you hoard of treasure trove,
    Salvation of my inmost soul and emperor of love !
    Come, hang your bag [1] around my neck all fair and square
      and level.
    LE.   For you to carry such a load would be the very devil !
    ARG.   But why not free yourself from toil and put it on to
      me ?
660 LE.   I'll be your porter, you go on in front ; so should it
       be.
    ARG.   Come, come ; what's this ? Why don't you give
      the bag to your poor master ?
    LE.   Then bid your sweetheart beg of me to save you
      from disaster ;
    For that's a steepish slope whereon you bade me place it *level.* [2]
    PH.   Thou apple of mine eye, my rose, my soul, in whom
      I revel,
    Leonida, O give it me ; let lovers' prayers prevail.
    LE.   Well, call me then your sparrow, and your chicken,
      and your quail ;

---

[1] The 20 minæ, being in silver, would weigh about 20 lbs.

[2] He means that the money will slide off his master's neck into the
hands of Philænium.

Your lambkin, and your kidling, and your calf that gaily
skips ;

And then catch hold of my two ears and kiss me on the lips.

ARG.   Must she kiss you, you worthless scamp ?

LE.   Pray why not, if you please ?

[*Phil. kisses him.*]

[*To Arg.*] By Pollux, you sha'n't have it, if you don't em-   670
brace my knees.[1]

ARG.   My need compels me ; I'll embrace your knees;
now hand it over.

PH.   Come, my Leonida, I pray, bring help to my dear
lover.

Buy both your freedom and his love by giving him the money.

LE.   What a sweet pretty girl you are !   If it were mine,
my honey,

I'd give it you without a word ; but *he's*[2] the man to dun ;

He only gave it me to keep.   Gently, my gentle one !

Here, Libanus, catch hold of this ! [*Giving him the bag.*]

ARG.   D'you mock me to my face ?

LE.   I wouldn't, but you clasped my knees with such a
sorry grace.

[*Aside to Lib.*] Now take your turn, and bubble him, and
kiss her, if you can.

LI. [*aside*].   Say nought, but watch me !

ARG. [*to Phil.*]   Come, my love, let us approach   680
this man,

For he's a very decent sort, not like that treacherous thief.

LI. [*aside*]. I'll strut about ; and in my turn they'll ask
me for relief.   .

ARG.   O save your master, Libanus, and hear him
humbly plead,

---

[1] As a suppliant.   [2] Pointing to Libanus.

Give me those fifty pounds ; you see my love and my sore
    need.

Li.   I'll see; I'd like to do it; come again to-morrow early.

Now let the lady beg and pray ; she will not find me surly.

Ph.   Shall I prevail by loving you or giving you a kiss ?

Li.   Why, both.

Ph.   Then, I beseech of you, save us from this abyss !

Arg.   O, Libanus, my patron, give it me ; 'twould be
    more meet

690 A freedman, not his patron, should bear burdens in the street.

Ph.   My Libanus, my eye of gold so precious, and my
    honey,

My darling, I'll do aught you like; but do give us the money.

Li.   Well, call me then your ducky, and your puppy, and
    your dovey,

Your swallow, and your jackdaw, and your sparrow, and your
    lovey !

Transform me to a serpent, let me have a double tongue ! [1]

And throw your arms around my neck and hug me ! come
    along !

Arg.   Shall she embrace you, hangman ?

Li.   Why, don't I deserve it, eh ?

                    [*Phil. embraces him.*]

[*To Arg.*]   And now as you've insulted me, I'll have to make
    you pay.

If you would have this money, you must just give me a ride.

Arg.   What, carry you?

700 Li.   Why, certainly ! There is no way beside.

Arg.   O hang it ! If you think it's right that I should
    carry you,

Mount up !

---

[1] *i.e.,* By putting your tongue between my lips as you kiss me.

LI.   This is a noble way proud spirits to subdue!
Stand up then as you used to, when once a boy at play.
Yes, so! that's it! you are the smartest horse I've seen to-day.
　ARG.   Mount up!
　LI.   I will.　[*Gets on Argyrippus's back.*]　Hallo,
　　　　　what's this?   You are a lazy lot!
I'll take away your corn, by Jove, unless you go full trot.
　ARG.   Sweet Libanus, come, that's enough—
　LI.   I want a bit more still,
For now I'm going to spur you on to gallop up the hill.
Then to the mill I'll send you where they'll flog you till
　　　　you go.
Woa up! I'll get down at this hill; you don't deserve it, 710
　　　　though!
　　　　　　　　　　　　[*Libanus gets off Arg.'s back.*]
　ARG.   Well, now you've fooled us both, I hope you'll not
　　　　prove a defaulter.
Pay up the cash!
　LI.   First put me up a statue and an altar,
And sacrifice a bull to me; for I am your *Salvation.*
　LE.   Here, master, shunt that fellow off, and hear *my*
　　　　application.
You'll pray to me and offer me the same things as he wishes?
　ARG.   And what, pray, is your godhead's name?
　LE.   'Tis *Fortune* and propitious.
　ARG.   So much the better.
　LI.   Why, what can be better than Salvation?
　ARG.   I do no wrong to her when I pay Fortune adoration.
　PH.   They both are good!
　ARG.   Yes, when they give me good, then
　　　　　　　I'll believe it.
　LE.   Now pray to me for what you want.
　ARG.   What then?

720   LE.   You shall receive it.

ARG.   I want to marry this dear girl.

LE.   And so you shall, say I !

ARG.   Do you say true ?

LE.   Of course I do.

LI.   Now come to me and try ;

Desire of me what most you wish to happen ; and it's done.

ARG.   What could I wish for more than that, of which,
    alas, I've none

Those fifty pounds in full to give to my dear sweetheart's
    mother.

LI.   They shall be yours ; cheer up, my boy, you're rid of
    all your bother.

ARG.   As usual, Fortune and Salvation make a mock of men.

LE.   I was the head to-day when we the money did obtain.

LI.   And I the tail.

ARG.   I can't make either *head* or *tail* of you.

730 Your speeches and your fooleries, I own, I can't see through.

    LE.   We've fooled enough, I think ; so now we'll tell you
    everything.

Hear, Argyrippus, what I say : your father bade us bring
This money to you.

ARG.   O, you've come just in the nick of time !

LE.   Well, here are fifty good true pounds, gained by a
    naughty crime ;

On certain terms he gives them you.

ARG.   What are the terms, I pray ?

LE.   That you should ask him to the feast.

ARG.   Go, bid him come away !

We never can repay him who has joined our severed lives.

740 Go, run, Leonida ; for I'm on pins till he arrives.

    LE.   He's in the house.

ARG.   He didn't come this way.

LE.   No ; he went round
And got in by the garden gate, for fear he should be found
By any of the slaves ; he doesn't want his wife to know,
For if your mother knew how we had got the cash—
ARG.   Hallo
Good words !
LI.   Come quickly in.
ARG.   Good-bye.
LE.   And may your love still grow !
                                    [*Exeunt omnes.*]

DIABOLUS. PARASITE.

[*Enter Diabolus and Parasite.*]

DI. Come, show me that agreement you've drawn up
Between me and my bride.   Read out the terms,
For you're a perfect artist in this kind.
PAR. 'Twill make the lady tremble when she reads.
DI. Well, read it to me.
PAR.   Are you listening ?
DI.   Yes.   750
PAR. " Diabolus, the son of Glaucus, gives
Cleæreta the sum of fifty pounds,
That he may wed Philænium, her daughter."
DI. She mustn't ever see another man.
PAR. Must that be in ?
DI.   It must, and write it plain !
PAR. " She shall not ever see another man,
Though she should say he is her friend or patron,
Or feign that he's the sweetheart of her friend ;
Her doors must be fast closed to all but you,   760
And she must always say she's ' not at home.'
Then, though she say it's come from foreign parts,

No letter shall be found in all the house,
Nor a waxed tablet ; [1] also any picture
From which wax might be got for writing letters,
She now shall sell ; and if they are not sold
Within four days from when she gets the money,
They shall be yours, to burn them, if you like,
That she may have no wax wherewith to write.
She shall invite no guest ; *you* shall do that.
If she catch sight of any other man,
770 She instantly shall look the other way.
She shall not drink with any one but you ;
Shall take the cup from you and hand it back ;
Nor drink a single drop without your knowledge."
    DI.   That's well.
    PAR.   "To turn suspicion from herself, [2]
She shall not tread on anybody's foot
When she gets up or crosses the next couch.
Nor in descending shall she take a hand.
She shall not give her ring to anyone
To look at, nor shall ask his in return,
Nor shall she challenge anyone but you
To play at dice ; and she shall name your name,
780 And not say, ' Thee,' [3] when challenging to throw.
And only goddesses shall she invoke,
And no male god ; but if she must do so,
She shall tell you, and you shall do it for her.

---

[1] I need hardly remind the reader that the Romans wrote their letters on thin boards or tablets smeared over with wax. The pictures referred to are pictures executed in coloured wax.

[2] The following directions refer to her behaviour at a banquet. In certain arrangements of the couches, she would have to step over the next one in order to get out.

[3] Which might be taken as referring to someone else.

She shall not nod, or wink her eye, or beckon
To any man ; and if the light goes out,
She shall not move a limb until it's lit."

Di. First-rate !

Par.   Well, hear the rest.

Di.   All right ; read on.   790

Par.   "She shall not utter an ambiguous word,
Or speak in any language but her own.
If she perchance must cough, she shall not cough
So as to put her tongue out when she coughs.[1]
If she pretends she wants to clean her lips,
She shall not do it so ; it would be better
For you to wipe her lips yourself than suffer
That she should show her open mouth to men.
Her mother never shall drop in to dinner,
Nor start to make complaints ; and if she does,   800
Her punishment shall be to have no wine
For twenty days."

Di.   Bravo ! a clever bond !

Par.   "Then, if she bids her maidens take to Venus
Or Cupid garlands, wreaths, or precious ointments,
Your slave shall see that Venus gets them all,
And not some man to whom she's sending tokens."
These are not trifles, nor mere funeral songs.[2]

Di. I'm satisfied.   Let's enter !

Par.   After you !

[*They go into Cleæreta's house, where they find
    Demænetus and Argyrippus celebrating the
    engagement of the latter with Philænium,
    and come out again, breathing fury.*]

---

[1] This might be regarded as an invitation to kiss.
[2] Funeral songs, in which, as in our funeral sermons, the *imaginary*
element was largely predominant.

I

DIABOLUS. PARASITE.

[Enter Diabolus and Parasite from Cleæreta's house.]

810   Di. Come on! Oh, shall I suffer this in silence?
I'll die but I'll go tell the villain's wife.
Shall you[1] sit there, kissing that lovely girl,
And tell your wife 'twas only fatherly?
Where did you get the money for her mother?
Didn't you steal it from your wife at home?
I'm hanged if I'll keep silence one more minute.
I go at once and tell her that I know
You'll quickly strip her bare, unless she stops you,
To furnish means for your extravagance.

820   Par. It should be done; but don't you think that *I*
Had better tell her, lest she should suppose
That you have done it more for your own passion
Than for her sake?
    Di.   By Jove! I think you're right.
You go and stir her up and make a row;
Tell her he's drinking with her darling son,
And with his sweetheart, and she's robbing him.
    Par. I'll see to it.
    Di.   And I'll go wait at home.

*[Exit Parasite into the house of Demænetus, and Diabolus
off the stage to his own house.]*

DEMÆNETUS. ARGYRIPPUS.

*[The front of Cleæreta's house is removed, and the marriage ban-
quet is disclosed, Demænetus reclining next to Philænium.]*

830   De. I hope that you don't mind, my boy, that I am sitting
by your wife.
    Arg. I honour you too much for that, although I love
her as my life;

---

[1] *i.e.* Demænetus, who is within.

And so I do not mind a bit, dear father, that she sits by you.

DE.   A youth, my Argyrippus, should be modest.

ARG.   Father, you say true ;
I only do as you deserve.

DE.   Then let us fall to this good cheer,
With draughts of wine and pleasant talk.   I want your love
   and not your fear,
My dearest son.

ARG.   By Pollux ! I would give you both, like a
                     good lad.

DE.   I should believe it if I saw you jolly.

ARG.   Do you think I'm sad ?

DE.   I don't *think* so ; I *see* you are, as if your neck were
   in the noose.

ARG.   O, don't say so !

DE.   Then don't *be* so, and I'll not say it.
                     What's the use ?   840

ARG.   Why, see, I'm smiling !

DE.   May my foes be always bless'd with
                     such a smile !

ARG.   Well, I'll confess that what you say is true.   I'm
   angry all this while,
Because she's sitting by your side ! for, father, the plain truth
   to say,
It *does* annoy me ; not because I don't want you to have your
   way,
But I love her ; and I should like another girl to sit by you.

DE.   But I want *her !*

ARG.   You have your wish ; but I should like to
                     have mine too.

DE.   You needn't grudge me this one hour, since I have
   found the means for you

To pay the money, and to have her for your own your whole
   life through.

  ARG. Ah! you are right; I see my folly.

850 DE. Then fire away, and let's be jolly.

ARTEMONA. PARASITE. DEMÆNETUS. ARGYRIPPUS.
     PHILÆNIUM.

*[Enter outside Parasite and Artemona from the house of
     Demœnetus.]*

 ART. Do you say you saw my son and my old husband
  drinking here?

That he's stolen fifty pounds of mine to give his sweetheart
  dear?

That my son knew all about it, whilst his father did the
  deed?

 PAR. Ne'er again believe my statements, though you find
  them in the creed,

Artemona, if deception in my present words you find.

 ART. Out, alas! I thought my husband was the noblest
  of mankind—

Sober, temperate, and saving, and devoted to his wife.

 PAR. Now you see that he has been a worthless rascal
  all his life—

Drunken, reprobate, intemperate, hating his poor wife like
  mad!

 ART. If it were not so, he'd never do as he does. Oh,
860 he's bad!

 PAR. Well, you know, I always took him for a decent,
  sober man.

But his present actions show he's built upon another plan.

 ART. This is what he meant by saying he was off, so
  serious,

Just to dine with Archidemus, Chærea, Chærestratus,

Clinias, Chremes, Cratinus, Dinias, Demosthenes ;[1]
All the time, no doubt, the scamp's been carrying on such
 games as these.
 Par. Why, then, don't you bid your maidens pick him up
  and take him home?
 Art. You be quiet ; he shall suffer !
 Par.   Ah, I knew that this would come,
From the day when you were married.
 Art.   Oh, dear me, I always thought 870
He was busy in the senate or with clients, as he ought ;
That exhausting toil in business made him snore the livelong
 night.
He was toiling at a business of a different nature quite ;
Going to other people's houses, whilst poor I sat all alone ;
Bad himself, he's not contented till he's taught it to his son.
 Par. Follow me then ; you shall catch him at it in the
  neatest way.
 Art. There is nothing I'd like better.
 Par.   Stay a minute !
 Art.   What d'you say?
 Par. Could you recognise your husband, if you saw him
  at a feast,
With a garland on his head and sitting by a girl, the beast ?
 Art. Yes, I could !
 Par. Well, there you see him !
   [*Bringing her where she can see the banqueters.*]
 Art. O, the wretch !
 Par.   Here, wait a bit ! 880
Let's observe them from our ambush, whilst they're not
 suspecting it.

---

[1] This alphabetical arrangement ingeniously suggests that these are
but the first names on a long list.

[*Art. and Par. keep out of sight and watch proceedings.*]

ARG.   Don't you think it's time we finished?

DEM.   Well, I must confess, my son—

ARG.   What?

DEM.   Your wife's the nicest girl that ever I set eyes
upon.

PAR. [*apart*].   Do you hear him?

ART. [*apart*].   Yes, I hear him.

DEM. [*to Phil.*]   Now I'll tell you what I'll do ;
I'll just steal my wife's best mantle as a wedding gift for you.
I would do it, even though it cost my spouse a year of life !

PAR. [*apart*].   Ah, I fear it's not the first time he has
robbed his wretched wife !

ART. [*apart*].   Yes, no doubt he was the robber, when I
thought it was my maids ;

Those poor innocents have suffered for their master's escapades.

ARG.   Father, set the wine a-going ; my next drink is over-
890   due.

DEM.   Waiter, take the wine to him ; meanwhile I'll have
a kiss from you.   [*Kisses Philænium.*]

ART. [*apart*].   Wretched me !   He's kissing her—a man
with one foot in the grave !

DEM.   Ah ! your kisses are much nicer than my lady ever
gave.

PH.   Don't you like to kiss your wife, then ?

DEM.   Bless you, no !   I'd much prefer,
If I must, to drink ditch-water, rather than be kissed by her !

PH.   How I pity you !

ART. [*aside*].   He'll need it !

ARG.   Hallo, father, what d'you say ?
Don't you love my mother ?

DEM.   Love her?   Certainly, when she's away !

ARG.   When she's there?

DEM.   I wish her dead!

PAR. [*apart*].   You see how much he loves 900
you, ma'am.

ART. [*apart*].   Oh, I'll make him pay for this with
interest, when I get him home!

Yes, I'll kiss him with a vengeance, as he seems so fond of
it!

Would you slander me, you villain?   All right, only wait a
bit.

Just come home to me!   I'll show you there are risks in
speaking ill

Of the woman whom you married for her money, that
I will!

ARG.   Now then, father! throw the dice and we'll throw
next.

DEM.   All right.   No tricks!

Here's to you, Philænium, and my wife's death!—Ah,
double six!¹

Cheer me, boys, and pass a goblet full of wine for that good
throw.

ART. [*apart*].   I can't bear it any longer.

PAR. [*apart*].   Well you haven't learnt, you know,

How to be a *porter*.²   Come on, let's go for him; now's your
chance.

ART. [*coming out*].   I *won't* die; and for that wish, sir,
I'll lead you a pretty dance.

PAR.   Please, will someone run and quickly bring an 910
undertaker here?

ARG.   Mother, hail!

---

¹ Literally, *Venus*; Demænetus has thrown the best throw.

² I venture to modify this joke (*fullonia*, 'the fuller's trade').

ART.   A truce to greetings!

PAR.   Poor old man! he's dead with fear!
Now it's time for me to toddle; ah, this quarrel's looking
    well!
I'll go to Diabolus and tell him how it all befel;
And I hope he'll stand a dinner for me, whilst they fight it
    out.
Then to-morrow I'll devise some dodge to get the girl, no
    doubt.
If I don't, I've lost my patron, for he's all on fire with love.
                              [*Exit Parasite.*]

ART. [*to Phil.*] What's your business with my husband?
    tell me that, miss!

920 PHIL.   Oh, by Jove,
She's half killed me, she's a nuisance!

ART.   Get up, gallant, come on home!

DEM. Oh! I'm nothing!

ART.   Yes, you are, for you're a scoundrel!
    Out you come!
See, the cuckoo still keeps sitting! Get up, gallant, come
    on home!

DEM. Woe is me!

ART.   O, truthful prophet! Get up, gallant, come
    on home!

DEM. Go away! I'll come directly!

ART.   Get up, gallant, come on home.

DEM. Pray you, wife—

ART.   O, *wife*, indeed! I *am* your wife, then, you
    allow!
I believe I was your pet aversion, not your wife, just now.

DEM. O, I'm done for!

ART.   Tell me, have you learnt to like my
    kisses yet?

DEM.   Yes, they smell of myrrh.

ART.   And did you steal my mantle for your
pet?

PHIL.   No, by Castor! ma'am, he only promised he *would* 930
steal me one.

DEM.   You be quiet!

ARG.   But I tried to hinder him.

ART.   A pretty son!
That's the way you think a father ought to teach his child to
do.
Don't you feel ashamed?

DEM.   I do, love! very much ashamed—*of you!*

ART.   Hoary-headed cuckoo, I will drag you from your
haunts.   Proceed!

DEM.   Mayn't I stay—the dinner's ready—just until I've
had my feed?

ART.   You shall have a dinner such as you deserve when
you get home.

DEM.   I shall have a poorish night; I see my wife's
pronounced my doom.

ARG.   If you plotted 'gainst my mother, didn't I a row
foretell?

PHIL.   Don't forget the cloak!

DEM.   I wish you'd silence in this jade compel!

ART.   Come on!

PHIL.   Give me one more kiss before we part.

DEM.   O, go to hell! 940

EPILOGUE [*by the Company*].

If the old man *did* deceive his wife and have a little game,
That is nothing new or wondrous; other people do the same;
No one has so strict a conscience or so resolute a breast

That, if once the chance is given, he won't do just like the
rest.

Now if you would save the old man from a beating, plead his
cause,

And he cannot fail to win it, if you give him your applause

AULULARIA;

OR,

THE POT OF GOLD.

INTRODUCTION.

NEITHER the Greek source of this play nor the date of its reproduction by Plautus at Rome is known. The name Aulularia signifies the Play of the Little Pot. The end of it has unfortunately perished along with the beginning of the next play, the Bacchides; but the prologue enables us to supply the deficiency, so far, at least, as the completion of the story is concerned. It has been frequently imitated; the adaptations of Molière and Fielding are best known. The plot requires very little modification in order to fit the play for general reading. The scene is laid in Athens. I have used Wagner's edition of this play as well as those enumerated in the General Introduction.

DRAMATIS PERSONÆ.

THE HOUSEHOLD GOD OF EUCLIO.

EUCLIO	-	*An old man.*
STAPHYLA	-	*An old woman, his housekeeper.*
EUNOMIA	-	*Sister of Megadorus.*
MEGADORUS	-	*An old man.*
STROBILUS	-	*Slave of Megadorus.*
ANTHRAX	-	*A cook.*
CONGRIO	-	*A cook.*
STROBILUS	-	*Slave of Lyconides.*
LYCONIDES	-	*A young man, nephew of Megadorus.*
[PHÆDRA	-	*A young lady, daughter of Euclio.]*

ARGUMENT I.

A MISERLY old man called Euclio,
Who hardly dares to trust himself, has found
Buried within his house, a Pot of Gold;
This Pot he hides again, and pale with fear
Keeps guard on it.   A youth, Lyconides,
Has won the love of Euclio's only daughter,
And secretly becomes engaged to her.[1]
Meanwhile, one Megadorus, an old man,
Persuaded by his sister to get married,
Demands the miser's daughter for his wife.
The hard old man reluctantly consents,
And, fearing for his Pot, takes it away,
And hides it, first in one place, then another.
10   The servant of that same Lyconides
Who loves the girl, lays plots against the miser.
The youth himself beseeches Megadorus,
Who is his uncle, to give up the girl.
When Euclio's been tricked out of his Pot,
He unexpectedly receives it back,
And gladly gives Lyconides his daughter.

ARGUMENT II. *(ACROSTIC).*

A Pot of Gold old Euclio preserves
U nsleepingly with anxious vigilance.
L yconides is plighted to his daughter.
U ndowered, Megadorus seeks her hand.
L iking the match, he sends both cooks and meat.
A nxious about his gold, old Euclio hides it.
R ight soon the lover's slave finds out and steals it,
I t is restored to Euclio by the lover,
A nd for his pains he gets both wife and gold.

---

[1] The original is slightly modified here for obvious reasons.

THE HOUSEHOLD GOD AS PROLOGUE.

[*The scene represents a street, with the houses of Euclio and
Megadorus side by side.   Enter the Household God*[1]
from Euclio's house.]

THAT none of you may wonder who I am,
I'll briefly tell you.   I'm the Household God :
This house from which you saw me coming out,
For many years I've occupied and guarded
For the sire and grandsire of its present owner.
His grandfather intrusted to my care
A secret treasure which he buried deep
Under the earth, and begged of me to keep it;
But when he died, so covetous was he,
He wouldn't show it even to his son,   10
But rather chose to leave him penniless
Than point him out the treasure.   So he left
That son of his a farm of no great size,
Whereon he lived in toil and wretchedness.
But when he died who'd hidden away the gold,
I began watching, if his son would pay
Greater regard to me than did his father ;
But he, with ever-growing carelessness,

---

[1] The Lar or Household God probably appeared as a youth, with
short tunic and buskins, and a horn in his hand. See the picture in
Rich's Dict. of Antiquities, S. v. Lar.

Neglected me and failed to do me honour;
20   So I neglected him; and soon he died.
He left a son behind him, who lives here,
As covetous as his sire and grandsire were.
He has one daughter, who from day to day
With frankincense or wine entreats my grace,
And gives me garlands.   So for her sweet sake
I've caused old Euclio to find the treasure,
To be a marriage portion for the girl.
A gentleman has fallen in love with her,
And has discovered who his sweetheart is;
30   But neither she nor Euclio knows his name.
To-day I'll make the old man from next door here
Ask her in marriage; I do it with this purpose—
That her true lover may secure her hand.
Now this old man who'll ask her for his wife
Is uncle to the youth I told you of,
Who fell in love with her at Ceres' feast.—
But hark! old Euclio shouting out, as usual,
And turning his housekeeper out of doors,
Lest she should get to know.   I guess he wants
To see his gold, whether it's not been stolen.

                         [*Exit Household God.*]

                 EUCLIO.   STAPHYLA.

     [*Enter Euclio, pushing out Staphyla from his house.*]

40   EUC.   Get out, I say, get out; out of this door!
You treacherous spy, with peeping, prying eyes!
     ST.   Why beat a *wretch* like me?
     EUC.   To make you *wretched*,
And give you a *bad* time, you *bad* old woman!
     ST.   But tell me why you've turned me out of doors.
     EUC.   Harvest of whips! and must I give you reasons?

Away from the door !—See how she crawls along !—
I tell you what it is : if I can get
A cudgel or a whip, by Hercules !
I'll see if I can't mend your tortoise-pace.
    St.   May Heaven grant me grace to hang myself,   50
Rather than be your slave on these hard terms !
    Euc.   Hark you, the hag is muttering to herself !—
By Hercules ! you wretch, I'll dig your eyes out,
So that you can't be watching all I do.
Go off now ! Further !
    St.   Further still ?
    Euc.   Well, well,
Stay there ! and if you move a finger's breadth,
Or even the width of a nail, from where you are,
Or look this way, until I give you leave,
I'll send you to the gallows for a lesson !—
[*Aside.*] I'm sure I never saw a worse old woman   60
Than this ; I'm horribly afraid of her ;
I fear she'll trick me with some plot or other,
And smell out where my gold is hidden away ;
Yes, in the back of her head the wretch has eyes.
And now to see whether the gold is safe
Where I have hidden it ; how it plagues my soul !

                        [*Exit Euclio into his house.*]

    St.   Alas, by Castor ! I cannot discover
What trouble has befallen my master here ;
Or madness is it ? Ten times in a day
He'll often turn me out in this same fashion.   70
By Pollux ! I can't guess what whims possess him.
He'll sit up all night long ; then all the day,
Like some lame cobbler, he will stay at home.
And then again, how I'm to keep from him

                             K

This foolish love affair of his dear daughter's,
I cannot think ; there's nothing left for me,
Except to make myself a capital I,[1]
And round my wretched neck a halter tie.

EUCLIO.   STAPHYLA.

[Re-enter Euclio from his house.]

EUC. [*aside*].   My mind's relieved, so I'll come forth
   again,

80   Now I have found that all is safe indoors.
[Aloud to Staphyla.] You come inside and keep a careful
   watch.

ST.   Keep watch on what?   That no one steals the house?
There's nothing else at all to tempt a thief ;
It's full of emptiness and spiders' webs.

EUC.   Doubtless, for your sake, Jupiter should make me
A Philip or Darius,[2] you old witch !
I wish those spiders' webs to be preserved !
I'm poor, I know ; what the gods send I bear.
Get in and shut the door.   I'll be back soon.

90   Take care you don't let anybody in.
They'll ask for fire perhaps, so put it out,
So there may be no reason for their asking ;
If one spark lives, *your* vital spark I'll quench !
If they want water, tell them it's cut off.
The knife, the axe, the pestle, and the mortar,
Which our good neighbours always want to borrow,
Tell them the thieves have been and stolen them.
No soul must be let in whilst I'm away.

---

[1] Literally, "make myself into one long letter ; " the resemblance of a
hanging man to the letter I is sufficiently obvious.

[2] Philip of Macedon and Darius of Persia were two proverbially
wealthy monarchs.

Yea, even this I charge you solemnly,—
E'en should Good Fortune come, don't you admit her.   100
  Sr. O, she'll take care of that herself, I'm sure ;
She never comes within a mile of us.
    Euc. Silence ! go in !
    St.   To hear is to obey.
    Euc. Mind, fasten both the bolts. I'll be back soon.

[Exit Staphyla into the house.]

It rends my heart to have to leave the house.
I go reluctantly ; though I've my reasons ;
The master of our ward has promised us
To give us each a drachma, man by man. [1]
If I neglect i· and don't go to get it,
They'll all suspect that I have gold at home ;   110
For 'tis not likely that a poor old man
Would miss a chance of getting e'en a trifle.
As it is, though I most carefully conceal it,
They all appear to know it, and they greet me
Far more effusively than was their wont ;
They come, they stop, they shake me by the hand ;
It's " How d'ye do ? " and " How are you, old man ? "
And " How are you getting on ? " from morn till night.
Now, I'll be going whither I set out
And come back home as quickly as I can.

[Exit Euclio to the market-place.]

EUNOMIA.   MEGADORUS.

[Enter from their house Eunomia and Megadorus.]

  Eu. 1 hope you'll believe that I say this, my brother,   120
As a matter of duty, for surely no other

---

[1] These distributions of money to the citizens were common enough at
Athens, as they became afterwards at Rome.

Should care for your welfare like me, your own sister.
I know you think woman a bore, and resist her
As one that is terribly given to chatter;
Indeed I remember I've heard some such matter
As that not one is born dumb in each generation;
Well, one thing I *will* say without hesitation,
You'll not find another who's nearer and dearer;
And so when I talk, you should be a kind hearer.
130 For surely we two should advise one another,
And not keep things back and in fearfulness smother
Our thoughts, but declare them, like sister and brother.
So I've brought you out here, and away from the clatter,
To discuss with you freely a family matter.

MEG.   Thou best of women, here's my hand!
EU.   Where is she? I don't understand.
MEG.   Yourself!
EU.   Not me!
MEG.   Oh, I'll withdraw!
EU.   You ought to make the truth your law.
        No woman's absolutely best;
140   All fail in something, 'tis confest.
MEG.   Oh, I'm with you there!
Never will I contradict you on that point, my sister dear!
EU.   Then listen, my treasure.
MEG.   I will; so employ and command me at pleasure.
EU.   What I think now would be just the best thing for
        you
                I'll tell you, if you've leisure.
MEG.   Oh, it's just like you, sister!
EU.   I wish you would do—
MEG.   Why, what, sister?
EU.   What I don't fear to aver
Would make your life blest and provide you an heir.

MEG.   Heaven grant it !

EU.   I want you to marry a wife.

MEG.   Oh, misery me, you've bereft me of life !   150

EU.   How's that?

MEG.   Oh, your words rattle round my poor bones,
And shatter my skull.   Sister dear, you speak stones !

EU.   Oh, do as I beg you !

MEG.   I would if I durst.

EU.   It would be for your good.

MEG.   Yes it would—to die first !
But hear the conditions I stipulate, pray !
She must marry to-morrow and die the next day.
If you'll find me a wife who on these terms will marry,
Get ready the feast, for no longer I'll tarry.

EU.   I'll find you one, who's quite a wealthy personage,
      Though you are getting on, and she's of middle age ;
      If you'll permit me, I will get her, I'll engage.   160

MEG.   May I be allowed a question ?

EU.   Yes, as many as you choose.

MEG.   If an old man marries one who's past her prime,
      see how he'll lose !
Even should a son be given them, and that's very dubious,
There's no doubt about his name, he must be christened
      Postumus.[1]
Now, dear sister, I'll relieve you of your care about the pelf ;
Thanks to heav'n and our forefathers, I am rich enough my-
      self.
I don't want your well-bred lady with a temper and a dower,
Shouting, ordering, riding in an ivory litter from her bower,
Clothed in purple ; these expenses turn a husband to a slave.

---

[1] *i.e.,* The last : the idea apparently being that it is not to be antici-
pated that more than one child will result from such a union.

170   Eu.   Tell me then, I do beseech you, who's the wife
you'd like to have?

Meg.   So I will.   You know old Euclio, our poor next-
door neighbour here?

Eu.   Yes; he's not so bad a fellow.

Meg.   Well, it is his daughter dear

That I want to get engaged to.   Sister, don't you raise objection.

She is poor, you'd say; she is! but, poor or rich, she's my
selection.

Eu.   Well, heaven bless you both!

Meg.   Amen!

Eu.   Then do you want me any more?

Meg.   No; good-bye!

Eu.   Good-bye, dear brother!

               [*Exit Eunomia into her house.*]

Meg.   Now I'll knock at Euclio's door.

Ah! I see him, coming home from somewhere; yes, it's he,
I'm sure.

EUCLIO.   MEGADORUS.

[*Enter Euclio, returning from the market-place.*]

Euc.   Ah, my mind misgave me sadly when just now I left
my home!

So I went reluctantly; and not a single wardsman's come,

180 Nor the master of the ward, who had to dole the money out.

Hastily I'll hasten home.   My soul is there, though I'm
without.

Meg.   May the gods bestow upon you, Euclio, their
benison.

Euc.   Heaven bless you, Megadorus!

MEG.   Well, how are you getting on ?

EUC. [*aside*].   Not for nothing does a rich man greet a
poor one civilly !

Oh ! he knows I've got that treasure, so he's affable to me.

MEG.   How d'you do, I say ?

EUC.   But poorly from the money point of view.

MEG.   Ah, well, if your mind's contented, you've enough
to see you through.

EUC. [*aside*].   Ah, that hag has doubtless told him of the
gold ; the secret's out !

I'll tear out her tongue and eyes, the miserable pry-about !

MEG.   What are you saying to yourself there ?

EUC.   Sighing o'er my poverty. 190

I've a grown-up girl who's dowerless, so she cannot married
be ;

I can't find a husband for her.

MEG.   Don't say so, good Euclio.

That's all right ; I'll see she's married ; I'm your friend, I'd
have you know.

EUC. [*aside*].   All these promises mean something ; he is
gaping for my gold.

Stones in one hand, bread in t'other ! no ! I'm not to be
cajoled !

I will never trust a rich man when he is so monstrous civil ;

Though he strokes you down so gently, he would send you
to the devil.

Ah, I know those cuttlefish, who stick to everything they
touch !

MEG.   Pray, attend to me a little ! just a word (it won't
be much),

I would say about a matter that concerns both you and me. 200

EUC. [*aside*].   Out alas ! he's hooked my treasure ! now he's
anxious, I can see,

To conclude some bargain with me; I must go and look
  inside.

[*Sets off towards his house.*]

MEG.   Where are you off to?

EUC.   Just a minute! I have something to provide.
[*Exit Euclio into his house.*]

MEG.   I'm afraid that when I tell him I desire to be his
  son,

And to marry his fair daughter, he will think I'm making fun.

Not another living man so harps upon his poverty.[1]

[*Re-enter Euclio.*]

EUC. [*aside*].   Heaven protects me; it's all safe! if that is
  safe which one can see.

I *was* scared before I went indoors! pale terror froze my
  blood!

[*Aloud.*] Now I'm back, good Megadorus! what's your
  wish?

MEG.   You're very good!

Now I hope you won't mind answering certain questions I
210   will ask.

EUC.   If I don't dislike the questions that will be an easy
  task.

MEG.   Tell me, what is your opinion of my family?

EUC.   Why, good!

MEG.   Of my honour?

EUC.   Good again!

MEG.   My acts?

EUC.   You act just as you should.

MEG.   Do you know my age?

---

[1] *i.e.*, He's so full of his own poverty that he'll never think it possible
that a rich man should marry his daughter.

Euc. You're pretty old, and have a pretty pile !

Meg. Well, I know that you're a man entirely free from guilty guile ;
So I think and always thought.

Euc. [*aside*]. Ah, he's got scent of that same gold !
[*Aloud.*] Is that all ?

Meg. Now our opinions of each other have been told,
Praying it may prove a blessing to your girl, yourself, and me,
I request your daughter's hand. Come, promise that it so shall be.

Euc. Megadorus, you are doing a deed unworthy of your 220
fame ;
Though I'm poor I never hurt you ; why should you of me make game ?
Ne'er by deed or word have I deserved that you should treat me so.

Meg. Nay, I didn't come to mock you, nor am I so doing.
No !
I should be ashamed to do it.

Euc. Why then ask my daughter's hand ?

Meg. That we all may make each other happier ; that's what I have planned.

Euc. It just strikes me, Megadorus, that you're rich, and what is more,
Occupy a high position ; I'm the poorest of the poor.
Should I now betroth my daughter unto you, I sadly fear
You're the ox and I'm the ass ; and if we're yoked together here,
Should the ass not pull up level, in the dirt he'll lie forlorn, 230
Whilst the ox no more regards him than if he had ne'er been born.
I can't pull with you, I fear ; and my old friends will mock at me,

So I'd have no stable stable, should she be divorced, you see.
Then the asses all would bite me, and the oxen gore me too;
If I leave my fellow-asses for the oxen, peace adieu!

MEG.   Nay, the closer you associate with the folk of good
    degree,

All the better for yourself! So take my offer, close with me,
And betroth your daughter to me.

EUC.   She's no dowry.

MEG.   I don't care ;

For her purity and sweetness are a dowry rich and rare.

EUC.   I just tell you that you mayn't suppose I've found
240   some treasure trove.

MEG.   Oh, of course !   Betroth her to me !

EUC.   So be it.—-But ah ! by Jove !

Am I ruined ?

MEG.   What's up now ?

EUC.   I heard a spade clink on a stone.

MEG.   Oh, it's only someone digging in my garden.

                [*Exit Euclio into his house.*]

          Where's he gone ?

Off he runs before it's settled !   I suppose he scorns me then.
When he sees I seek his friendship, he just does like other
    men :
If a wealthy man endeavours to be friends with one that's
    poor,
They can hardly come to terms ; the poor man thinks he's
    not secure.
When the chance has gone for ever, then he wants it back
    too late.

EUC. [*coming out again, to Staphyla within*].
250 Oh, if I don't tear your tongue out by the roots, you reprobate,
I myself will give you leave to send me to the gallows straight!

MEG. So it seems, by Hercules! friend Euclio, you think
me fit
To be mocked in my old age; I don't see how I merit it.

EUC. No, by Pollux! Megadorus! How could I do such
a deed?

MEG. Well, will you betroth your daughter to me?

EUC. Yes, if we're agreed
On the dowry that I mentioned.

MEG. You betroth her then?

EUC. I do.
Heaven approve it!

MEG. May it be so!

EUC. Pardon my reminding you
Of the compact, that my daughter shouldn't bring you any
dower.

MEG. I remember.

EUC. Ah, but you will shift about from hour to hour.
It's off and on, and on and off with you, exactly as you please. 260

MEG. Well, with you I'll have no quarrel. Now for the
festivities!
Make to-day the wedding day.

EUC. Yes, that will suit me splendidly.

MEG. I'll get ready. Is that all?

EUC. It is.

MEG. Then that's all right. Good-bye!
Ho, Strobilus, come you quickly with me to the market-place!

[*Exit Megadorus.*]

EUC. Ah, he's gone! By heaven, I pray you, just observe
how gold brings grace!
There's no doubt he's heard a whisper of the treasure I have
got;
That is what he's gaping after; that's the reason he's so hot!

EUCLIO. STAPHYLA.

Euc. Where are you, who've been a-blabbing to our neighbours one and all,
That my girl will have a dowry?   Staphyla, don't you hear
me call?

[*Enter Staphyla from Euclio's house.*]

Listen !   Go and get your dishes washed up and in due
270   array.
I've betrothed my daughter ; Megadorus marries her to-day.
STA.   Heaven approve it ! but it cannot be ! too sudden
has it come !
Euc.   Silence ! go and have all ready when from market I
get home.
Shut the door ; I'll soon be back.

[*Exit Euclio to the market-place.*]

STA.   O, bless my soul !   What shall I do ?
Utter ruin overhangs us, me and master's daughter too.
She's in love with that young fellow, though his name we do
not know ;
We can't hide it any longer ; O dear, here's a pretty go !
I must do what master told me ; so I'll go inside, I think.
Ah, by Castor ! I'm afraid I have a dreadful draught to drink.

[*Exit Staphyla into the house.*]

STROBILUS. ANTHRAX. CONGRIO.

[*Enter Strobilus, with Anthrax and Congrio (cooks), Phrygia and
Eleusium (music girls), and other slaves from the market.*]

280   STR.   When master'd done his shopping at the market,
And hired these cooks and dancing girls, he bade me
Divide all he had bought into two parts.

CONG.   By Hercules! you sha'n't cut *me* in two !
But if you want me *all*, I'm at your service.

ANTH.   Why, if he wants your *awl*,[1] you idiot,
You can't oblige him ; for you're not a cobbler.

CONG.   I didn't mean that kind of awl at all,
But something different, Anthrax.

STR.   Well, my master
Is marrying to-day.

ANTH.   Whose daughter is it ?

STR.   Old Euclio's, our next-door neighbour here.   290
Half the provision is to go to him :
One of the cooks, one of the music-girls.

ANTH.   What, half to him and only half to you ?

STR.   Exactly so.

CONG.   What, couldn't the old man
Pay for a wedding feast for his own daughter ?

STR.   Bah !

CONG.   Well, why not ?

STR.   Why not ? you want to know ?
A stone is not as dry as this old fellow.

CONG.   Do you say so ?

STR.   Yes, and you'd best believe it.
Why, he will call all gods and men to witness
That he is ruined and utterly destroyed,   300
If a puff of smoke escapes from out his chimney.
Nay, when he goes to bed he ties a bag
Over his mouth.

CONG.   What for ?

STR.   Lest he should lose
His breath whilst he's asleep. Oh, it's a fact !

CONG.   Nay, I believe you !

---

[1] This is not a translation of the original joke, but an equivalent.

STR.   Ah, but that's not all ;
He weeps to pour away his dirty water.

CONG.   Do you think that we could coax from the old
310   man
A cool two hundred pounds to buy our freedom ?

STR.   He wouldn't lend his hunger, if you asked him.
Why, yesterday the barber trimmed his nails ;
And he picked up and carried off the clippings !

ANTH.   By Pollux ! he's a mighty stingy man !

STR.   Would you believe a man could live so
    meanly ?
A kite once snatched a scrap of meat from him ;
Away he runs in tears to the magistrate ;
With sighs and groans he starts to beg of him
To send a summons out against the kite !
320 A thousand things I'd mention if we'd time.
But tell me, which of you's the smarter man ?

CONG.   I, much the better !

STR.   *Cook*, not *thief*, I mean.

CONG.   Well, so do I.

STR.   And you ?

ANTH.   I'm what you see.

CONG.   *He* only cooks on market days ;[1] he gets
A job but once a week.

ANTH.   Man of five letters ![2]
You slander *me?* thief ! thief ! thrice thievish thief !

STR.   Be quiet now, and take the fatter lamb.

ANTH.   All right.

STR.   You, Congrio, can take the other,

---

[1] He's so bad a cook that he is only hired on market days, when there
is a rush, and so only gets a job once a week (lit., once in nine days).

[2] Lit., of three letters, *viz.* FUR (=thief).

And go in there ;[1] and do you follow him.
You others come with me.

  Cong.   O, that's not fair !   330
By Hercules ! they have the fatter lamb.

  Str. Then you shall have the fatter music girl !
Phrygia, go with him ; and you, Eleusium,
Come here with me.

  Cong.   Strobilus, you're too smart !
You've pushed me off to this old miser's house,
Where I shall have to shout, until I'm hoarse,
For everything I want.

  Str.   O, you're a fool !
To do you favours is to throw 'em away.

  Cong. How so?

  Str.   Well, first of all, there's no crowd there
To get in your way. If you want anything,   340
Fetch it from home ; don't waste your precious time
In asking for it. In *our* house you'd find
A crowd of servants, heaps of fancy things,
And gold, and silver plate, and costly robes.
If anything got lost—(O yes, I know
You never think of filching—where there's nothing !)
They'd say, " The cooks have stolen it ! collar them !
Tie them up, thrash them, throw them in the well."
Now you are safe from this ; there's nothing there
For you to steal. So follow me !

  Cong.   I follow !

    Strobilus. Staphyla. Congrio.

  Str. Ho, Staphyla ! undo the door !
  Sta. [*within*].   Who calls ?   350

---

[1] *i.c.*, To Euclio's house. There are other slaves present besides the cooks and dancing girls, who are addressed in the next clauses.

STR.   Strobilus.

STA. [*coming out*].   Well, what is it ?

STR.   Please let in
These cooks, this music girl, and these provisions,
Which Megadorus sends to Euclio
Against his marriage feast.

STA.   But, good Strobilus,
Is it for Ceres that this feast's prepared ?

STR.   Why do you think so ?

STA.   Well, I see no wine.[1]

STR.   The master's bringing that along himself.

STA.   We have no firewood.

CONG.   Have you any laths ?

STA.   Of course.

CONG.   They'll do, you needn't send for more.

STA.   What, filthy wretch !   Because you want a fire
360 To cook the dinner and discharge your function,
Do you demand that we should burn our house ?

CONG.   O no !

STR.   Well, take them in.

STA.   Pray, follow me.
[*Exeunt Staphyla, Congrio, Phrygia, etc., into Euclio's house.*]

STROBILUS.[2]

STR.   Push on !   I'll go see what the cooks are doing.
To watch those rascals needs the greatest care,
Unless I make them cook down in the well,
And then in baskets haul the dinner up.
But if down there they eat up what they've cooked,
The gods above will go without their dinner—
The gods below get theirs !   But here I'm chattering,

---

[1] It would appear that no wine was used at the festivals of Ceres.

[2] This speech is assigned in the MSS. to " Fitodicus (= Pythodicus),
a slave ; " I follow Ussing in giving it to Strobilus.

As if I'd nothing in the world to do,   370
With all these sons of thievery in the house.
                    [*Exit into the house of Megadorus.*]

ErcLIO. CONGRIO.

[*Enter Euclio from the market-place.*]
Euc. I wished to be magnanimous to-day,
And show up well at the marriage of my daughter.
I go to market, ask for fish, and find
It's dear; and lamb is dear, and beef is dear;
And veal, and pork, and cod, they all are dear;
And all the dearer that I had no money.
There's nothing I can buy, so, in a rage,
I come away, and cheat the paltry rogues.
Then on my way I started meditating—
" What you have lavished on a festival,   380
You'll want on common days, if you're not careful."
Thus spake I with my stomach and my soul,
Until I was resolved to spend as little
As I could help upon my daughter's marriage;
And so I bought this incense and these flowers,
To put, in honour of our household god,
Upon the hearth, that he may bless the wedding.—
Hallo! do I behold my house door open?
And what a noise inside!   Am I being robbed?
    CoNG. [*within*].   Borrow a larger pot amongst your neigh- 390
        bours;
This is too small.   It will not hold the stuff.
    Euc.   Alas! my gold is stolen; he wants my Pot!
Apollo, I beseech thee, come and help me!
Pierce with thine arrows those who steal my treasure,
If e'er before thine aid has thus been given!
But I'll rush in before I'm wholly ruined.
                    [*Exit Euclio into his house.*]
                                                  L

ANTHRAX.

[Enter Anthrax from the house of Megadorus.]

ANTH. Come, Dromo, clean the fish! And you, Machærio,
Just bone the conger and the eel; be quick!
I'll go next door and borrow a bread-pan
400 From Congrio.   You'd better get that cock
Plucked cleaner than a maiden's face for me.
But what's this uproar going on next door?
The cooks, by Jove, are doing their duty well!
I'll hurry back, or we shall have a row!

[Exit Anthrax into Megadorus's house.]

CONGRIO.

[Enter Congrio, rushing in terror from Euclio's house.]

CONG. Help me, clear the streets,[1] ye citizens, natives,
neighbours, strangers, aliens.
Ne'er before have I been hired to cook a feast for baccha-
nalians—[2]
How he banged us with his cudgels, me and my disciples
making
410 Into pads to try his strength on.   Oh, my wretched back is
aching!
I never knew a day when wood was offered at a lower rate;
He loaded us with cudgels first, then turned us out of his
front gate.
Alas! I die!   From out his den the Fury comes with
furious look!
He's after me!   Well, never mind!   I'll take a leaf out of
his book.

---

[1] *i.e.*, To give room to run.   [2] See note on *Bacchides* 53, p. 192.

EUCLIO. CONGRIO.

[Enter Euclio from his house.]

EUC. [1] Come back, you runaway! Stop, thief! stop!

CONG. Oh! stop your jaw, sir!

EUC. I'll report your name to the magistrates, you scamp!

CONG. What for, sir?

EUC. You've got a knife.

CONG. A cook should have.

EUC. My life you threaten!

CONG. It's a pity I didn't take it too, before I was beaten.

EUC. You're the vilest wretch alive to-day; and that is true, sir!
There's none I would more readily help to punish than you, 420 sir!

CONG. O, you needn't tell me; I know it all; the proof is the licking
I've received from your cudgels; I'm as tender as any chicken.
What business have you to meddle with me, you beggarly miser?

EUC. Do you ask? By Jove, if I'd hit you harder, 'twould have been wiser. *[Euclio strikes him again.]*

CONG. Very well! But I'll make you pay, as sure as my head's got sense in't.

EUC. I believe it has—a sense of my stick! or there's something dense in't.
I should like to know what you were after, making a riot,

---

[1] The metre of lines 415—446 is as follows :—

$$\smallsmile\, \underline{}\!\smallsmile\! - |\smallsmile\, \underline{}\!\smallsmile\! - ||\smallsmile\, \underline{}\!\smallsmile\! - \smallsmile$$

with the usual licences (anapæst or spondee for iambus). I have imitated it as well as I could. At 447 the trochaics begin again.

When I was away, within my house !

Cong.   Well then, be quiet !

I came to cook for the wedding feast.

Euc.   And pray, with your pardon,

430 What does it matter to you what I eat ?   You're not my
   guardian.

Cong.   Well, I want to know if we're to stay to cook your
   dinner !

Euc.   And I want to know if my things are safe from you,
   you sinner !

Cong.   I only want to remove my pots, if I can do it !

I'm quite content without taking yours.

Euc.   No more ! or you'll rue it.

Cong.   Why on earth prevent us cooking the feast ?
   That is our mission.

Have we said or done a single thing to cause suspicion ?

Euc.   Do you ask ? you villain, you who've found out ways
   to be spying

Into every cupboard in the house, peeping and prying !

If you'd done your duty and not moved a step away from
   the fireplace,

440 You'd have saved yourself a broken head; you deserve it, you
   scapegrace !

Now to make my fixed determination even still clearer,

If, without my orders, you dare to come a single step nearer,

I'll just make your back as raw as a steak, thwack here and
   thwack there !

You know now what you've got to expect.

                         [*Exit Euclio into his house.*]

Cong.   Hallo ! come back there !

Well, help me, Laverna![1]   If you don't give up my pans, sir,

---

[1] The goddess of thieves.

I'll just raise the deuce in front of the house! Then, perhaps, you'll answer!
  What's a man to do, I wonder? I've no luck to-day,
that's sure!
  I was hired for eighteenpence;[1] my doctor's bill will come
to more!
    [*Re-enter Euclio, with the Pot of Gold under his cloak.*]
  Euc. [*aside*]. Ah, my Pot, I'll never leave thee, take thee
with me everywhere!
Never more shalt thou be periled by such dangers, I'll take
care.
[*Aloud.*] Now then, enter, if you like, you cooks and
music girls, and all!
Take in with you, if you wish, your flock of hirelings, great
and small.
Cook away and work away as much as you like, and slave
like blacks!
  Cong. Very fine, when with your cudgel you have crammed
my crown with cracks!
  Euc. Get inside, now; you were hired to do your work
and not to chatter.
  Cong. Come, old man, I'll make you pay for thrashing
me! That's what's the matter.
I was hired to cook your dinner, not to be your whipping
post.
  Euc. Go to law, then! Stop your clamour! Now, go
boil, and fry, and roast,
Or be off and hang yourself.
  Cong.   The same to you, my worthy host!
    [*Enter Congrio into the house of Euclio.*]

---

[1] Lit., for a *nummus*, = a drachma or didrachma, *i.e.*, about nine-
pence or eighteenpence of our money.

460   Euc. Gone at last ! Ye gods immortal, it's a perilous affair
When a poor man gets entangled with a wealthy millionaire.
See how Megadorus tries to catch me every kind of way !
He pretends 'twas in my honour that he sent those cooks
    to-day ;
Don't believe it ! No ! he sent them just to steal my little
    stock.
Then, as might have been expected, my confounded dung-
    hill cock,
Bought with the old woman's savings, ruined me within an
    ace ;
For the wretch began a-scratching with his claws all round
    the place
Where the gold was lying buried ; piercing anguish thrilled
    my breast,
So I took a stick and slew him as a burglar manifest.
470 I've no doubt the cooks had promised they would pay him
    handsomely,
If he'd show them where the gold was !   Now I've put them
    up a tree !
Why say more?   The fight is finished 'twixt the dunghill cock
    and me !
See, my kinsman, Megadorus, coming from the market-place !
Well, it wouldn't do to cut him ; I must stop and do him
    grace.

MEGADORUS.   EUCLIO.

*[Enter Megadorus from the market-place ; he does not at first
see Euclio.]*

    MEG.   I've told my plan to many of my friends
About my marriage with old Euclio's daughter ;
They praise the girl, and say I've done right well.
In my opinion, other wealthy men

Should do the same, and take to them in marriage   480
The daughters of the poor without a dowry ;
So would the State be more harmonious,
For we[1] should lose the odium we've incurred ;
Our wives would dread us more than they do now,
And our expenses would be greatly lessened.
As this would please the great majority,
Our only quarrel would be with a few
Of greedy and insatiable soul
Whom neither law nor magistrate can limit.
But if you say, " Whom will the rich girls marry,
Those who have dowers, if this be made the law ? "   490
Let 'em marry where they will, but without dowry.
If this were so, they'd seek instead of dower
To bring us sweeter tempers than they do.
I'll cause that mules,[2] dearer than horses now,
Shall be sold cheaper than your Gallic geldings.[3]

    Euc. [*aside*].   God bless my soul, this is a pleasant hearing !
How kindly does he speak of us poor folk !

    Meg.   No wife would say, " I brought you, sir, a dowry
Far greater than the income you possessed ;
Therefore, it's fair I should have robes, and gold,   500
Maidens, and mules, and mule-drivers, and footmen,
Pages to serve, litters to carry me."

    Euc. [*aside*].   How well he knows the ways of married
        ladies !
They ought to make him censor of the women.

    Meg.   Now you can see more carts[4] at your house-door

---

[1] *i.e.*, The wealthier classes.

[2] Mules were very costly, being in great demand for the use of ladies of wealth and rank. Megalorus says he will put a stop to the demand.

[3] Which were considered very inferior.

[4] Bringing home your wife's shoppings.

Than in the country when you're at your farm.
But that is nought compared with the sad day
On which the tradesmen come to get their money.
There stand the fuller, the embroiderer,
Hairdressers, border-makers, violet-dyers,
510 Dealers in underclothes and bridal veils,
Dyers in yellow, sleeve-makers, perfumers,
Sellers of linen garments, slipper-makers,
Cobblers that squat at ease, and shoemakers ;
There stand the sandal-dealers, there the dyers ;
The milliners and tailors want their cash ;
There stand the belt-makers and girdle-sellers.
You've got these paid ; a thousand more press on ;
They stand, your gaolers, all about your hall,
Weavers, and fringe-dealers, and cabinet-makers.
520 You pay them and you think the list's exhausted ;
But no ! the saffron-dyers march along,
Or some new plague or other with his bill.

    Euc. [*aside*].   I'd speak to him, but that I fear he'd stop
His tale of women's manners ; so I'll wait.
    · Meg.   When all these hucksters have been duly paid,
Last comes a soldier, asking for his money.[1]
You go and have a reckoning with your banker,
The hungry soldier waiting for the cash ;
And when the banker's got it reckoned up,
530 You find that your account is overdrawn.
The soldier has to wait till another day.
These are a few out of the many troubles
And heavy costs that go with all large dowries.
The undowered wife is in her husband's power ;

---

[1] The tax for the support of the army, which, when assessed on the wife's property, the husband had to pay.

But dowers bring loss and ruin to the husband.
[*Catches sight of Euclio.*]
Why, here's my relative before the house !
How are you, Euclio ?

EUCLIO. MEGADORUS.

Euc.   With infinite pleasure
I have devoured your speech.
    MEG.   What, did you hear me ?
    EUC.   Yes, every word, right from the very first.
    MEG.   Excuse me, don't you think it would be fitter
To get yourself a little better dressed   540
Against your daughter's wedding ?
    EUC.   Megadorus,
I cut my coat according to my cloth.
Let those who've wealth and means remember well
From what they've risen.   And pray, don't think that I
Or any other poor man have at home
More than appearances would seem to show.
    MEG.   Nay, don't be down !   May Heaven smile on your
      store,
And bless with growing increase all you have.
    EUC. [*aside*].   I don't like that expression, "all you have ; "
He knows, as well as I do, what I've got.
That wretched hag has told him everything.
    MEG.   Why do you silent leave our conference ?
    EUC.   I have a fault to find with you.   550
    MEG.   What is't ?
    EUC.   What is it? why, you've filled my house with thieves ;
They swarm in every corner, woe is me !
You've sent into my house five hundred cooks
With six hands each, true sons of Geryon. [1]

---

[1] A giant with three bodies and, therefore, six hands.

Though Argus watched them, who's all over eyes,
Whom Juno set to keep a watch on Jove,
He couldn't do it ; then the music-girl
Would drink the fountain of Pirene dry,
At Corinth there, that's if it flowed with wine !
The fish she'd—

560   MEG.   There's enough for a regiment !
I sent a lamb too.
       EUC.   Yes, and that same lamb
Is the most care-worn beast I ever saw.
       MEG.   I'd like to hear you prove the lamb is care-worn.
       EUC.   Why, he's all skin and bone ; he's thin with care.
Nay, you can see right through him in the sunlight.
He's as transparent as a Punic lantern. [1]
       MEG.   I bought him to be *killed*.
       EUC.   Then you had better
Arrange for his funeral ; he's already dead.
       MEG.   Well, come, we'll have a gay carouse together.
       EUC.   I haven't any wine.

570   MEG.   Oh, I will order
A cask of fine old wine from my own cellar.
       EUC.   I'd rather not ; I drink nothing but water.
       MEG.   Ah, if I live, I'll make you drunk to-day,
You water-drinker !
       EUC. [*aside*].   Yes, I see his dodge.
He's trying now to bury me in drink,
That he may change the home of this. my gold.
I'll stop that game ; I'll hide it somewhere else ;
And so he'll lose his labour and his wine.
       MEG.   Excuse me, I must bathe for the sacrifice.

                          [*Exit Meg. into his house.*]

---

[1] Perhaps made of glass, which was invented by the Carthaginians.

Euc.   My Pot, how many enemies thou hast,   580
And that sweet gold that is shut up in thee !
Now this is my best plan, to carry thee,
My Pot, to the shrine of Faith,[1] and there to hide thee.
Oh, Faith, we know each other ; take good heed
That thou change not thy name, if I do trust thee.
I trust me, Faith, unto thy faithfulness.

[*Exit Euclio to the temple with the Pot.*]

STROBILUS.

[*Enter Strobilus,[2] the slave of Lyconides.*]

STR.   All good slaves may take example, how they should
  behave, from me ;
And not think their master's orders are a bore or injury.
If a slave would serve his master just according to his mind,
He will put his master's interests first and keep his own 590
  behind.
Even in the deepest slumber he'll remember he's a slave ;
[3]And his eyes will learn to tell him what his master's looks
  would have ;
Then he'll execute his orders faster than with race-horse 600
  speed.
If he does so, then the ox-hide ne'er will make his shoulders
  bleed ;

---

[1] Fides, whose temple stands near Euclio's house.

[2] This Strobilus is not the same as the Strobilus of the first three acts.
The identity of name is probably due to the fact that the same actor
played both the parts.

[3] Seven lines are inserted here in the MSS. apparently from some
other play.   They are inappropriate to the situation, and end abruptly in
the middle of a sentence.   I have therefore followed Brix and Wagner in
omitting them.

He won't spend his time in making fetters bright with constant wear.

Well, my master loves the daughter of poor Euclio, who lives
there ;

He's just heard that Megadorus is about to wed his dear ;

So to spy out what they're after, he's dispatched and sent me
here.

Ah ! I'll lounge beside this altar ;[1] no one will suspect me
then ;

Hence I'll see what they are doing and take my master word
again.

Euclio.   Strobilus.

*[Enter Euclio returning from the temple of Faith where he has
hidden the Pot.]*

Euc. Now, good Faith, don't tell a soul that I have put
my gold in there ;

Nobody will find it now or drag it from its secret lair.

610 Though if anyone *did* find it, he would get a noble spoil,

For the Pot is crammed with gold. O Faith, frustrate their
wicked toil !

Now I'll bathe for sacrifice, that I mayn't cause the least delay

When my kinsman comes to carry my dear daughter home
to-day.

Once again, O Faith, I pray thee, keep me safe that Pot of
mine ;

To thy faith my gold I've trusted, placed it in thy grove
and shrine.

[Exit Euclio into his house.]

---

[1] There was always an altar upon the stage. Strobilus intends to
appear in the character of an idle loafer who has nothing to do but to
bask in the sun.

STR. O ye gods immortal, what a tale is this I've just
    heard told !
That he's hidden in the temple some big Pot that's crammed
    with gold !
Faith ! to him do thou prove faithless, but be faithful unto me !
Why, I guess, this is the father of my master's love. 'Tis he !
I'll go in and search the temple, see if I can find the gold,   620
While the old man's busy yonder. Help, O Faith, my theft
    so bold ;
Then a bowl of wine I'll offer, if I only get the pelf,
First I'll offer it to you, and then I'll drink it up myself.

                   [Exit Strobilus to the temple.]

EUCLIO.

[Enter Euclio from his house.]

EUC. Hist ! a raven's crying harshly on the left ; oh, it's
    no joke !
First he cawed and scratched the gravel, then he gave a
    solemn croak.
Oh, the minute that I heard him, how my heart went pit-a-
    pat !
I must run and see about it ! something's wrong, I'm sure of
    that.

                   [Exit Euclio to the temple.]

EUCLIO. STROBILUS.

*[Re-enter Euclio, dragging after him Strobilus, who has not
succeeded in finding the Pot.]*

EUC. Out, come out, you worm, you, creeping secretly
    from underground !
You were hiding just now, were you ? Oh, you're done for,
    now you're found !
Ah, by Hercules ! you swindler ! see if I don't make you rue.   630

Str.   What the devil is the matter?   What have I to do with you?
What are you hitting *me* for, sirrah?   Just let go my necker-chief!

Euc.   Why, most thrashable of mortals! thief, and thief, and three times thief!

Str.   What have I stolen?

Euc.   Give it up, sir!

Str.   Give *what* up?

Euc.   Come, come, you know!

Str.   I've not stolen aught of yours.[1]

Euc.   You'll give it up before you go!
Come, get on.

Str.   Get on with what?

Euc.   You can't escape me!

Str.   What do you want?

Euc.   Hand it over!

Str.   That's a phrase with which you're doubtless conversant.[2]

Euc.   Hand it over! no more chaffing! I've no time for fooleries.

Str.   Hand *what* over?   Name it, man! come, tell me plainly what it is.
Nothing have I touched or taken that is yours.

640   Euc.   Then show your hand.

Str.   There you are!

Euc.   The other!

---

[1] There is a joke here which I cannot get into English.   The line runs:
Str.   Nil equidem *tibi* abstuli.
Euc.   At illud quod *tibi* abstuleras, cedo.
[2] I take Ussing's reading as being the sweeter of the two.   He means that Euclio is a foot-pad.

STR.   There, then!

EUC.   Now the third one I demand!

STR. Poor old chap, he's very bad! His wretched wits
    are quite unsteady.

Sir, you do me wrong!

EUC.   I do, that I've not had you hanged already.

But you shortly will be if you don't confess.

STR.   Confess to what?

EUC. Tell me what you've stolen from me.

STR.   Hang me, if I've stolen a jot,

Or have wished to do so, either.

EUC.   Come on then, shake out your cloak.

STR. As you like! [*Shaking his cloak.*]

EUC.   It's in your shirt, then!

STR.   Feel me! Have your little
    joke!

EUC. Bah! How ready is the wretch to have his inmost
    secrets scanned!

But I'm up to all your tricks. Again, sir, show me your right
    hand.

STR. There!

EUC.   And now the left one show me!

STR.   Both at once, sir, certainly.   650

EUC. This is useless. Give it here!

STR.   Give what?

EUC.   Ah, you are mocking me!

You have got it.

STR.   Got it? what?

EUC.   O yes, no doubt you'd like to hear!

Give me all you've got of mine.

STR.   You're mad! Why, isn't it quite clear

That I've naught at all about me? You have searched me
    through and through.

Euc.   Stay, stay! Who's the other fellow who was there
    inside with you?
[*Aside.*] 'Sdeath! he's in there robbing me!   This fellow
    will run off, I know,
If I let him.[1] But I've searched him. He's got nothing.
                           [*Aloud.*]   Off you go!
    Str.   Heaven's best curses light upon you!
    Euc.   He's the gratefullest of men!
I'll go in and drag your comrade by his throat from out his den.
Won't you leave my sight?   Begone!
    Str.   I'm off!
660   Euc.   And don't come back again!
                        [*Exit Euclio to the temple.*]

                STROBILUS.

Str.   I'd rather die outright in agonies
Than fail to catch the old man in my wiles.
Now he'll not dare to hide his money here;
I guess he'll bring it out to some new place.
Ha, ha! I hear him.   There! he's got it with him!
Meanwhile I'll hide myself beside this door.[2]

        EUCLIO.   STROBILUS.

[*Enter Euclio bringing his Pot from the temple.*]

Euc.   I thought I might have put more faith in Faith,
But she has very nearly blacked my nose![3]
Had not the raven helped me, I'd been ruined!
670 I wish that raven could come here to me,

---

    [1] Euclio imagines that Strobilus has a partner who is still in the temple
looking for the Pot. He is satisfied that Strobilus hasn't got it; and
therefore thinks it best to let him go, and return to the temple himself to
look for his imaginary accomplice.   I read with Wagner " hinc abierit."
    [2] The door of Megadorus' house.
    [3] To blacken a sleeper's nose with a burnt cork is a trick that still
survives.

Who warned me ; I would *tell* him something good.
To *give* him food would be as good as lose it.—
I've hit upon the very place of safety !
Outside the walls there is a pathless grove
Filled with dense willows, sacred to Silvanus ;
There will I find a spot ; I am resolved ;
Silvanus will I trust rather than Faith.

                       [Exit Euclio to the grove.]

   STR.   Bravo ! bravo ! the gods are on my side !
I'll run on first and climb up in a tree ;
Thence I shall see where Euclio hides his gold.
My master bade me stay *here*, certainly.   680
But if I get the cash, I'll stand a thrashing.

                       [Exit Strobilus to the grove.]

              LYCONIDES.   EUNOMIA.

     [Enter Lyconides and Eunomia from the town.]

   LYC.   Mother, I've told you all ; you know as much
As I, about old Euclio's daughter here.
Now I adjure and pray you once again
Go tell it to my uncle, mother dear !

   EU.   You know that I am heart and soul with you ;
I trust I shall prevail upon my brother ;
The thing's a fair one, if, as you affirm,
You are engaged to marry Euclio's daughter.

   LYC.   D' you think I would deceive you, mother mine ?   690

   EU.   Come in with me, my son, and see my brother ;
I'll beg him earnestly to grant your prayer.

   LYC.   Go in, I'll follow you directly, mother.

               [Exit Eunomia into Megadorus' house.]

I wonder where my slave Strobilus is.
I bade him wait me here ; but now I think on't,

                             M

If he's at work for me, I won't be angry.
700 I'll go in where my fate is being discussed.

> [*Exit Lyconides into Megadorus' house.*]

STROBILUS.

> [*Enter Strobilus from the grove with the Pot of Gold.*]

    STR. I'm richer than the fabled woodpeckers
Who guard the hills of gold ! Those other kings,
They're not worth mentioning, the beggarly rascals !
I am the great King Philip ! [1] O happy day !
When I'd left here, I got there long before him,
And took my station in a lofty tree,
And there I saw where Euclio hid his gold.
When he was gone, I scrambled down the tree,
Dug up the Pot of Gold. But then I spied
710 The old man coming back ; he didn't see me,
For I had slipped a little to one side—
Ha ! here he comes ! I'll go hide this at home !

> [*Exit Strobilus to the house of Lyconides.*]

EUCLIO.

> [*Enter Euclio from the grove.*]

    EUC. Oh, I'm lost and undone and destroyed ! Where to
run ? Where to stand ? Stop a thief ! Ah, but who's
to stop whom ? [2]
I don't know ! I can't see ! I've gone blind ! Where I
am, where to go, who I am, I don't know ! All is gloom.
Oh, my mind is distracted, I can't see my way ! O help me,
O help me, good people, I pray ! [3]

---

[1] Philip of Macedon, whose gold mines gave him the reputation of
great wealth.

[2] Lines 713—725 are anapæstic octonarii :—

    ⏑⏑– | ⏑⏑– | ⏑⏑– | ⏑⏑– || ⏑⏑– | ⏑⏑– | ⏑⏑– | ⏑⏑–

This is addressed to the audience.

O I beg and beseech you to show me the villain who's taken
   and stolen my money away.
There is nothing to laugh at.   I know you, you wretches !
   There's lots of you thieves there, in spite of your bluff,
A - sitting and hiding yourselves in dress clothes so that
   strangers would think you were honest enough !—[1]
Did you speak, sir?   Ah, yes, I am sure I can trust *you !*   I
   see you're a good man.   Your face tells me so.—
What, none of you has it?—O sir, you have killed me !
   Pray tell me who has it ?—What's that ?—You don't
   know ?—   720
O wretch that I am!   I'm destroyed!   I am ruined !   There
   never was man in so sorry a plight !
Such hunger and poverty, groaning and sorrow, this day has
   brought on me, most pitiful wight !
I'm the woefullest creature alive !   what's the use of his life
   to a man who has lost all his pelf?
I've watched it and guarded it, O so devoutly ! labour all lost!
   I've but cheated myself,
Yea, my heart and my soul !   And, at this very moment,·
   another's rejoicing and shouting, the thief,
(Oh, it's past all enduring !) o'er *my* loss and grief !

LYCONIDES.   EUCLIO.

[*Enter Lyconides from the house of Megadorus.*]

  Lyc.   Who is this who's bawling out before our house
   like some sad lover ?
Why, it's Euclio, I believe !   It's all got out !   My game is
   over !
He's found out that we're engaged.   Well, I am in a pretty
   mess !

---

[1] Only the wealthier people had seats.   *See* General Introduction.

730 Which is best, to go or stay? to speak or run?   Oh, I can't
   guess !
   Euc.   Who's that speaking?
   Lyc.   I, poor wretch !
   Euc.   Nay, I'm the wretch who'm standing here !
Woes and troubles rush upon me in such force.
   Lyc.   Be of good cheer !
   Euc.   How can that be, I beseech?
   Lyc.   The crime that troubles you to-day [1]
I committed, I confess it.
   Euc.   What is that I hear you say?
   Lyc.   Simple truth.
   Euc.   And, pray, what evil have you e'er
   received from me
That you should attempt to ruin me and all my family?
   Lyc.   It was Heaven that drove me to it and enticed me
   thereto.
   Euc.   How?
   Lyc.   I confess that I'm a sinner, and my grievous fault
   avow,
And I'm come to you a suppliant who your pardon now im-
   plores.
   Euc.   How could you have dared to do it and to touch what
740   wasn't yours?
   Lyc.   What would you have me do?   The thing is done
   and can't be undone now.
Heaven willed it; naught can happen if the gods do
   not allow.

---

[1] The confusion between the Pot and the young lady, which gives the
point to this dialogue, is greatly helped by the fact that in Latin the same
pronoun serves for both, Pot *(Aula)* being feminine. I have had to translate very freely to keep up the misunderstanding.

Euc.   Yes, and Heaven also willed that I should set you
in the stocks.

Lyc.   Don't say that.

Euc.   What business had you meddling with my
things, you fox?

Lyc.   It was love and wine that made me.

Euc.   Wretch of triple insolence!
Do you dare to come and tell me such a tale? What im-
pudence!
Why, if people are permitted in that way to make things right,
We shall steal our ladies' jewels from them in the broad day-
light;
Afterwards, if we are caught, we'll make a fine excuse and
weep,
Say for love and wine we did it! Love and wine are far too
cheap,   750
If all's lawful to a man, provided he's in love and tight!

Lyc.   But I've come to beg your pardon and to set the
matter right.

Euc.   I hate men who first do wrong and afterwards apologise.
You'd no business touching what was mine, that's how the
matter lies.

Lyc.   True, I dared to go so far, sir; and I know 'twas
wrong; but still,
I'm prepared to stick to it.

Euc.   What, stick to it against my will?

Lyc.   O no, not against your will; but still, I think it
should be so;
And I think you'll come to see it in that light, good Euclio.

Euc.   Give it back, or else—

Lyc.   Give *what* back?

Euc.   Why, what you have stolen from me.   760

Or I'll drag you to the judge and enter action presently.

Lyc. *I* have stolen from *you?* What is it?

Euc.   O, Jove bless your innocence!
You don't know!

Lyc.   Of course I don't, unless you speak some
clearer sense.

Euc. It's that Pot of Gold I'm wanting, which you just
confessed to me
You had stolen.

Lyc.   Never! never!

Euc.   You deny it?

Lyc.   Certainly!

Why, I never knew or dreamt about your money or your Pot.

Euc. Give it me, I say; the one that from Silvanus' grave
you got.

Go and fetch it! See, look here, I'll give you half on't
willingly;

Though you've thieved I'll keep it quiet; only bring it back
to me.

Lyc. O, you're mad to call me thief! The fact was,
Euclio, I thought

770 You'd found out another matter of a very different sort.
I would willingly discuss it at your leisure, if I might.

Euc. On your honour, have you stol'n that gold of mine?

Lyc.   No! honour bright!

Euc. Do you know who stole it?

Lyc.   No, sir!

Euc.   And if you should get to know
Who has stolen it, will you tell me who it is?

Lyc.   Yes, I'll do so.

Euc. And you'll never help the thief or share it with him?

Lyc.   Certainly.

Euc. If you break your word?

Lyc.   Then Heaven lay what curse it will on me !

Euc.   That'll do.   Now to your story.

Lyc.   As you may not be aware
From what family I spring, my uncle's Megadorus there.
I'd Antimachus for father ; my own name's Lyconides,
And my mother is Eunomia.

Euc.   That I knew.   Your business, please !   780

Lyc.   You've a daughter, I believe.

Euc.   I have, she lives in there with me.

Lyc.   You've betrothed her to my uncle.

Euc.   Yes, you have it perfectly.

Lyc.   He has sent me word to tell you he repudiates the
      girl.

Euc.   What, when everything is ready and the feast's pre-
      pared, the churl ?
Oh, may all the gods in Heaven curse him with a curse un-
      told !
Him through whom I've lost to-day, poor luckless wretch,
      my store of gold !

Lyc.   Come, cheer up, don't speak of cursing !   There's
      a thing I hope may be
Good for you and her as well.   Heav'n grant it ! please, say
      after me.

Euc.   Well, Heav'n grant it.

Lyc.   Yea, Heav'n grant it.   Listen, now, to
      me a while.
When a man has done a wrong, there's no one so entirely   790
      vile,
But he blushes when he makes apology ; then, hear my plea !
If I've done a wrong to you or to your daughter thoughtlessly,
Pray you, pardon me, and give me for my wife your daughter
      fair !
It is true, without your knowledge I became engaged to her

At the feast of Ceres, driven by the force of youth and wine.

EUC.   Woe is me, what deed is this I hear you tell?

LYC.   Come, don't repine !

For my uncle gave her up just so that she might marry me.

800 Go in, ask if it's not true.

EUC.   Alas, I'm ruined utterly !

One misfortune on another comes and sticks to me like glue.

I'll go in and ask about the truth of this.

LYC.   I'll follow you.

                         [*Exit Euclio into his house.*]

I'm nearly in the harbour now !   I *am* a lucky lover !

But where my slave Strobilus is, I really can't discover ;

I'll wait for him a little while ; and then I'll just step over

And follow Euclio ; meantime he'll find, if he should doubt it,

From the old nurse that I spoke truth ; for she knows all about it.

STROBILUS.   LYCONIDES.

[*Enter Strobilus.*]

STR.   Gods immortal, ye have blessed me with illimitable joy !

I've a four-pound Pot of Gold ; there's not a richer man than I !

810 Of all men who live in Athens I'm the luckiest by far !

LYC.   Surely I can overhear the voice of someone speaking.

STR.   Ah !

Do I see my master there?

LYC.   Is that my servant that I see ?

STR.   It is he !

LYC.   It is no other !

STR.   I'll accost him !

Lyc.   Yes, it's he !
I expect that he's been talking, as I bade him, to her nurse.
   Str.   Why not tell him that I've found this booty and my
     news disburse ?
Then I'll ask to be set free.   Yes, now I'll go and tell him
   all.
I have found—
   Lyc.   What have you found ?
   Str.   Not what the urchins shout and bawl
They've found in the bean ! [1]
   Lyc.   I see you're chaffing in your usual way, sir !
   Str.   Stay, I'll tell you all.
   Lyc.   Get on then, tell me !
   Str.   I have found to-day, sir, 820
Boundless riches !
   Lyc.   Where ?
   Str.   I've got a four-pound Pot that's full of
   money !
   Lyc.   What do you say ?
   Str.   I've stolen it from old man Euclio !   Ain't
   it funny ?
   Lyc.   Where's the gold ?
   Str.   In a box at home.   So please now,
   master, set me free !
   Lyc.   Set you free !   A likely thing ! you lump of foul
   iniquity !
   Str.   O get out ! your dodge I see !
Cunningly I tried your temper ! You'd soon find the gold a
   lodging !

---

[1] *i.e.*, Not something of trifling importance.   The editors don't seem
quite certain what the boys *did* find in the bean.   Some say it was a
little worm, called " Midas ; " others a certain number of beans, say
seven, or nine, which was supposed to be lucky.

What if 1 had *really* found it?

LYC.   Come, sir, it's no use your dodging.
Fetch the gold !

STR.   The gold ?

LYC.   Go, take it to old Euclio !

STR.   Where'll I get it ?

LYC.   From the box you told me of.

STR.   My tongue *does* run on, if I let it !
830 I've a way of talking nonsense.

LYC.   Come, sir, fetch it, or you'll see—

STR.   You can kill me if you like ; but you'll not get it
out of me !

[Here, through an unfortunate gap in the MSS., the play
ends. A few fragments of the later portion have survived,
from which and the prologue we can gather that Lyconides
restored the Pot of Gold to Euclio on condition of receiving
his consent to marry his daughter ; and that Euclio subse-
quently bestowed the money upon the young couple to start
them in life. This may have been part of the bargain made
by Lyconides, or the result of a sudden change in the old
miser's temper. Strobilus was doubtless emancipated ; and
so all ended happily.]

BACCHIDES;

OR,

THE SISTERS.

INTRODUCTION.

THIS play is based upon the Δὶς 'εξαπατῶν of the famous poet Menander. Its date is to some extent determined by the reference to the multiplication of triumphs in line 1074. This indicates that it was written somewhere between 190 and 185 B.C. It was certainly later than the Epidicus, as will be seen by a reference to line 211. It is one of the most brilliant of the comedies of Plautus; but the objectionable character of the plot has caused it to be less read than some other inferior specimens of the poet's art. I have tried to preserve the wit and grace of the original, whilst so far modifying the story as to omit what is most offensive. The scene is laid at Athens.

DRAMATIS PERSONÆ.

PISTOCLERUS   *Son of Philoxenus, in love with Bacchis Attica.*

BACCHIS ATTICA ⎱
BACCHIS SAMIA ⎰   *Sisters.*

CLEOMACHUS -   *A Captain, in love with Bacchis Samia.*

LYDUS -   -   *A Slave, Tutor to Pistoclerus.*

CHRYSALUS   -   *Slave of Nicobulus.*

NICOBULUS   -   *A Citizen of Athens.*

MNESILOCHUS -   *Son of Nicobulus, in love with Bacchis Samia.*

PHILOXENUS -   *A Citizen of Athens.*

A PARASITE.

[A BOY.]

[ARTAMO   -   *An Executioner.*]

THE beginning of this play has perished along with the end of its predecessor. But it is easy to supply what is lacking from the remainder of the play. The prologue probably related how, two years before the opening of the play, Nicobulus, a citizen of Athens, had sent his son Mnesilochus to Ephesus to collect a debt owed to him by Archidemides, a citizen of that place. Calling at Samos on his way, Mnesilochus fell in love with a girl called Bacchis, who was, however, hired for a year by a certain military captain, Cleomachus, and taken away by him to Athens. Mnesilochus, hereupon, writes to Pistoclerus, a friend of his in Athens, begging him to find the girl, and, if possible, release her from the captain's service. Hereupon followed the first scene in which Pistoclerus is introduced, reading and commenting on his friend's letter. To him enters Bacchis Attica, and informs him that she is expecting a visit that day from her sister, who has come from Samos, and who bears the same name as herself. Pistoclerus tells her of his friend's commission, and is overjoyed at having found so readily the object of his quest. The Samian Bacchis now enters along with Cleomachus, who gives her permission to visit her sister, and leaves her at the house. The two sisters greet one another, Pistoclerus having retired into the background, or left the stage. It is at this point that the play, as we have it, begins.

PISTOCLERUS. BACCHIS ATTICA. BACCHIS SAMIA.

[*Scene: a street in Athens, with the houses of Bacchis Attica and of Nicobulus side by side. Enter Pistoclerus, Bacchis Attica, and Bacchis Samia.*]

ATT.   Is it best for me to speak, and you be silent?

SAM.   Yes, that's clear.

ATT.   Well, then, if my memory fails me, you must help me, sister dear.

SAM.   Nay, love, if I tried to help you, I'd be sure to do it wrong.

ATT.   Sooner would the nightingale forget the way to sing her song.

Come with me.

PIST.   [*aside*].   What are they after, these twin sisters with one name?

[*Aloud.*] What are you discussing?

ATT.   Something good.

PIST.   That's not your usual game.   40

ATT.   O how wretched is poor woman !

PIST.   As she merits, I aver.

ATT.   This, my sister, begs of me to find someone who'll rescue her

From that captain,[1] make him send her home when she has served her time.

Do this, pray !

PIST.   Do what ?

---

[1] This is Thornton's rendering of "miles," and commends itself by reason of its constant use in the earlier English comedy.

ATT.   Just see that she's sent to her native clime,
So that when her year is ended, he mayn't keep her as his maid.
If she'd only gold to give him, he'd release her and be glad.
   PIST.   Where's the man ?
   ATT.   He'll be here shortly.   Meanwhile you will
      serve us best,
Till he comes, by going indoors and sitting down to take a rest.
You shall have a glass of wine, and after that a loving kiss !
   PIST.   Ah ! your flattery's nought but bird-lime !
   ATT.   What do you mean?
50   PIST.   Why, I see this,
You two want to catch a pigeon; if your lime-twig touch his wing,
I can well foresee, my lady, all the trouble it will bring.
   ATT.   How ?
   PIST.   Ah, Bacchis, I don't like your Bacchæ and your
      Bacchanal.[1]
   ATT.   What do you fear ?   To ask you in to take a seat's
      not criminal.
   PIST.   Not your *seat* but your *deceit* is what I fear, you
      naughty girl !
I am young, and your attractions set my senses in a whirl.
   ATT.   Oh, you silly goose, don't fancy I am making love
      to you.
When the captain comes, I want you to be here and help us
      through.
You'll protect us from the insults which that fellow may intend;
60   You'll prevent him ; at the same time you will serve your
      worthy friend.[2]

---

[1] The Bacchic mysteries were introduced at Rome during the time of
Plautus, and became the occasion of such infamous crimes that in 186 B.C.
they were declared illegal, and those participating in them were rendered
liable to capital punishment.   "Bacchanal" means "bacchanalian den."
   [2] *i.e.*, Mnesilochus, who had commissioned Pistoclerus to find and take
care of Bacchis Samia.

And the captain, when he comes, will think that I'm engaged
    to you.
Won't you answer?

    PIST.   Ah, your words are nice enough to listen to;
But one finds when put in practice they've a sharp point, all
    the same!
Pierce one's soul, goad through one's goods, and wound one's
    doings and good fame.

    SAM.   Why are you afraid of her?

    PIST.   Do you ask?   What should a lad be doing
With your boudoir for gymnasium, where he'll only sweat
    to ruin?
For my quoits I shall get losses, and for running shame
    abhorr'd.

    ATT.   Hear him talk!

    PIST.   Within my hands you'll put a dove and not a sword.
When I want my boxing-gloves, I'll get a drinking-cup instead;
For my helm a wine-bowl, for my crest a garland round my   70
    head,
For my spear the dice-box, for my breastplate some luxurious
    weed,
With a girl upon my shield-arm, and a sofa for my steed.
Hence, avaunt!

    ATT.   Ah, you're too savage!

    PIST.   Never mind, I know my way.

    ATT.   I must take in hand and tame you.

    PIST.   No! there'd be too much to pay.

    ATT.   Feign to love me!

    PIST.   Shall I feign in jest, or do it seriously?

    ATT.   Ah, well, we must get to business.   Kindly put your
    arm round me
When the captain comes.

    PIST.   What for?

                                   N

ATT.   For him to see.   I have my plan.

PIST.   And, by Pollux! I've my fear!   But, here, I say—

ATT.   What ails the man?

PIST.   What if I drop in upon you when a luncheon or carouse

80 Or a dinner party's on?—You often have them at your house.
—Where's my seat?

ATT.   By me, my darling! jolly lad by jolly lass!

Come at any time; you'll always find by me a plate and glass.

When you want a jolly time, just say to me, " My rose of grace,

Make me welcome!" and I'll do it, and find you a jolly place.

PIST.   Here's a madly-rushing torrent! and it can't be lightly crossed.

ATT. [aside].   And, by Castor! in this torrent something shall by you be lost!

[Aloud.] Take my hand and come along.

PIST.   No, no!

ATT.   Why not?

PIST.·   Because, in sooth,

Evening hours and wine and ladies are too tempting to a youth.

ATT.   Very well! so let it be! It is for you alone I care.

90 Let the captain take her with him; you can go if you prefer.

PIST.   Nay, I'm helpless, for I cannot quell my passion's rising wave!

ATT.   What are you afraid of?

PIST.   Nothing! Lady, I'm your willing slave!

Yours I am for any service!

ATT.   Now you're jolly! Listen here.

I should like to give a feast to welcome home my sister dear.

I will bid them bring you money, then I'll ask you to be pleased

Just to go to market for me and provide a sumptuous feast.

PIST.   Nay, *I'll* pay.   It would be shameful that you
    should find out a way,
For my sake, to do me kindness, and then have the cost to pay.

ATT.   But I don't want *you* to give it.

PIST.   Let me !

ATT.   All right, if you please
Be quick, darling !

PIST.   I'll be back before my love has time to freeze.   100
                   [*Exit Pistoclerus to the market.*]

SAM.   So my coming brings you luck, dear sister.

ATT.   How is that, I pray ?

SAM.   Why, in my opinion, you have made a splendid
    catch to-day.

ATT.   Oh, he's mine !   But we must see about Mnesi-
    lochus, my dear ;
We must save you from the captain that ou may earn
    money here.

SAM.   It's my wish.

ATT.   We'll see to it.   Now, let's go in to bathe
    and dress.
You'll be feeling squeamish from your voyage.

SAM.   Yes, dear, more or less.

ATT.   Come along and have a bath, 'twill take away your
    weariness.   [*Exeunt into the house of Bacchis.*]

LYDUS.   PISTOCLERUS.

[*Enter from the market Pistoclerus, preceded by a crowd of slaves
carrying food, flowers, wines, etc., for the feast; Lydus[1]
following him.*]

LYD.   For some time, Pistoclerus, I've been following
In silence at your heels, intent to see   110

---

[1] Lydus is the pædagogus or tutor of Pistoclerus ; he is, as men of his
profession usually were, a slave.

What you are going to do with all this gear.
God bless my soul ! Lycurgus'[1] self, I think,
Might well have been debauched by such a show.
Where are you going now, away from home,
With this procession ?

    PIST.   Here [*pointing to the house of Bacchis*].

    LYD.   Why, who lives there ?

    PIST.   Why, Love, Delight, and Charm and Grace and Joy,
And Jest and Sport and Chat and Kissy-kissy !

    LYD.   What business have you with those cursed gods ?

    PIST.   Cursed is he who curses at the good.
Yea, you blaspheme the gods ; it's very wrong.

120   LYD.   What, is there any god called Kissy-Kissy?

    PIST.   Didn't you know? O Lydus, you barbarian !
I used to think you wiser far than Thales.[2]
Fie ! you've less wits than a Poticius.[3]
So old, and not to know the names of the gods !

    LYD.   I do not like this gear.

    PIST.   It wasn't meant
For you, but me ; I like it well enough.

    LYD.   O, you begin to flesh your wit on *me !*
Had you ten tongues, silence becomes your youth.

    PIST.   Come, Lydus, I'm too old to go to school.

130 I care for nothing in the world just now
But that the cook mayn't spoil these luscious viands.

    LYD.   Alas ! you've ruined both yourself and me !

---

[1] The famous Spartan legislator.

[2] The famous philosopher of Miletus, and one of the seven sages.

[3] The Poticii had charge for some centuries of the sacred rights of Hercules ; but in the time of Appius Claudius they handed over their duty to the public officials, and as a result the family shortly became extinct. Liv. i. 7, ad. fin. Verg. Aen. viii. 281.

My toil and all my lessons are in vain.

PIST.   I've lost my labour just as much as you ;
Your teaching's been no good to either of us.

LYD.   O heart of steel !

PIST.   Come, you're a nuisance, Lydus !
Be still, and follow me.

LYD. [*To the spectators.*]   O, did you hear?
He doesn't call me "tutor," but plain " Lydus !"

PIST.   Of course ! it's quite absurd and out of place,
When a young fellow goes to see his sweetheart,   140
And sits by her, and other guests are present,
That any " *tutor* " should be standing by.

LYD.   Is *that* what all this preparation's for?

PIST.   I hope it is ; but Heaven determines all.

LYD.   Have you a sweetheart ?

PIST.   When you see, you'll know.

LYD.   You sha'n't !   I won't allow it !   Go back home !

PIST.   Drop that, or you'll be whipped !

LYD.   What !   *I* be *whipped ?*

PIST.   Yes ; I'm too old for you to school me now.

LYD.   Find me a gulf wherein to fling myself!
I've seen more than I ever wished to see.
Better that I had died than lived for *this !*   150
A pupil utter threats against his master !
Save me from pupils of such lusty blood !
His vigorous youth bullies my age and weakness.

PIST.   I shall be Hercules, I guess !—you Linus ! [1]

LYD.   Nay, but I fear that I shall be your Phœnix, [2]

---

[1] Linus taught Hercules to play the lyre ; but when Linus found fault
with him, Hercules killed him.

[2] Phœnix brought the news of the death of Achilles to his father,
Peleus.

To tell your father of your early death !

    Pist.   O, drop ycur history !

    Lyd.   He's lost to shame !—

The gross impertinence that you've assumed

160 Ill suits your youth.—He's thrown his life away !—

Do you remember that you have a father ?

    Pist.   Am I your slave, or are you mine, good sir ?

    Lyd.   A viler master taught you this, not I.

More readily you learn his shameful lessons

Than those I taught you with such fruitless toil.

Oh, it was villainously done by you,

To hide these sins from me and from your father !

    Pist.   So far, good Lydus, I have let you talk ;

But that will do.   No more ! but follow me.

                    [*Exeunt into the house of Bacchis.*]

CHRYSALUS.

[*Enter Chrysalus from the harbour.*]

170   Chr.   Land of my master, hail ! I'm glad to see thee

After my two years' stay in Ephesus.

Neighbour Apollo,[1] thee I greet, who dwellest

Next door to us, and beg thee, of thy grace,

Not to permit my master Nicobulus

To come across me, till I first have met

The comrade of Mnesilochus, Pistoclerus,

And given him the letter he has sent

To tell him all about his sweetheart, Bacchis.

---

[1] The altar of Apollo stood in the centre of the stage, and so adjoined the house of Nicobulus. Aul. 598, Merc. 667.

PISTOCLERUS.   CHRYSALUS.

[*Enter Pistoclerus from the house of Bacchis.   He addresses her as he comes out.*]

PIST.   You needn't beg so hard that I'll come back,
For I can scarcely tear myself away.
You hold me fast in love's sweet bonds and fetters.   180
CHR.   By the immortal gods, it's Pistoclerus !
Hail, Pistoclerus !
PIST.   Chrysalus, all hail !
CHR.   I'll tell you briefly what you want to say :—
You're glad I've come : and I am duly grateful.—
You ask me in to dinner, as you ought
On my return from foreign parts : I'll come.—
I bring you hearty greeting from your friend :
You ask me where he is : he lives.
PIST.   How is he ?
CHR.   That's just what I was going to ask of *you.*
PIST.   How can *I* know ?
CHR.   None better.
PIST.   Why, how's that ?   190
CHR.   He's alive and well, if you have found his sweet-
    heart ;
If not, he's ill and very like to die.
His sweetheart is her lover's very soul ;
If she's away, he's nought ; and if she's there,
She makes his money nought, poor wretched fellow !
But have you executed his commission ?
PIST.   Rather than he should come and find I've failed
To do what he requested in his message,
I'd go and dwell in the infernal shades !
CHR.   Then you've found Bacchis ?
PIST.   Yes, the Samian one.   200

CHR.   Take care that no one touch her heedlessly.
You know your Samian ware [1] is precious brittle!
    PIST.   At your old games again!
    CHR.   But where is she?
    PIST.   Here, where you saw me coming out just now.
    CHR.   How jolly! why, that's just next door to us!
Does she remember her Mnesilochus?
    PIST.   Nay, he's her only darling!
    CHR.   Oh, indeed!
    PIST.   Nay, trust her! Oh, she loves to sheer distraction.
    CHR.   That's right.
    PIST.   Nay, Chrysalus—
    CHR.   Well?
    PIST.   Not a moment
210 Passes, but she is mentioning his name.
    CHR.   So much the better she!
    PIST.   Nay—
    CHR.   Nay, I'm off!
    PIST.   Why, aren't you pleased to hear of his good luck?
    CHR.   O yes, but I can't stand your wretched acting! [2]
Why, the Epidicus, [3] my favourite play,
I can't endure, if Pellio's [4] acting it.—
So Bacchis is a fine brave lass?
    PIST.   She is.
Were mine not Venus, I would call her Juno. [5]

---

[1] Samian pottery was famous for its beauty and brittleness. Capt. 290, Mer. 177.

[2] This very unexpected turn must have been very amusing to the audience.

[3] Another of Plautus' plays.

[4] Pellio was an actor with whom we may suppose that Plautus had some fault to find.

Bacchis Attica being Venus, he can't call her sister Juno; as Juno was not the sister of Venus.

Chr.   This then is how it stands, Mnesilochus!
You've got your love ; now find the wherewithal.
She'll need some gold perhaps.

Pist.   Of Philip's [1] coinage.   220

Chr.   Perhaps she needs it now.

Pist.   Nay, before now.
The captain's coming soon—

Chr.   A captain too ?

Pist.   Who wants the gold for setting Bacchis free.

Chr.   Well, let him come; the sooner 'tis, the better !
I have it with me.   I'm afraid of no one,[2]
Nor will I ask for anybody's help,
If but my heart be firm in my design.
Go in ; this is *my* business.   And tell Bacchis
Mnesilochus is coming.

Pist.   So I will.
                   [*Exit Pistoclerus into the house of Bacchis.*]

Chr.   This business of the gold belongs to me.
We've brought from Ephesus twelve hundred Philips   230
Which our host owed to my old master here.
Some trick I'll forge to-day to get the money
For my young master, him who is in love—
I hear our door ! [3]   Who is it coming out?

NICOBULUS.   CHRYSALUS.
[*Enter from his house Nicobulus.*]

Nic.   I'll go to the Piræus [4] and enquire
If any ship has come from Ephesus ;

---

[1] Philip of Macedon's gold coinage was current throughout Greece and
Italy at this time.   [2] Cf. Asin, I., 1, 110.

[3] The doors opened outwards ; and it was customary to knock at the
door before coming out, so as to warn passers-by to get out of the way.

[4] The harbour of Athens, in which city the scene is laid.

My mind misgives me that my son is taking
So long a holiday and not returning!
    CHR. [*aside*]. Heaven helping me, I'll rob the old man
    finely.
I mustn't be caught napping; I want gold;
240 Now is the *crisis, Chrysalus,*[1] my boy!
I will accost him; he shall prove to-day
The ram of Phrixus,[2] and his fleece of gold
I'll shear to the very quick, or I'm mistaken.
[*Aloud.*] Chrysalus, his slave, salutes good Nicobulus!
    NIC. Good heavens! why, Chrysalus, where is my son?
    CHR. I think you might return my greeting first.
    NIC. Well, how d'ye do? but where's Mnesilochus?
    CHR. Alive and well.
    NIC.   He's come?
    CHR.   He has.
    NIC.   Bravo!
Your news is water to a thirsty man.
And is he well?
    CHR.   Fit as a prize-fighter.
    NIC. And how's the business gone at Ephesus?
250 Has he got the gold from Archidemides?
    CHR. My heart and head are split, good Nicobulus,
To hear the mention of that wretch's name.
Call him not *friend:* a *fiend* he's proved to you.
    NIC. Why so, I pray you?
    CHR.   Nay, I'm confident,
Fire, Moon, Sun, Day, four gods of mickle might,
Have never shone upon a greater villain!
    NIC. Than Archidemides?

---

[1] This is not the pun of the original, but may serve in its place.
Phrixus was the owner of the famous ram with the golden fleece.

CHR.   Than Archidemides.

NIC.   What has he done?

CHR.   Nay, what has he *not* done?
First, he began to wrangle with your son,
And said he didn't owe a single penny.   260
Mnesilochus then summoned to his aid
Pelagones, who's our old and trusty friend.
Then in his presence he produced the seal
Which you had given your son to bring to him.

NIC.   Well, when he'd shown the seal?

CHR.   He starts to say
That it's a forgery, not your seal at all.
What insults on your guiltless son he heaped!
[Charged him with forgeries in other cases.] [1]

NIC.   Have you the gold?   That's what I want to know.

CHR.   The magistrate appointed arbitrators; [2]   270
He lost his case and so perforce he paid us
Twelve hundred Philips.

NIC.   Yes, that was the debt.

CHR.   But hear about the trick he tried to play us!

NIC.   What, is there more?

CHR.   Yes, this was a kite's swoop.

NIC.   I've been deceived, and trusted all that gold
To an Autolycus. [3]

CHR.   But, pray you, listen.

---

[1] A doubtful line.

[2] Lit., The prætor appointed recuperators.   This was the custom at
Rome in all cases of dispute between foreigners and citizens.

[3] The Autolycus referred to was the grandfather of Odysseus, and a
prince of thieves.   Hom. Od. xix. 395 :—

> " Autolycus . . . who very far before
> All men in sleight of oaths and dexterous skill
> Ranked by the gift of Hermes."—(Worsley's translation.)

Nic.   I didn't penetrate his greedy soul.

Chr.   After we'd got the gold, we straight embarked,
Longing for home.   But sitting on the deck
And looking round, I saw a privateer
280 Being fitted out for sea.[1]

Nic.   Alas ! I'm ruined !
That privateer has pierced me to the heart.

Chr.   Your friend and certain pirates owned her jointly.

Nic.   O what a dolt I was to trust to him !
The very name of Archi*demides*
Declares the "*damned ease*" with which he cheats.

Chr.   The privateer lay waiting for our ship,
And I began to watch what they would do.
Meanwhile our ship sets sail to leave the harbour.
When we had got outside, they followed us
290 Swifter than birds or winds.   When I perceived
What they were doing, we stopped our ship at once.
But when they saw us stop, they set to work
To row about the harbour.

Nic.   O the villains !
What did *you* do ?

Chr.   O, we put back to port.

Nic.   'Twas wisely done.   And what did they do then ?

Chr.   When evening fell, they made for land once more.

Nic.   They meant to steal the gold ; that was their aim.

Chr.   I saw that well enough, and was alarmed.
Well, when we saw them plotting for the gold,
300 We straightway laid our plans ; and the next day
Removed the gold in presence of them all,
Plainly and openly, that they might know it.

Nic.   A clever trick !   What's next ?

---

[1] I give this line up.

CHR.   That hipped them sadly.
When they had seen us take the gold away,
They beached the privateer with furious looks.
We placed the gold in Theotimus' care,
Who is Diana's priest at Ephesus.
    NIC. Who's Theotimus?
    CHR.   Megalobulus' son,
And quite the dearest man in Ephesus.
    NIC. By Jove! but he'd be *dearer* still to me   310
If he should swindle me of all that gold.
    CHR. O, but it's stored in great Diana's temple,
In public keeping.
    NIC.   O, you've ruined me!
I'd rather have it in my *private* care.
But didn't you bring any of it home?
    CHR. Why, yes, but I don't know how much he brought.
    NIC. What, you don't know?
    CHR.   No, for Mnesilochus
Went secretly by night to Theotimus,
And neither told to me nor anyone
How much he got from him; so I don't know.
But certainly it was not very much.   320
    NIC. Was it half, do you think?
    CHR.   I really couldn't say;
But I don't think so.
    NIC.   Would it be a third?
    CHR. I don't think so; but really I don't know.
All that I know is that I do not know.
Now you will have to take your passage thither,
To bring the money back from Theotimus.
And, oh, I say—
    NIC.   What's that?
    CHR.   You'll not forget

To take your son's ring with you.

Nic.　　　　　'Why his ring?

Chr.　Because we gave that sign to Theotimus,
That he who brought the ring should have the gold.

330　Nic.　I'll not forget, and thanks for your advice.
Is Theotimus rich?

Chr.　　　　　I guess he *is;*
I tell you, sir, he soles his shoes with gold.

Nic.　Why's he so dainty?

Chr.　　　　　He's so very rich
He don't know what to do with all his gold.

Nic.　I wish he'd give it *me!*　But who was there
When Theotimus had the gold from you?

Chr.　All Ephesus: there's not a man but knows it.

Nic.　Well, that at least was wisdom in my son,
To give the gold to a rich man to keep;
For he can get it back upon demand.

340　Chr.　Nay, he won't keep you waiting for a minute.
You'll have it the same day that you arrive.

Nic.　I thought that I had done with going to sea,
For I am getting old to take a voyage.
But in this case I see I have no choice;
My fine friend Archidemides compels me.—
But tell me, where's my son Mnesilochus?

Chr.　I think he's gone down to the market-place
To greet his friends and the gods on his return.

Nic.　Well, I'll be off and find him if I can.

　　　　　　　[*Exit Nicobulus to the market-place.*]

Chr.　I've put a pretty load upon his back!

350　My plot I've woven not altogether badly.
It's gained my love-sick master what he wants;
For he can take as much as he requires
Of that same gold, and only give his father

Just what he likes.   Now the old gentleman
Will go to Ephesus to fetch his gold.
Meanwhile, we'll pass the time in pleasant fashion,
Unless, indeed, he doesn't leave us here,
But takes Mnesilochus and me with him !
O, what a jolly coil it is I'm making !
But what will happen when he finds it out ?
When he discovers that he's gone for nothing,
And that we've used the gold, alas for me !   360
I guess when he comes back, he'll change my name
And make me *Crossalus*, not *Chrysalus*.
I'll run away, if that should prove the best.
If I am caught, I'll give him trouble yet ;
If he has rods in the field, well, I've a back ! [1]
But now I'll go and tell my master's son
About the gold and how his sweetheart's found.

> [*Exit Chrysalus to the market-place.*]

LYDUS.

[*Enter Lydus from the house of Bacchis, where the feast is now
going on.*]

   LYD.   Throw wide open, I beseech you, and unclose this
      door of Hell !
It deserves no better name; it doesn't need a sage to tell
He who enters must abandon every hope of temperance ;   370
Bacchanals,[2] not Bacchides, are ye who lead this frenzied
      dance.
Hence, avaunt, ye fatal sisters, drinking up the blood of men !
Fitted up with costly baits to lure to ruin is your den.

---

[1] He means that he can stand a flogging.   Cf. Asin. 317.
[2] See note on v. 51 above; p. 192.

Soon as I had seen them, straightway I betook myself to flight.
Shall I keep all this in secret, hiding from your father's sight,
Pistoclerus, your excesses, follies, and extravagance?
Ah, you'll lead me, and your father, and your friends, a pretty
    dance,
Driving us to shame and sorrow, and inextricable ruin!
For you've no regard for me or for yourself in what you're
    doing;
380 Both your father and myself, your friends and all who bear
    your name,
By your conduct you'll make aiders and abettors of your
    shame.
No, you sha'n't! I'll tell your father all about this little
    game.
I myself will stop your nonsense, and inform your father
    straight;
Then he'll come and drag you from this swinish feast, ere 'tis
    too late!   [*Exit Lydus to tell Philoxenus.*]

MNESILOCHUS.

[*Enter from the harbour Mnesilochus, who has just landed from
his voyage.*]

MNES. After much consideration, hither my conclusions
    tend;
Nothing, save the gods, is better than a tried and trusty
    friend,
One I mean who really is so; and I'll tell you how I know:
When I'd gone to Ephesus, which happened some two years
    ago,
To my comrade, Pistoclerus, I despatched a messenger,
390 Begging him to find my sweetheart, Bacchis; now with joy I
    hear

He has found her, so my servant Chrysalus brings word to
    me.
Then against my worthy father he's devised some trickery,
To procure me all the money I require.   ¹[Why, there's my
    friend !]
Well, by Pollux, in my judgment thanklessness I'd ne'er de-
    fend :
Better to let off a foe than slight a man who's done you good;
Yes, extravagance is nobler than such base ingratitude.
Good men praise the one ; the other even wicked men will
    blame.
So that I must watch and labour, lest I injure my good name.
Now your *side* must be *decided*, now's the testing time, my lad,
Whether you are what you should be, whether you are good 400
    or bad,
Just or unjust, mean or generous, gentlemanly or a clown ;
Don't you let your slave surpass you in the kindnesses he's
    shown.
What you are, you can't conceal. — But who come here ?
    Yes, without doubt,
My friend's father and his tutor ! Let me hear what they're
    about.

LYDUS.   PHILOXENUS.   MNESILOCHUS.

[*Enter Lydus and Philoxenus.*]

Ly.   Now, I'll see if I can't rouse your indignation, worthy
    sir !
Follow me !
    Ph.   Where shall I follow ? where are you taking me ?
    Ly.   To her
Who alone has brought to ruin and destroyed your only son.

---

¹ The last words of line 393 must be wrong ; for Pistoclerus does not
come on at this point.

Pн.   Gently, Lydus !   Keep your temper, and much folly
you will shun.

At his age we mustn't wonder if he plays a trick or two ;

410 Greater wonder if he *didn't !*   Why, it's what *I* used to do.

Ly.   Out, alas ! it's your complaisance ruins him ; yes,
you're too kind.

But for you I should have brought him quickly to a better
mind.

Now by your extreme indulgence you've reduced to utter
shame
Pistoclerus.

Mn. [*aside*].   O, good heavens ! do I hear my comrade's name ?

What has Pistoclerus done to put old Lydus in a rage ?

Pн.   Everybody's swayed by passion for a little at his age ;

Soon he'll loathe himself for doing it.   Lydus, treat him
tenderly ;

If he doesn't carry matters to extremes, why, let him be !

Ly.   No, I won't ! while I have life, I won't permit it to
be done !

420 Listen, you, who plead the cause of your abandoned foolish
son !

Had you such indulgence granted, when you were as young
as he ?

I'll engage, when you were twenty, you had not the liberty

E'en to stir a finger's breadth, without your tutor, from your
home.

If, before the day had dawned, you weren't at the gymnasium,

You were punished most severely by the trainer of the youth ;

Yea, in such a case, the trouble went still further ; for, in
sooth,

On the pupil and his tutor, both alike, the blame would fall.

Then in racing, wrestling, boxing, hurling spear, and quoit,
and ball,
And in leaping they were practised, not in courting and in
kisses ;
There they spent their youth, and not in quiet corners with 430
the misses.
When from race-course or gymnasium you had got back
home again,
Neatly dressed, upon your stool you sat beside your tutor then,
Reading in your book, and if you missed a single syllable,
You were striped like any tiger, for your tutor whipped you
well.
   Mn. [*aside*].   How I'm grieved that these reproaches fall
upon him in mistake !
Though he's innocent he suffers this suspicion for my sake.
   Ph.   Ah, but, Lydus, times are altered.
   Ly.   Yes, I'm well aware of that !
In the good old times a man would oft be made a magistrate,
Ere he ceased to pay obedience to his tutor's least command ;
Now, before a lad is seven, if you touch him with your hand, 440
He will seize his slate and with it break his tutor's head
straightway.
If you go and tell his father, this is what you'll hear him
say—
" That's my brave boy ! I'm delighted you defend yourself
so well."
Then the tutor gets a rating : " You old wretch, incapable,
Don't you punish him for doing it, he's a brave and merry
wag.
Go, sir master, patched up like a lantern with a greasy
rag ! " [1]

Both the reading and interpretation of this line are doubtful.   I have
taken what seems to me to give the best sense.

That's the end of your appeal.   I ask how any tutor durst
Exercise authority when he himself is beaten first ?

MN. [*aside*].   Eh, but his complaint is bitter!   After hearing what he's said,

450 I should guess that Pistoclerus has been punching Lydus'
head.

PH.   Who is this, whom I see standing at the door ?

LY.   Philoxenus,

Why, not even an apparition of the gods could please me
thus !

PH.   Who is it ?

LY.   Mnesilochus, the friend and comrade of your boy !

But how different !   Other things than ladies' love his
thoughts employ.

Happy, happy Nicobulus, to have got a son so dear !

PH.   Ah, Mnesilochus, good morning!   I'm right glad to
see you here.

MN.   Thanks, Philoxenus !   Heaven bless you !

LY.   Ah, how is his father blessed !

Here's a son who's crossed the ocean in his father's
interest,

Always thoughtful and attentive to his every wish and word.

460 He and Pistoclerus in their boyhood childish friendship
shared.

He's not more than three days older, if you judge them by
their age ;

But in sense and wit he's thirty years his senior, I'll engage.

I would rather trust my troubles than my money to your son.

PH.   Why ?

LY.   Because, a few days after, all my troubles would be
gone ! [1]

---

[1] *i.e.*, If he got rid of them as quickly as he does of money.

Pн. You'll be whipped, if you don't stop your unjust
    charges !

Lv.   You be quiet !
You're a fool if you refuse to hear the story of his riot.

Mn. What's my friend been doing, Lydus, that you
    blame him in this way ?

Lv. Your friend's ruined.

Mn.   Heaven forbid it !

Lv.   O you'll find it as I say.
Nay, I saw him in the act ; it's not from hearsay that I'm
    talking.

Mn. What's he done ?

Lv.   He's fallen in love with a young girl !

Mn.   O dear, how shocking ! 470

Lv. One who sucks in like a whirlpool everyone she
    glances on.

Mn. Where's her house ?

Lv.   Why, here [*pointing*].

Mn.   And where's she come from ?

Lv.   She's a Samian.

Mn. What's her name ?

Lv.   It's Bacchis.

Mn.   You're mistaken, Lydus ; I know well
All about it ; Pistoclerus really isn't culpable.
He was only executing a commission, as I'll prove,
For his friend with faithful zeal ; so don't imagine he's in
    love.

Lv. Must he then, to execute with faithful zeal his friend's
    commission,
Take the lady on his knee and kiss away sans intermission ?
Couldn't it be executed any other way than this,
With his arm around her waist, with lip to lip in one long
    kiss ?

480 Nay, I'd be ashamed to tell you all I saw him doing there,
In my presence, without blushing. But your feelings I will
     spare.
He is ruined, my poor pupil, your companion, and his son,
For I say a man is ruined when his modesty is gone.
[Why say more? If I'd been willing to remain and see his
     ruin,
I'd have had a better chance of watching what the lad was
     doing;
But I fear I should have seen more than I ought in that mad
     wooing].[1]
   Mn. [*aside*]. Ah, my heart is broken, comrade! Shall
     I go and kill the girl?
490 If I don't, I'd rather die myself! My brain is in a whirl!
All my confidence is shattered, all my trust in men is gone!
   Ly. See, how bitterly he's grieving at the ruin of your son!
How his comrade's bad behaviour robs his soul of all her
     joy!
   Ph. Come, Mnesilochus, I pray you, try to save my
     naughty boy.
He's my son and your companion; rescue him!
   Mn.   I hope I may!
   Ly. Don't you think it will be better, if along with him I
     stay?
   Ph. No, Mnesilochus will manage.
   Ly.   Well, then, let him have it hot!
For on you and me and all his friends he's put a shameful
     blot.
   Ph. Well, to you I trust this business. Come on, Lydus!
   Ly.   Right! we'll trot.
       [*Exeunt Philoxenus and Lydus to the town.*]

      These three lines are doubtful.

MNESILOCHUS.

Mn.   ¹I wonder which of them's my deadliest foe,   500
My comrade, or my Bacchis?   I can't t ll!
Does she love him the best?   Then let her have him.
By Hercules! the curse shall fall on her!
For never be my word again be'ieved,
If I don't in a thousand fashions—love her!
She shall not make a laughing stock of me;
For I'll go home—steal something from my father
And give it her!--Oh, but I'll be revenged!
Yes, though I make—my father beg his bread!
But what a senseless idiot I am
To babble here all I am going to do!   510
If I know anything, I'm sure I love her.
But I'll take precious care that she shall never
Be a lead filing wealthier for me!
Rather than that I will outbeg a beggar!
She shall not live to mock me!   I'm resolved
To pay back all the money to my father.
Then shall she flatter me all penniless
When all her flattery is of no more use
Than to crack jokes with dead men in their graves.
Yes, certainly, I'll take the money back,   520
And beg my father for my sake to pardon
Poor Chrysalus, and not be angry with him,
Since for my sake it was he hocussed him.
I must look after him, who for my sake
Told him the lie.   You slaves, come after me!
[*Exeunt Mnesilochus and his Attendants into the house of
     Nicobulus.*]

---

¹ The unexpected turns which Mnesilochus gives to his threats against
Bacchis may be taken as the result of the conflict between his anger
which prompts revenge, and his love which will not allow him to carry
out his denunciations.

PISTOCLERUS.

[*Enter Pistoclerus from the house of Bacchis, addressing her as he leaves.*]

PIST. Everything shall be postponed to what my Bacchis bids me do.
I'll go seek Mnesilochus and bring him back with me to you.
But I'm very much astonished, if he's met my messenger,
What he's stopping for. I'll go right to his house. Perhaps he's there.

MNESILOCHUS. PISTOCLERUS.

[*Enter Mnesilochus from the house of Nicobulus.*]

530 MN. All the gold I've given my father. Now, then, I should like to see,
When I've nothing left to give, the girl who so despises me.
It was hard to get my father to forgive old Chrysalus!
But at last I did succeed in making him less furious.
PIST. [*aside*]. Ah, is that my comrade?
MN. [*aside*].   Ah, is that my enemy I see?
PIST. [*aside*]. Yes, 'tis he!
MN. [*aside*].   'Tis he!
PIST. [*aside*].   I'll run to meet and greet him lovingly.
[*Aloud.*] Hail, Mnesilochus!
MN.   Good morning.
PIST.   Now you're back from your exile,
We must have a dinner!
MN.   No, sir! it would only stir my bile.
PIST. Have you caught some illness since returning?
MN.   Yes, pain without end!
PIST. Where've you got it?

MN.   From a man whom up to now I thought
my friend.

PIST.   Ah, too many of that pattern live amongst us now- 540
a-days.

Friends you think them, but they're shown up traitors by
their treacherous ways ;

Full of talking, never doing, their honour is a broken reed ;

Others' better fortune never fails their envious thoughts to
feed.

No one ever envies *them*, their idleness takes care of that !

MN.   Ah, I see you've studied them, and know their prac-
tices quite pat.

From their cursed disposition this one curse will still arise ;

No one loves them, they may reckon all mankind their
enemies.

When they think they're cheating others, it's themselves the
fools are cheating !

That's the sort of man he is, whom as a brother I've been
treating.

He, as far as in him lay, has done me all the harm he could, 550

And confounded my resources to my harm and not my good.

PIST.   He must be a worthless scoundrel.

MN.   I confess I think so too.

PIST.   Tell me who he is, I beg you ?

MN.   Softly, he's a friend to you.

If he were not, I would beg you, to the utmost of your power,

To avenge me.

PIST.   Tell me who he is, and if that very hour

I don't make him suffer, let me take the prize for laziness.

MN.   He's a worthless wretch, but yet a friend of yours.

PIST.   Still, none the less,

Tell me who he is ; a worthless villain's friendship I dis-
claim.

MN.   Well, I see I can't avoid it ; I shall have to tell his
    name.

560   Pistoclerus, *you* have ruined me, your comrade, utterly !
    PIST.   What's that ?
    MN.   What ? Why, didn't a letter come from Ephesus
        from me
Asking you to find my sweetheart ?
    PIST.   Yes, and I have found her, too.
    MN.   Tell me, weren't there girls enough in Athens to
    suffice for you
To go courting, but you needs must choose one trusted to
    your care ;
Lay your wicked plans against me, and go fall in love with
    her ?
    PIST.   Are you mad ?
    MN.   Nay, don't deny it, for your tutor's told me all;
You've betrayed me.
    PIST.   Do you want to anger me beyond recall?
    MN.   You love Bacchis.
    PIST.   Yes, but there are *two* girls here who bear
    that name.
    MN.   Two?
    PIST.   Yes, sisters.
    MN.   Now you know you're talking nonsense ;
    oh, for shame !

570   PIST.   Look you here, if you continue thus my honour to
    gainsay,
I shall take you on my back and bear you in.
    MN.   Nay, I'll come.   Stay !
    PIST.   No, I won't ; you sha'n't suspect me falsely.
    MN.   All right, lead the way.

        [*Exeunt into the house of Bacchis.*]

PARASITE.

[Enter from the town a Parasite with a boy.]

Par.   I am the Parasite of that worthless rascal
The captain, him who brought the girl from Samos.
Now he has bid me come to her and ask
Whether she'll pay the gold or go with him.—
You came with her, my boy, not long ago ;
You know which house it is ; go straight and knock.

> *[The boy knocks gently at the door of Bacchis.]*

Come back, you scamp !   How modestly he knocks !
Though you can eat a good three feet of loaf,   580
You don't know how to knock !

> *[The Parasite goes and knocks furiously himself.]*

> > Ho ! who's within ?

Hallo ! who's here ?   Who'll open me this door ?
Come, somebody !

PISTOCLERUS.   PARASITE.

[Enter Pistoclerus from the door.]

Pist.   What's all this knocking for ?
Come, what the deuce do you mean by practising
Your strength in battering other people's doors ?
You've nearly smashed the panel !   What do you want ?
Par.   Good day, young sir !
Pist.   Good day !   But whom do you seek ?
Par.   Bacchis.
Pist.   But which ?
Par.   Bacchis is all I know.
In brief, Cleomachus, the captain, sent me
To say that she must pay two hundred Philips,   590
Or go with him to Elatia[1] to-day.
Pist.   O no !   Say she won't go !   Go back and tell him.

---

¹ A city in Phocis.

She has a lover here.   So you be off !
 PAR.   Don't lose your temper !
 PIST.   *Won't* I lose my temper ?
By Hercules ! your jaw is near to trouble ;
My tooth-crackers are itching to be at it.
 PAR. [*aside*].   I gather from his words that I must mind
He doesn't knock out all my nut-crackers !
[*Aloud.*]   I'll tell him what you say, but at *your* peril !
          [*The Parasite moves off.*]
 PIST.   Look here !
 PAR.   I'll tell him what you say.
600 PIST.   But tell me,
Who are you ?
 PAR.   I'm the captain's body-guard.
 PIST.   He must be a scamp, his body-guard's so vile.
 PAR.   He'll come, swelling with rage.
 PIST.   I hope he'll burst
 PAR.   There's nothing else ?
 PIST.   Be off, and quickly too !
 PAR   By-bye, tooth-cracker !
 PIST.   By-bye, body-guard !
      [*Exit Parasite back to the soldier.*]
Well, things have got to this, that I don't know
How to advise my friend about his sweetheart.
The angry fool has given his dad the gold,
And hasn't got a cent to pay the captain.
610 But I'll stand on one side.   I hear the door.
See where Mnesilochus comes sadly forth !

MNESILOCHUS.   PISTOCLERUS.

[*Enter Mnesilochus from the house of Bacchis.*]
 MN.   Pettish, hasty, fool, and nought less !
  Hot, ungovernable, thoughtless !

> Acting without law or measure,
> Scorning right and faith at pleasure !
> Powerless to control my passion,
> Full of hateful, vile suspicion,
> That's my wretched, sad condition.
> Would that someone else were me !

How *can* I have done it ?   Ah, none could be worse,
Or more richly deserve the gods' bitterest curse !
To be hated and cut is my fate, I can see.
Yes, it's foes, not friends, I deserve to have !
The bad, not the good, must befriend such a knave.

> All the reproaches deserved by the shameless,   620
> I deserve better ; my folly is nameless !
> Madman ! to give back my father the gold
> When I had got it !   O sorrow untold !
> Myself and good Chrysalus too I have sold !

PIST. [*aside*].   I must comfort him, I'll try it.
[*Aloud.*]   Mnesilochus, what's up ?
MN.   I'm done for !
PIST.   Heaven forbid !
MN.   I say I'm done for !
PIST.   Be quiet, madman !
MN.   How be quiet ?
PIST.   Have you lost your wits ?
MN.   I'm done for !

> Many keen and bitter woes
> Rend my heart with piercing throes !
> To think that I believed that lie !
> I blamed you undeservedly.

PIST.   Come, cheer up !
MN.   No use to try !
          A corpse is worth far more than I.   630
PIST.   The parasite of the captain bold

Came here just now to get the gold.
I sent him off with a flea in his ear
Away from the door, away from here;
I drove him off.

MN.   That doesn't help *me*.
What can I do? O misery!
He'll take her away with him, I see.

PIST.   Had I the cash, I'd not *promise*, by Jove!

MN.   You'd *give* it me; yes: if you weren't in love
I'd trust your friendship through and through;
But you've enough of your own to do!
How can I look for help from you?
You are helpless.

PIST.   Say no more. Some god will sure look after us.

MN.   Nonsense!

PIST.   Stay!

MN.   What is it?

PIST.   See, here comes your saviour, Chrysalus.

CHRYSALUS. MNESILOCHUS. PISTOCLERUS.
[*Enter Chrysalus.*]

CHRY.   Ah, I'm worth my weight in gold! I ought to
640   have a golden image;
Yes, I've done a double crime, got double plunder from this
        scrimmage!
Poor old master! how I've paid him!
What a jolly fool I've made him!
Clever old man! But my clever plan
Forced him and drove him to trust all I told to him.
Now for that bold man, son of the old man,
My partner in larking, and guzzling, and sparking,
I have brought royalest treasures of gold to him
Of his own store, he's not got to go fetch it round.
        Not good enough are

Slaves who can get but some two or three wretched pound;   650
   I'm no such duffer!
  There's nothing worse than a slave without sense,
  With a head that's totally thick and dense,
  Who can't get all he wants from thence.
  For nobody is any good,
  Who cannot rapidly change his mood;
  A villain with villains, a thief among thieves;
    There's not much *he* leaves!
  If a fellow's worth a pin,
  He can always change his skin;
  With the good or the bad he'll take a hand;
  And always steer as the times demand.
 But I must find out how much money the lad
 Has kept, and how much he's returned to his dad;   660
 To treat him as Hercules [1] surely was best;
 Just pay him a tithe, and then collar the rest!
 But see where he's coming of whom I'm in quest.
Have you dropped your money, master, that you're gazing
 on the ground?
Well, you *are* a sad and melancholy couple I have found!
I don't like it; it means mischief. Come, let's have the   670
 reason told.
 Mn. Chrysalus, I'm ruined!
 Chry.   What! perhaps you took too little gold?
 Mn. Curse on it, too little? Nay, but many times much
  less than that!
 Chry. Why, you fool, when I had gained an opportunity
  so pat
By my skill, for you to take as much as you could e'er desire,
Did you take it with your finger-tips as if it were on fire?

---

[1] It was customary to dedicate a tenth of any unexpected gain to Hercules. Nicobulus should have received the same fraction.

Did you think a chance like this would *often* come to you,
you muff?

MN.   No, you're wrong.

CHRY.   Nay, *you* were wrong; you didn't dip in deep
enough.

MN.   You'd accuse me far more strongly, if you knew the
whole affair.

CHRY.   O, I'm ruined! by your words you fill me with
foreboding care.

MN.   I'm undone!

CHRY.   How so?

680   MN.   Because I've given my father every cent.

CHRY.   Given it?

MN.   Yes.

CHRY.   What, all?

MN.   Yes, every penny!

CHRY.   O, my heart is rent!

What on earth possessed you, man, to do a deed so villain-
ous?

MN.   I suspected him [1] and Bacchis on a false charge,
Chrysalus,

That they'd laid a plot against me; so, enraged, I gave the
gold

To my father.

CHRY.   When you gave it to him, what's the tale you told?

MN.   O, I said I'd got the money straight from Archidemides.

CHRY.   If you said so, sorest torments on poor Chrysalus
must seize!

When the old man sees me, he will have me bound and
flogged straightway.

MN.   I've prevailed upon my father—

---

[1] *i.e.*, Pistoclerus.

CHRY.   What, to do just what I say?

MN.   No, to let you off entirely, and his anger to dismiss! 690
With much trouble I succeeded.   Now, you must look after
this—

CHRY.   What?

MN.   To find some other way of catching the old
          gentleman.

Set your wits to work, contrive, concoct, fix up some know-
          ing plan.

Skilfully deceive the old man's skill, and carry off the gold.

CHRY.   Oh, it hardly can be done.

MN.   Yes, easily, if you are bold.

CHRY.   Easily, the deuce! when he's just caught me lying
          plump and flat.

If I told him I was lying, he'd not dare to credit that.

MN.   Oh, you should have heard him telling me about
          you!   It was fun!

CHRY.   What did he say?

MN.   That if you told him that the sun there was
          the sun,

He'd believe it was the moon, and that the day was really 700
          night.

CHRY.   He sha'n't talk like that for nothing; oh, I'll pay
          him out all right!

MN.   What are we to do?

CHRY.   Oh, nothing; go on loving as you do.

Tell me how much gold you're wanting; I'll engage to give
          it you.

As my name is *Chrysalus*, I'll prove a golden *butterfly!* [1]

Come, Mnesilochus, inform me what you want, and don't be
          shy.

---

[1] This is not Plautus' pun, of course; which depends upon the deriva-
tion of Chrysalus from χρυσός (gold).

Mn. Well, the captain wants two hundred Philips for
my Bacchis there

Chry.   You shall have it !

Pist.   And there'll be some more expenses—

Chry.   Steady, sir !

One thing at a time ! when *this* is finished, then I'll tackle
that.

For two hundred Philips first I'll aim at our old plutocrat.

710 If my shot should bring his tower and his outworks toppling
down,

I shall straight march through the breach upon his old time-
honoured town ;

If I take it, you shall carry gold to your girls by baskets
full,

As I hope.

Pist. Our hopes are with you, Chrysalus most bounti-
ful !

Chry. Pistoclerus, go to Bacchis' house and quickly
bring me here—

Pist. What ?

Chry.   A pen, some wax, and tablets, and some
tape.

Pist.   Oh, never fear !

[*Exit Pistoclerus into the house of Bacchis.*]

Mn. What are you going to do?

Chry.   Just tell me ; is your luncheon all prepared ?

There'll be two of you, I reckon, and your sweetheart makes
the third.

Mn. As you say.

Chry.   Has Pistoclerus got a sweetheart ?

Mn.   Never fear !

He loves one and I the other of two sisters who live here.

Chry. What is that you're telling me ?

MN.   Our number.

CHRY.   Where's your luncheon set?   720

MN.   Why do you ask?

CHRY.   ˉ   Because it's information I desire to get.

You don't know what I'm intending and am going to begin.

MN.   Take my hand and come up with me to the door.

 [He takes Chrysalus to the door of Bacchis' house.]

       Now then, look in!

CHRY.   Bravo, that's a splendid place, the very one I

would desire.

 [Re-enter Pistoclerus with the writing materials.]

PIST.   Give a decent fellow orders, and you'll get what

you require.

CHRY.   What have you got?

PIST.   Why, everything that you just asked me to

obtain.

CHRY. [*to Mnes.*]   Now, then, quickly take the pen and

tablets in your hand.

MN.   What then?

CHRY.   Write down there what I shall tell you; *you* must

write it, understand,

So that, when your father reads it, he may recognise the 730

hand.

Write!

MN.   Write what?

CHRY.   O, say you hope he's well, just in your

usual way.

PIST.   Rather write you hope he's dead and buried, if the

truth you'd say!

MN.   Don't confuse me! [*Writes.*]   There, that's written!

CHRY.   Come, then, let's hear what it is.

MN. [*reading*].   "I, Mnesilochus, send greeting to my

father."

CHRY.   Now add this :—

> "Father, Chrysalus is plying me with taunts and gibes
>   untold,
> All because I wouldn't cheat you, but restored you
>   all the gold."

PIST.   Give him time to write it !

CHRY.   Why, a lover's hand should not be slow !

PIST.   Oh, it's not so quick at writing as at spending cash,
you know.

MN.   Get along ; that's written.

CHRY.   " Father, keep an eye upon that man ;

> He is laying plots to get the money from you, if he
>   can;

740

> And he swears and vows he'll get it."—Please take
>   care to write it plain.

MN.   Go ahead !

CHRY.   " And then he says he'll give the gold to
>   me again

> To be spent on girls and banquets and on going
>   all the pace ! [1]
> Mind, dear father, have a care, or he will cheat you
>   to your face."

MN.   What's the next ?

CHRY.   O write away !

MN.   Well, tell me what I have to write.

CHRY.   " But, dear father, keep the promise that you made
>   me in your sight.

> Pray, don't flog him ; only bind him and detain
>   him safe at home."

Where's the wax and tape ?   Just tie and seal the letter.
Make haste !   Come !

---

[1] Lit., "On playing the Greek."

Mn.   O, but tell us why you want a letter written in this
   way,
Telling him to bind you fast, and not believe a word you 750
   say.
   Chry.   It's my whim !   So will you kindly look to your-
   self, and don't mind me !
I've contracted for this job, and at my peril it shall be.
   Mn.   Right you are !
   Chry.   Give me the tablets.
   Mn.   Take them !
   Chry.   Now, attention, please.
You, Mnesilochus, you, Pistoclerus, go, and at your ease
Sit down and enjoy your banquet, with your sweethearts at
   your side,
And then drink at the same table where the banquet is
   supplied.
   Pist.   Is that all ?
   Chry.   No, one thing further ; when you've once
              sat down, d'you see,
Don't rise up again from table, till you get the sign from
   me.
   Pist.   Noble general !
   Chry.   Get along ! you should have had two drinks
                 by now.
   Mn.   Let's be off !
   Chry.   *You* do your duty ; *I'll* do mine, I dare avow ! 760
[*Exeunt Mnesilochus and Pistoclerus into the house of Bacchis.*]

CHRYSALUS.

   Chry.   Ah, it's a mad design I have in hand,
And like enough it will be overthrown.
Well, now I want the old man in a fury,

For it won't suit this trick of mine at all,
If he's not out of temper when he sees me.
Oh, if I live to-day I'll cheat him finely!
I'll do him browner than a roasted pea.
I'll walk to the door, and then when he comes out,
At once I'll place the tablets in his hand.

NICOBULUS.   CHRYSALUS.

[Enter Nicobulus from his house.]

770   NIC.   It fills me with vexation when I think
How Chrysalus has dodged me all this day.
   CHRY.   That's right! The old man's angry. Now's my
      time
To go and meet him.
   NIC.   Who's that talking there?
It's Chrysalus, I think.
   CHRY.   Now I'll approach him.
   NIC.   All hail, *good* slave! How goes it? Is it time
For me to sail for Ephesus and bring
My money home again from Theotimus?
You're silent?   O, by all the gods I swear
That, if I didn't love my son so well,
And wish to grant him all that he desires,
780   I'd have you flayed with rods and put in irons,
And sent to spend your life in grinding corn.
Mnesilochus has told me all your crimes.
   CHRY.   He's charged me, has he! Very fine indeed!
Yes, I'm a villain, curséd and abhorred!
Well, just take care! that's all I have to say.
   NIC.   What, do you threaten me, you scoundrel,
      you!

CHRY.   You'll find out what he is, before so long.
He ordered me to bring these tablets to you,
And prayed that you would do what he has written.
  NIC.   Give them to me.
  CHRY.   Observe the seal !
  NIC.   I do.
But where's my son ?
  CHRY.   O, I don't know ; my duty
Is to know nothing, and remember nothing.   790
I know I'm a slave ; but what I know, I know not.
                    [*Nicobulus reads the letter.*]
[*Aside.*]   Ah, now, my thrush is getting near the trap,
He'll soon be hanging in the noose I've set !
  NIC.   Just wait a minute.   I'll be back directly.
                         [*Exit Nicobulus into his house.*]
  CHRY.   Hark, how he tries to cheat poor simple me !
I don't know what he's gone for ! not at all !
He's gone to fetch the slaves to bind me fast.
Yon portly galleon's getting finely tossed !
Meanwhile, my little skiff speeds bravely on.
But hush ; I hear the door's about to open.

NICOBULUS.   CHRYSALUS.

[*Re-enter Nicobulus with Artamo and other slaves.*]

  NIC.   Now seize him, Artamo, and bind his hands !
  CHRY.   What have I done?
  NIC.   Strike him if he but mutters !   800
What does this letter say ?
  CHRY.   How should I know?
I brought it sealed to you, as I received it.
  NIC.   So *you're* the man who with your vile abuse

Annoyed my son for bringing back my gold?
It's *you* that said you'd get it back again
By trickery!

 CHRY.   Did I say so?

 NIC.   Yes, you did.

 CHRY. What man is he who says so?

 NIC.   O, be quiet!

No *man* says so; this *letter* proves you guilty,
Which you have brought; yes, bids me bind you.

 CHRY.   Ha,

810 Your son has made me a Bellerophon;[1]
I've brought the letter that condemns me. Right!

 NIC. Besides you've been persuading my weak son
To live a life of riot, you venomous wretch!

 CHRY. Poor fool, you little know you're being sold!
You're on the block,[2] the crier calls your name.

 NIC. Tell me who's selling me?

 CHRY.   Whom the gods love

Dies young, whilst yet he's strength and sight and
 sense.
If any god loved *him*, [*pointing to Nic.*] ten years ago,
Nay, rather, twenty years since he'd have died.

820 Too long he walks a burden to the earth;
A senseless, tasteless, worthless, stinking toad-stool!

 NIC. You dare call me a burden to the earth!
Go take him in, and bind him to a pillar.

---

[1] Hom. Il. vi. 168.

  " Yet he shrank from his blood, for it seemed to his soul an unlucky
   thing,
  But to Lycia he sent him, and baleful tokens he gave him to bear,
  A folded tablet with many a death-fraught sign traced there."—

          (Way's translation.)

  As a slave ready to be sold.

No, you shall never steal the gold away !
   CHRY.   And yet you'll give it me !
   NIC.   I give it you !
   CHRY.   Yes, and beseech me, too, to kindly take it ;
When you find out the danger and the peril
Which threatens him who now accuses me,
Then you'll give liberty to Chrysalus,
But he won't take it.
   NIC.   Tell me, prince of rascals,
What danger threatens my Mnesilochus ?   830
   CHRY.   Follow me here ; I'll show you.
   NIC.   But how far ?
   CHRY.   Only three steps.
   NIC.   Ten, if you like.
      [*Chrysalus leads the way to the door of Bacchis' house.*]
   CHRY.   Now then,
Artamo, push this door a little open ;
Gently, don't let it creak.—There, that'll do.—
Come here, sir, now !   Do you behold this banquet ?
   NIC.   Bacchis and Pistoclerus I can see.
   CHRY.   But who's on t'other side ?
   NIC.   O, you have killed me !
   CHRY.   Do you know the man ?
   NIC.   I do !
   CHRY.   But tell me, pray,
Isn't the girl a beauty ?
   NIC.   O, no doubt !
   CHRY.   Surely you don't suspect her ?
   NIC.   Yes, I do.
   CHRY.   You're wrong then.
   NIC.   Well, who is she ?
   CHRY.   O, find out !   840
For I won't tell you any more about it.

CLEOMACHUS. NICOBULUS. CHRYSALUS.

[*Enter Cleomachus.*]

CL. And so Mnesilochus, Nicobulus' son,
Would keep my girl by force. What does he mean?

NIC. Who's this?

CHRY. [*aside*]. In good time has my captain come.

CL. He thinks I am a woman, not a soldier,
And can't defend myself and what is mine.
Mars and Bellona never trust me more,
If I don't take his life, if once I meet him,
And disinherit him of vital breath.

850   NIC. He threatens my son ! Who is he, Chrysalus?

CHRY. The husband of the girl he's feasting with.

NIC. Her *husband?*

CHRY.   Yes, her husband.

NIC.   Is she married?

CHRY. You'll know ere very long !

NIC.   Oh, I'm undone !

CHRY. Now then ! is Chrysalus so great a villain?
Yes, listen to your son, and bind me fast !
I told you you'd find out his character.

NIC. What shall I do?

CHRY.   Tell them to let me go ;
For if you don't he'll surely murder him.

CL. There's nothing I would rather do to-day

860 Than catch him with the girl and kill them both.

CHRY. D'you hear him speak? Why don't you let me
go?

NIC. Here, loose him ! Oh, I'm dead, I'm mad with
fear !

CL. Yes, that bold girl, so lavish of her smiles,
Shall never make a laughing-stock of me.

CHRY. You might be able for a trifling sum

To buy him off.

NIC.   O do it, at any price !
If only he won't kill and murder him.

CL.   Unless I get two hundred Philips down,
I'll drain to the dregs the blood of both of them.

CHRY.   Ah, you can buy him off for that !

NIC.   Do so,   870
At any cost you like.

CHRY.   I'll go and do it.

    [*Chrysalus crosses the stage to Cleomachus.*]

What are you bawling at ?

CL.   Where is your master ?

CHRY.   Nowhere ! I cannot tell.   But are you willing,
Upon the promise of two hundred Philips,
To stop your shouting and your quarrelling ?

CL.   There's nothing I'd like better, I assure you.

CHRY.   And will you let me curse and blackguard you ?

CL.   At your discretion !

NIC.   How the rogue's wheedling him !—[1]

CHRY.   Yonder's the father of Mnesilochus.
So come with me and he will give his bond.
You ask for gold ; that's all that need be said.—

                    [*Chrysalus returns to Nicobulus.*]

NIC.   How goes it ?

CHRY.   Well, sir, for two hundred Philips
I've settled it !

NIC.   My saviour, you've preserved me !
I'm all impatience till I've said, " I'll pay ! "

CHRY. [*to Cleo.*]   You ask !   [*To Nic.*]   You promise !   880

NIC.   I'll promise ; ask away.

---

[1] Nicobulus is at one end of the stage, Cleomachus at the other ; so that neither hears what Chrysalus says to the other.

CL.   Will you give me two hundred sterling Philips?

CHRY.   "They shall be given," say! answer him!

NIC.   I'll give them.

CHRY. [*to Cleo.*]   How now, you filthy wretch! do we
  owe you aught?

How dare you be a nuisance to my master,

And threaten him with death?   We'll make you suffer!

If you've a sword, we have a spit at home,

With which, if you provoke me any more,

I'll prod you into mouse holes for your pains.[1]

890 I long ago have seen the foul suspicion

That tortures you.   You think he's with the girl.

  CL.   Nay, but he *is*.

  CHRY.   By Jupiter, Juno, Ceres,

Minerva, Latona, Spes, Ops, Virtus, Venus,

Castor and Pollux, Mars and Hercules,

Mercurius, Summanus, Sol, Saturnus,

And all the other gods, I vow and swear,

He's neither sitting with her, no, nor walking,

Nor kissing her, nor any other thing.

  NIC. [*aside*].   Hark how he swears!   His perjury has
    saved me!

  CL.   Then where's Mnesilochus?

  CHRY.   He's in the country;

His father sent him there.   The girl is gone

900 To the Acropolis, to see the temple

Of great Minerva.   Go and see yourself

If she's not there; the doors are open now.

  CL.   I'll to the market-place.

  CHRY.   Nay, to the gallows!

  CL.   I shall demand the money, though, to-day.

---

[1] An obscure line.   I fail to make any tolerable sense of it as it stands.

CHRY.   Demand it and be hanged! and don't suppose
We would come begging to a wretch like you.
                    [*Exit Cleomachus to the market-place.*]
He's gone! now, master, by the immortal gods,
I beg you, let me go in to your son.
    NIC.   Why go in there?
    CHRY.   To castigate him soundly,
For doing such things as this in such a way.
    NIC.   Nay, do so, Chrysalus, and, I beseech you,
Don't fail to let him have it.
    CHRY.   Don't tell me!   910
I shall reproach him far more bitterly
Than e'er Demetrius did Clinia.[1]
                    [*Exit Chrysalus into the house of Bacchis.*]
    NIC.   This slave's exactly like a blood-shot eye;
If you've not got one, you're not anxious for it;
But if you have, you can't help rubbing it.
For if he hadn't happened to be here,
The captain would have caught Mnesilochus,
And killed him on the spot, without a doubt.
Now I've redeemed him for two hundred Philips,
Which I have promised I will give the captain.   920
But I won't pay them till I've seen my son;
I'll never lightly trust that Chrysalus.
But let me read this letter once again;
One ought to trust a letter signed and sealed.
                    [*Exit Nicobulus into his house.*]

CHRYSALUS.

[*Enter Chrysalus from the house of Bacchis, with a letter in his hand.*]

The sons of Atreus gained great fame,
When Priam's town they overcame,

Apparently characters in some well-known play.

And levelled the proud walls of Troy,
Whose building was the gods'[1] employ ;
With foot and horse, an army stout,
And warriors famed the world about,
And a good thousand ships to boot,
It took them ten full years to do't.
But Priam knew no such disaster
As I've inflicted on my master.
Without a fleet, without an army,
930 Or host of soldiers to alarm ye,
His father's gold I've stormed and won
To give it to his love-sick son.
Before he comes, my feelings urge
That I should sing the old man's dirge :—

O Troy, my home !   O Pergamum !
O Priam old ! alack the day !
Thou hast a fearful fine to pay !
Four hundred Philips is the sum.

This letter, which I here present,
All signed and sealed in proper course,
Is not a letter, but a horse,
The horse of wood the Grecians sent.[2]

Our Epius[3] is Pistoclerus ;
I've left Mnesilochus, our Sinon,[4]

---

[1] *viz.*, Neptune (Poseidon) and Apollo. Hom. Il. vii. 452.

[2] It must be remembered that the letter was written on a tablet of *wood*, smeared over with wax.

The maker of the famous wooden horse. Verg. Æn. ii. 264.

[4] Sinon was left behind by the Greeks when they sailed away from Troy, and was found by the Trojans lying on the tomb of Achilles. He represented himself as having been maltreated by the Greeks, was admitted into Troy, and let the soldiers out of the horse.

No hero's barrow to recline on,
But in the house of Bacchis near us.

Bacchis, who's with him, is the fire [1]
For flashing signals ; but her kisses
Burn *him* instead !   I am Ulysses,
Who formed the plan at their desire.   940

The letters written hereupon
Are soldiers hidden in the horse,
All clad in arms and full of force ;
So far the thing goes bravely on.

Not his stronghold but his strong-box
Shall feel my horse's bold attack ;
Destruction, death, damnation black,
Shall seize his gold in spite of locks.

The old man's watchfulness remiss is ;
I'll call him Ilium suitably ;
The captain's Menelaus ; I
Am Agamemnon and Ulysses.

Mnesilochus is Alexander,[2]
Who made his ruined country quake ;
He ravished Helen, for whose sake
Poor Ilium's wealth I soon shall squander.

Now, as I've heard, Ulysses cherished
A spirit, bold and bad, like mine.

---

[1] It had been arranged that Sinon should give a signal to the Greeks
by lighting a fire.

[2] Better known as Paris, whose rape of Helen was the cause of the
Trojan war.

As I was caught in bold design,
950   So he, caught begging, nearly perished,[1]

Seeking the state of Troy to learn.
My hap was just like his to-day;
Being bound, by craft I got away;
So he used craft to serve his turn.

At Troy three fatal signs were reckoned
To indicate her coming doom;
The loss of the Palladium;[2]
The death of Troilus, the second.[3]

The third, when at the Scæan gate,[4]
The upper lintel should be riven;
So three like signs to us were given
To show our Ilium's coming fate.

The first one was the monstrous hum,
Which to the poor old man I told,
About the pirates and the gold;
Then stole I the Palladium.

Two signs of fate did still remain;
The city wasn't taken yet.
But when I got that letter writ,
960   And given him, Troilus was slain.

---

[1] Hom. Od. iv. 242.

[2] The Palladium, an image of Pallas. Troy could not be taken whilst this image remained in the city; Ulysses and Diomede stole it.

[3] Troilus was the youngest son of Priam, and was slain by Achilles.

[4] One of the gates of Troy.

Then, when he thought Mnesilochus
Was sitting with the captain's wife,
I had a job to save my life ;
And with Ulysses it was thus.

For Helen recognised his face,[1]
And told Queen Hecuba his name ;
But by the same old wily game
He wrought on her to grant him grace.

So *I* escaped the pressing throng
Of perils, and deceived my lord.
Then with that braggart man o' the sword,
Who captures cities with his tongue,

I next engaged, and won the day ;
Then met the old man merrily,
And conquered him with one big lie ;
At one blow bore the spoils away.

Two hundred Philips 'twill employ
To satisfy the captain's greed ;   970
Two hundred more we then shall need
To spend when we have taken Troy.

Our soldiers all are thirsty ones,
And wine should always follow war ;
' Our Priam beats the old one far—
He doesn't stop at fifty sons.[2]

---

[1] Eur. Hec. 243.
[2] Priam had fifty sons ; Nicobulus four hundred Philips.

He's got four hundred, all in rows,
Without a flaw, of sterling worth ;
But spite of their illustrious birth
I'll kill them all with two strong blows. [1]

If anybody wants our Priam,
I'm quite prepared to knock him down,
As soon as I have stormed the town,
In a job lot,[2] if you will buy him !
        [*Enter Nicobulus from his house.*]
But there stands Priam at our door ;
I'll go and talk to him some more.

NICOBULUS.   CHRYSALUS.

NIC.   Who's that I hear talking near me? Ah! What
news have you to tell?
Have you done the work I bade you?
    CHRY.   Yes ; come nearer.
980   NIC.   Very well.
    CHRY.   I'm a noble orator ; my speech begat in him such
loathing
Of his crimes, he fairly wept.
    NIC.   What did he say?
    CHRY.   O, he said nothing.
Silently in tears he listened, while I tried to make him better ;
Then in silence wrote and sealed, and put into my hands this
letter,
Bade me give it you.   But I'm afraid it sings the same old
song.
Look at the seal.   Is it his ?
    NIC.   I know it.   Let me read it.
    CHRY.   Read along.

---

i.e., The two letters.
[2] He's too worthless to be put up alone.

[*Aside.*] Ah, now the upper lintel's riven; and Troy's de-
    struction is at hand.

My wooden horse will make a stir!

NIC.   Stay, till this letter I have scanned.

CHRY. Why should I stay?

NIC.   I want you to know
    What's written here before you go.

CHRY. I have no wish to hear it, though!

NIC.   Yet stay!

CHRY.   Why should I stay at hand?

NIC. Be still and do what I command.

CHRY. Right, I'll stay.

NIC.   The writing's small.

CHRY.   O, that's because you cannot see; 990
If your sight were good, it's big enough.

NIC.   Look here, attend to me.

CHRY. No, I won't!

NIC.   You shall, I say.

CHRY.   What for?

NIC.   Just do as you are told.

CHRY. Well, that's fair; for by his master every slave
    should be controlled.

NIC. Come here, now.

CHRY.   Well, read away, sir; and my ears shall wait
    on you.

NIC. He didn't spare the wax or pen; but anyhow I'll
    read it through—

[*Reads.*] "Dear father, pray you give two hundred Philips
        To Chrysalus, if you would save my life."

CHRY. O, that's a serious loss!—Look here!

NIC.   .   What is it?

CHRY. Doesn't he greet you first?

NIC.   No, I don't see it. 1000

CHRY. Why then, the letter starts with impudence.
Don't give it, if you're wise ; but if you do,
You'd better get another porter for it ;
For I won't take it, order as you will ;
My innocence has borne enough suspicion.

NIC. But listen whilst I read what's written next—
[*Reads.*] " Father, I blush to come into your sight.
I've heard you know about my monstrous crime,
How I've been dining with the captain's wife."
1010 Ah ! that's no joke !   It cost two hundred Philips
To save your life, sir, after what you'd done !

CHRY. Yes ; all those points I duly placed before him.

NIC. [*reads*]. " I own I've been a fool ; but, father dear,
Do not desert me though I've stooped to folly.
'Twas my hot passion, my unchastened eyes,
Persuaded me to what I now regret."
Better be prudent first than sorry after !

CHRY. Those are the very words I used myself.

NIC. [*reads*]. " Pray you, be satisfied that Chrysalus
1020 Has plied me with a thousand keen reproaches,
And by his warnings led me to repentance.
It's only right that you should thank him for it."

CHRY. Does he write that?

NIC.   There, look, see for yourself.

CHRY. Ah ! how a guilty conscience humbles him !

NIC. [*reads*]. " Now, if I have a right to ask you, father,
Give me two hundred Philips, I entreat ! "

CHRY. No, not a penny, if you're wise !

NIC.   Be quiet !
[*Reads.*] " I've sworn an oath in set and formal terms
To pay it to the woman, ere night falls,
1030 Before she leaves me.   Father, save your son
From being forsworn !   O rescue me from her,

Through whom I've suffered so much loss and shame.
You needn't let the money worry you.
I promise to pay back *six* hundred Philips,
Upon my life.   Farewell, and help me, father."
Well, Chrysalus, and what is *your* opinion ?

CHRY.   O, I'm not going to give you any counsels ;
I won't commit myself.   If aught goes wrong,
I'll take care you sha'n't say that I advised it.
But, as I think, if I were in your place,
I'd rather pay the gold than see him ruined.   1040
One of two things must be ; so take your choice ;
To lose the gold, or let him be forsworn.
But I say nothing, neither yea, nor nay.

NIC.   I pity him.

CHRY.   No wonder ! he's your own !
And if you must lose more, that's pleasanter
Than that his shame should be the common talk.

NIC.   I wish the lad had stayed at Ephesus
Where he was safe, and not come home at all.
Well, as it's lost, let's get it quickly over.
I'll go and fetch out twice two hundred Philips ;   1050
Two that, alas ! I promised to the captain,
And two beside.   Stay here : I'll soon be back.

[*Exit Nicobulus into the house*].

CHRY.   Troy is destroyed, the chiefs are sacking her ;
I knew that I should ruin Pergamum.
By Jove ! if anybody says that I
Deserve the gallows, I won't contradict him.
I'm making such confusion !   Hark ! the door !
The spoil's being brought from Troy.   I'll hold my
     peace.

[*Re-enter Nicobulus with the money.*]

NIC.   Here, take the money ; bear it to my son.
1060 I'll to the market-place, and pay the captain.

CHRY.   I won't receive it ; go find someone else
To take it ; I would rather not be trusted.

NIC.   Here, take it ; or you'll vex me.

CHRY.   No, not I.

NIC.   But I beseech.

CHRY.   I mean just what I say.

NIC.   You're keeping me.

CHRY.   I will not have that gold
Entrusted to me ; or find someone else
To watch me well.

NIC.   O dear, you *are* a nuisance !

CHRY.   Well, give it me, if you must.

NIC.   Take care of it !
I'll not be long before I'm back again.

                [*Exit Nicobulus to the market-place.*]

CHRY.   I've *taken care* to make you miserable !
This is the way to carry out your plans !
O happy fate ! in triumph I retire,
Loaded with spoil.   The victory is ours ;
1070 The city's taken by my stratagems,
And I lead home my army all complete.
But, gentle hearers, don't you be surprised
That I don't have a triumph ; I don't care to :
The thing has grown too common.[1]   Nevertheless,
My soldiers shall not go without their wine.
Well, now I'll take our paymaster the spoil.

                [*Exit Chrysalus into the house of Bacchis.*]

---

[1] Up to the year 200 B.C. triumphs were rare ; but between 197 and
187, no less than fourteen triumphs were celebrated.   This helps to fix
the date of this play.

PHILOXENUS.

[Enter Philoxenus from the town.]

PHIL.   The more I consider the racket and row
  My poor silly son has been making,
The sort of amusement he goes in for now,
  And the rash headlong course he is taking,
The greater my care and anxiety grows
  Lest he should be wrecked by his passion.
I once was his age and did just what he does,
  But in a much modester fashion.
I loved and I courted, I feasted and drank,
  Gave presents, though that was but rarely.   1080
To be overstrict is the mark of a crank ;
  Modern fathers don't treat their sons fairly.
So I have determined to give my son rope,
  And permit him to follow his sparking ;
I think I've done right ; at the same time I hope
  He won't go too far with his larking.
So now I am off to Mnesilochus' house
  To see if he's done my commission.
I hope that his words have been able to rouse
  My son to a lively contrition.
I know he'll do all that occasion allows,
  For that is the lad's disposition.

NICOBULUS.   PHILOXENUS.

[Enter Nicobulus from the market-place.]

NIC.   Of all the men who ever were, or e'er shall be here-
  after,
Muddling mules, fat-headed fools, soft, silly subjects for
  laughter,
I freely confess I'm ahead of them all

In folly and downright stupidity ;
A man of my years, too ! I blush at my fall !
1090 Twice choused in my utter stolidity !
The longer I think of the deeds of my son,
The hotter's my just indignation ;
I'm ruined, destroyed, and completely undone ;
I cannot express my vexation.
    All woes are hastening on my track,
    All misery's piled upon my back.
    Chrysalus stabbed me to death to-day ;
    Chrysalus plundered me as I lay ;
    Chrysalus fleeced me of my gold,
    Fool that I was, by his tricks so bold !
Just think !   The captain informs me that she
They said was his wife, is his slave ; and that he
Had simply engaged her to serve him a year ;
In fact, he has made the thing perfectly clear ;
The money I promised to pay for my son
Was to compensate him for the months yet to run. [1]
This is the trouble that pierces my heart,
This is the cause of my bitterest smart ;
That I at my age should be made a fool,
1100 And sent, by Pollux ! again to school ;
When my head is white and my beard is grey
Should see my money filched away !
O to think that that worthless slave
Should dare to do it ! 'zounds I could rave !
I wouldn't have minded losing much more ;
It's the way he did it that makes me sore.

---

[1] He had paid for the girl's services for the year ; and hence wanted compensation for the months yet unexpired before he would release her and let Mnesilochus have her.

PHIL.   I certainly thought that I heard someone speak.
              Bless me! it's Mnesilochus' father!
NIC.   A companion in trouble I'll not have to seek;
              Here's someone to share with me, rather!
       Philoxenus, hail!
PHIL.   Same to you! Where've you been?
NIC.   With a wretched, unfortunate fellow!
PHIL.   I'm the wretched, unfortunate fellow you mean!
              For I have been there, I can tell you.
NIC.   It seems we're alike both in fortune and age.
PHIL.   Indeed, that's a fact. But the cause of your
       rage,
          Tell it me.
NIC.   Certainly; just what makes *you* so mad!
PHIL.   What! you don't say it's your son that makes *you*
              so sad?   1110
NIC.   Yes, it is.
PHIL.   *That's* the disease that's tormenting me.
NIC.   Chrysalus, sharper, has been circumventing me,
       Ruining my son, and myself, and my property.
PHIL.   What's wrong with your son?
NIC.   The truth I'll tell.
       He's fallen in love, and your son as well.
PHIL.   Your proof?
NIC.   I saw them.
PHIL.   That ends doubt.
NIC.   Come, then, hesitate no longer, let us knock and
       bring them out.
PHIL.   Oh, I'm ready.
NIC.   [*knocking at the door*].   Hallo, Bacchis, bid this door
       be opened straight!
If you don't, I'll get an axe and smash it open; I won't wait!

The Bacchides.   Nicobulus.   Philoxenus.

[*Enter to the door the two Bacchides.*]

1120   Att. Who's this that is shouting and bawling like thunder,
                Stirring up such a dither?

Nic. It's I and my friend.

Att.   What's their business, I wonder?
    Who drove these sheep hither?

Nic. They're calling us sheep!

Sam.   Sure their shepherd is sleeping,
To let them go wandering away from his keeping.

Att. But are they not fat and in splendid condition?

Sam. They both have been close shorn!

Phil. [*aside*].   I have a suspicion
They're mocking us.

Nic.   Let's take no notice, but scorn them.

Att. I wonder if three times a year they have shorn them.

Sam. There's one has been twice shorn to-day, dear! I
    fancy.

Att. They're old.

Sam.   But they once have been frisky I *can* see!

1130   Att. But look, sister dear, how they're leering and wink-
    ing!

Sam. They're meaning no harm by it, sister, I'm thinking.

Phil. It serves us just right, we were asses to venture.

Att. Let's drive them indoors.

Sam.   What's the use, if they enter?
They've got neither milk nor yet wool.   Let them stay there!
They've lost all they had; and no fruit can we gather
From them.   Don't you see how they're aimlessly straying?
They're dumb with old age.   What's the use of our staying?
They don't even bleat for the flock they have left; they seem
    to be utterly silly.

Att. Come, let's go in, sister.

Nic.   These sheep are desiring your company;
  stay with us, will ye?   1140

Sam.   Hark, the sheep like men are talking; miracles will
  never cease![1]

Phil.   Yes, these sheep will pay you back the ill they owe
  you, if you please.

Att.   I forgive you all you owe us; keep it, I don't want
  it back.

But I'd like to know the reason of your menacing attack.

Phil.   Why, because two lambs of ours are shut in here;
  we know your larks!

Nic.   And beside the lambs, a dog of mine that bites
  before he barks.[2]

Now, if you don't bring them forth and send them out of
  doors with speed,

We shall turn to savage rams and butt you; so you'd best take
  heed.

Att.   Sister dear, just a word with you.

Sam.   Sister, say on. [*They retire.*]

Nic.   I'd like to know what they are after.

Att.   The further old man[3] I put into your hands
    To move him to sweetness and laughter.   1150
  This angry old fellow I'll tackle myself.
    I think we can get the old boys in.

Sam.   Oh, I'll cheerfully manage the task you have set,
    Though I hate the old rascal like poison.

Att.   Take care that you do.

Sam.   You take care of yourself!
    As I promised the thing, I shall do it.

Nic.   Those two are concocting some villainy now;

---

[1] Lines 1141—1148 are trochaic.   [2] Chrysalus of course is meant.
  [3] *i.e.* Philoxenus.

What is it?　I wish that I knew it.

PHIL.　Old fellow, I say!

NIC.　　　　　　　　　Well, what do you want?

PHIL.　　　I'm afraid what I say will disgust you.

NIC.　Come, why are you blushing?

PHIL.　　　　　　　　I know you're my friend,
And so I'm determined to trust you.
I'm an ass!

NIC.　　　　　　O, I knew that a long time ago!
But speak, let me hear your confession.

PHIL.　The bird-lime has got on my feathers, I fear!
I'm pricked to the heart!

NIC.　　　　　　　　O, a prick in the rear
Would better assist your progression!
But what are you wanting to tell me? although
1160　　　　I think I can guess pretty fairly.
Still, I'd like you to tell me.

PHIL.　　　　　　　You see her? [*Pointing to Attica.*]

NIC.　　　　　　　I do.

PHIL.　　Well—she's not such a bad sort of girl, eh?

NIC.　She *is*, though, and you are an ass.

PHIL.　　　　　　　　Never mind!
I like her.

NIC.　　　You like —?

PHIL.　　　　　　　*Evidemment!* [1]

NIC.　What! changing your mind for a girl's pretty face!
And at your time of life, too!

PHIL.　　　　　　　O gammon!

NIC.　It's scandalous.

PHIL.　　　There! there's no need to say more.
My wrath with my son is all over—

---

[1] Philoxenus replies in Greek, ναὶ γάρ: the French word gives
much the same effect.

And don't you be angry with yours any more,
 For no one's so wise as a lover.

ATT. Well, what are we waiting for?   Sister, come on !
      [They return to the old gentlemen.]

NIC.   See there ! they're returning to floor us,
 Those pestilent girls who can wheedle so well !
  Come now ! are you going to restore us
 Our sons and my slave?   If you don't, I must try
  What force can effect.

PHIL.   You be quiet !
 You're no man, sir, I say, to address a sweet girl
  So unsweetly ; you'd better not try it.

ATT. You darling old man ! you're the best in the world !
  Now surely you'll grant me this favour :— 1170
 Desist from your savage intemperate wrath
  And pardon your son's bad behaviour.

NIC. Be off, or in spite of your sweet, pretty face
  I'll strike you directly.

ATT.   No matter !
 I don't think you'd strike me so hard as to hurt.

NIC.   Just hark how the lady can flatter !

ATT. Oh, dear, I'm afraid !

SAM.   *My* man's quieter, much !

ATT.   Come, lay aside all your suspicion,
 And please to walk into the house ; when you're
   there,
  You can talk your son into contrition.

NIC. Go, leave me, you wretch !

ATT.   Nay, but, reverend sir,
  Be persuaded !

NIC.   Persuaded by you, miss?

SAM. *My* man I'll persuade !

PHIL.   Nay, indeed, I entreat
  That you'll show me at once where the room is.

NIC.　Well, I've often seen men that were weak, but I ne'er
　　　　Saw a weaker than you.

1180 PHIL.　　　　　　　　　　　　I admit it.

ATT.　O come in with me! there are ointments in there,
　　　　And a banquet, and good wine to fit it.

NIC.　Enough of your banquet! It's no little loss
　　　　With which you already afflict me;
　　　　Out of four hundred Philips, my treacherous son
　　　　And Chrysalus, villain, have tricked me.
　　　　But I wouldn't accept as much money again
　　　　To grant those two wretches remission.

ATT.　But, supposing a half of the money's restored,
　　　　Won't you come in upon that condition,
　　　　And try to persuade yourself, hard as it is,
　　　　To grant them forgiveness?

PHIL.　　　　　　　　　　　　　He'll do it.

NIC.　Not a bit of it! No! Not a moment I'll wait!
　　　　Let me be! Oh, I'll see that they rue it!

PHIL.　Well, you are an ass, when the gods send you
　　good,
　　　　And you throw it away in your folly!
　　　　She'll give you the half of your gold. Take it, man!
　　　　And come in and let's drink and be jolly.

NIC.　Shall *I* go in there, where my son has been gulled,
　　　　And drink?

1190 PHIL.　　　　　　　You must drink, that is certain!
　　　　I'm rather ashamed of my weakness, I own;
　　　　But still, after all, it won't hurt one!

NIC.　Oh, how my head itches! [1] I cannot say no.

ATT.　And this is a thing should be thought on,
　　　　That though, whilst you live, you indulge your desires,
　　　　Your life after all is a short one.

---

[1] *Caput prurit* = I am puzzled.

  If you pass by the chance that is offered to-day,
    When you're dead, you will ne'er get another.

NIC. O what shall I do?

PHIL.   Why, there's no need to ask.

NIC. I'd like but I fear—

PHIL.   What's your bother?

NIC. I can't help being vexed with my son and his slave.

ATT. My honey, my dearest, forgive him!
  He's yours: do you think he would take anything
    Except what he's sure you would give him?
  Come, let me persuade you to pardon them both!

NIC.   Confound her! She won't take an answer! 1200
  What I have refused, she persuades me to do!
  Well, if I do wrong, it's entirely for you.

ATT. Nay, I'd rather it was for your son, sir!
  But can I believe you will stand to your word?

NIC. When I've once said a thing, I will do it.

ATT. The day is declining; come in now and dine,
  Your sons are expecting you over the wine.

NIC. Yes, expecting our deaths, if we knew it.

ATT. The evening's at hand; come along.

PHIL.   Lead the way,
  For we are your prisoners ever.

ATT. And thus the old men who laid snares for their sons
  Are captured themselves. Ain't I clever?

THE COMPANY. EPILOGUE.

Had these old men not remembered certain follies of their
  youth,

Their sons' escapades would not have gained a pardon
  here to-day,

But the scene we've played before you is a common one
    in sooth ;

Sons oft find their fathers kindly, even though their hairs
1210   are grey.

    Now farewell, good gentle hearers ; lift your hands and clap
        away !

CAPTIVI;

THE PRISONERS OF WAR.

R

INTRODUCTION.

THE original of this comedy is not known. It is conspicuous amongst the plays of Plautus by the absence of love-motive and the purity both of the story and the language. The praise bestowed upon it in the Epilogue is well deserved. The plot, though ingenious,[1] affords small scope for humour ; to supply this, the parasite Ergasilus is introduced. There is nothing to determine the date of the play. The Prologue, like that to the Amphitryon, is of later date ; probably about 150-140 B.C. The scene is laid in Ætolia.

I have found the editions of Brix and Sonnenschein of great service in translating this play. I have also consulted Prof. Strong's translation.

---

[1] Lessing considered it the best play ever written from the point of view of plot construction.

DRAMATIS PERSONÆ.

ERGASILUS — *A parasite.*

HEGIO — *An old gentleman.*

PHILOCRATES — *An Elian Knight* ⎫
⎬ *The prisoners.*
TYNDARUS — *Son of Hegio* ⎭

ARISTOPHONTES — *A prisoner.*

PHILOPOLEMUS — *A young man, son of Hegio.*

STALAGMUS — *A slave.*

OVERSEERS OF SLAVES.

A BOY.

ARGUMENT (*ACROSTIC*).[1]

C APTURED in fight was one of Hegio's sons,
A nother sold by a slave when four years old.
P risoners from Elis now the father buys,
T o give them in exchange for him who's ta'en ;
E nrolled amongst them is the son he'd lost.
I n hope of freedom he's changed with his master
V estments and name ; the old man is deceived.
E ager he [2] brings the prisoner and the slave ;
I n him the slave points out the long lost son.

[1] *Capteivei*, the spelling of the acrostic, is merely another form of *Captivi*.

[2] *i.e.*, Philocrates.

PROLOGUE.

[*The scene represents the house of Hegio in Ætolia. Before the house are seen standing in chains the two prisoners, Philocrates and Tyndarus.*]

PROL. You all can see two prisoners standing here,
Standing in bonds; they stand, they do not sit;[1]
In this you'll witness that I speak the truth.
Old Hegio, who lives here, is this one's father;
  [*Pointing to Tyndarus.*]
But how he's come to be his father's slave
My prologue shall inform you, if you'll listen.
This old man had two sons; the one of whom
Was stolen by a slave when four years old.
He ran away to Elis and there sold him
To this one's father. [*Pointing to Philocrates.*]
　　　　　—Do you see?—That's right !　　　　10
Yon fellow in the gallery [2] says he doesn't?
Let him come nearer, then !　What, there's no room?
If there's no room to sit, there's room to walk ![3]
You'd like to send me begging, would you, sir ![4]

---

[1] This is obviously meant for a joke, but none of the editors seem to see where it lies. May there not be a reference to the agitation which was going on about the middle of the 2nd century B.C. for the introduction of seats into the theatres? There is an allusion to this again in the twelfth line.

[2] Lit., In the farthest part of the house.

[3] *i.e.*, Outside, perhaps in the portico behind the stage.

[4] *i.e.*, By compelling me to strain my voice, and so render myself incapable of acting any longer.

Pray, don't suppose I'll crack my lungs for *you !*
You gentlemen of means and noble rank [1]
Receive the rest ; I hate to be in debt.
That run-a-way, as I've already said,
When in his flight he'd stolen from his home
His master's son, sold him to this man's father,

[*Pointing to Philocrates.*]

Who, having bought him, gave him to his son
20 To be his valet ; for the two lads were
Much of an age.   Now he's his father's slave
In his own home, nor does his father know it ;
See how the gods play ball with us poor men !
Now then, I've told you how he lost *one* son.
The Ætolians and the Elians being at war,
His *other* son, a not uncommon thing
In war, was taken prisoner ; and a doctor
At Elis, called Menarchus, bought him there.
His father then began to buy up Elians,
To see if he could find one to exchange
Against his son,—the one that is a prisoner ;
The other, who's at home, he doesn't know.
30 Now, only yesterday he heard a rumour
How that an Elian knight of highest rank
And noblest family was taken prisoner ;
He spared no cash if he might save his son ;
And so, to get him home more readily,
He bought these two from the commissioners.
But they between themselves have laid a plot,
So that the slave may get his lord sent home.
Thus they've exchanged their clothing and their names ; —

---

[1] *i.e.,* The senators and equites who occupied the orchestra and front
seats.

He's called Philocrates [*pointing to Tyndarus*], *he* Tyndarus
   [*pointing to Philocrates*],
And either plays the other's part to-day.
The slave to-day will work this clever dodge,   40
And get his master set at liberty.
By the same act he'll save his brother too,
And get him brought back free to home and father,
Though all unwitting : oft we do more good
In ignorance than by our best-laid plans.
Well, ignorantly, in their own deceit,
They've so arranged and worked their little trick, [1]
That he [*pointing to Tyn.*] shall still remain his father's slave.
For now, not knowing it, he serves his father.   50
What things of naught are men, when one reflects on't !
This story's ours to act, and yours to see.
But let me give you one brief word of warning :
It's well worth while to listen to this play.
It's not been treated in a hackneyed fashion,
Nor like the rest of plays ; here you'll not find
Verses that are too nasty to be quoted.
Here is no perjured pimp, or crafty girl,
Or braggart captain.—Pray, don't be afraid
Because I said a war was going on
Between the Ætolians and the Elians ;
The battles won't take place upon the stage.   60
We're dressed for comedy ; you can't expect
That we should act a tragedy all at once.
If anybody's itching for a fight,
Just let him start a quarrel ; if he gets
An opposite that's stronger, I dare bet
He'll quickly see more fighting than he likes.

---

[1] A doubtful line is omitted.

And never long to see a fight again.
I'm off.   Farewell, ye most judicious judges
At home, most valiant fighters in the field !

[*Exit Prologue.*]

ERGASILUS.

[*Enter Ergasilus from the town.*]

ERG.   *Grace* is the name the boys have given me,
70 Because I'm always found *before the meat !* [1]
The wits, I know, say it's ridiculous ;
But so don't I !   For at the banquet-table
Your gamester throws the dice and asks for *grace.*
Then is *grace* there or not ?   Of course she is !
But, more of course, we parasites are there,
Though no one ever asks or summons us !
Like mice we live on other people's food ;
In holidays, when folks go out of town,
Our teeth enjoy a holiday as well.
80 As, when it's warm, the snails lie in their shells,
And, failing dew, live on their native juices ;
So parasites lie hid in misery
All through the holidays, living on their juices,
Whilst those they feed on jaunt it in the country.
During the holidays, we parasites
Are greyhounds ; when they're over, we are mastiffs,
Bred out of " Odious " by " Prince of Bores."
Now here, unless your parasite can stand
Hard fisticuffs, and has no strong objection

---

[1] This pun is untranslatable ; I have, therefore, attempted some sort
of an equivalent.   Literally it runs, " The young fellows call me
' mistress,' because I am always present *invocatus* at the feast ; " *invocatus*
meaning both *unasked* and *invoked.*   Ergasilus justifies the name on the
ground that the lover in throwing the dice *invokes* the name of his mistress, and therefore she is *invocata* at the feast.

To have the crockery broken on his pate,
He'd better go and take a porter's billet
At the Trigeminal gate ;[1] which lot, I fear,   90
Is not at all unlikely to be mine.
My patron has been captured by the foe—
The Ætolians and the Elians are at war,
(This is Ætolia) ; Philopolemus,
The son of Hegio here, whose house this is,
In Elis lies a prisoner ; so this house
A house of lamentation is to me ;
As oft as I behold it, I must weep.
Now for his son's sake, he's begun a trade,
Dishonourable, hateful to himself ;
He's buying prisoners, if perchance he may   100
Find any to exchange against his son.
O how I pray that he may gain his wish !
Till he's recovered, I am past recovery.
The other youths are selfish, hopelessly,
And only he keeps up the ancient style.
I've never flattered him without reward ;
And the good father takes after his son !
Now I'll go see him. Ha ! the door is opening,
Whence I have often come, just drunk with gorging.

HEGIO. OVERSEER: ERGASILUS.

[*Enter from the house Hegio and an Overseer.*]

HEG.   Attend to me ; those prisoners that I bought   110
A day ago from the Commissioners
Out of the spoil, put lighter fetters on them ;
Take off these heavier ones with which they're bound,

---

[1] The scene is laid in Ætolia ; but Plautus does not hesitate to intro-
duce the Roman localities familiar to his audience.   The Trigeminal gate
lay between the Aventine and the Tiber, in the busiest part of the city ;
porters would, therefore, be in demand at this point.

And let them walk indoors or out at will ;
But watch them with the utmost carefulness.
For when a free man's taken prisoner,
He's just like a wild bird ; if once he gets
A chance of running off, it's quite enough ;
You needn't hope to catch your man again.

OVER.   Why, all of us would rather far be free
Than slaves.

120   HEG.   Why not take steps, then, to be free ?[1]

OVER.   Shall I give *leg-bail ?*   I've naught else to give !

HEG.   I fancy that in that case you would *catch it !*

OVER.   I'll be like that wild bird you spoke about.

HEG.   All right ; then I will clap you in a cage.
Enough of this ; do what I said, and go.

                  [*Exit Overseer into the house.*]

I'll to my brother's, to my other captives,
To see how they've behaved themselves last night,
And then I'll come back home again straightway.

ERG. [*aside*].   It grieves me that the poor old man should
    ply

130 This gaoler's trade to save his hapless son.
But if perchance the son can be brought back,
The father may turn hangman : what care I?

HEG.   Who speaks there?

ERG.   One who suffers in your grief.
I'm growing daily thinner, older, weaker !
See, I'm all skin and bones, as lean as lean !
All that I eat at home does me no good ;
Only a bite at a friend's agrees with me.

HEG.   Ergasilus ! hail !

ERG. [*crying*].   Heav'n bless you, Hegio !

---

[1] *i.e.*, Save up and buy your freedom. The Overseer intentionally
misunderstands Hegio's meaning (" take steps ").

HEG. Don't weep!

ERG.   Not weep for him?   What, not bewail
That excellent young man?

HEG.   I always knew   140
You and my son to be the best of friends.

ERG. Alas! we don't appreciate our blessings
Till we have lost the gifts we once enjoyed.
Now that your son is in the foeman's hands,
I realise how much he was to me!

HEG. Ah, if a stranger feels his loss so much,
What must *I* feel?   He was my only joy.

ERG. A stranger?   I a stranger?   Hegio,
Never say that nor cherish such a thought!
Your only joy he was, but oh! to me
Far dearer than a thousand only joys.   150

HEG. You're right to make your friend's distress your own;
But come, cheer up!

ERG.   Alas! it pains me here,
              [*laying his hand on his stomach.*]
That now the feaster's army is discharged.

HEG. And can't you meantime find another general
To call to arms this army that's discharged?

.ERG. No fear! since Philopolemus was taken,
Who filled that post, they all refuse to act.

HEG. And it's no wonder they refuse to act.
You need so many men of divers races
To work for you; first, those of Bakerton;   160
And several tribes inhabit Bakerton;
Then men of Breadport and of Biscuitville,
Of Thrushborough and Ortolania,
And all the various soldiers of the sea.

ERG. How oft the noblest talents lie concealed!
O what a splendid general you would make,

Though now you're serving as a private merely.

HEG.   Be of good cheer ; in a few days, I trust,
I shall receive my dear son home again.
I've got a youthful Elian prisoner,
170 Whom I am hoping to exchange for him,
One of the highest rank and greatest wealth.

ERG.   May Heaven grant it !

HEG.   Where've you been invited
To dine to-day ?

ERG.   Why, nowhere that I know of.
Why do you ask ?

HEG.   Because it is my birthday ;
And so, I pray you, come and dine with me.

ERG.   Well said indeed !

HEG.   That is if you're content
With frugal fare.

ERG.   Well, if it's not *too* frugal ;
I get enough of that, you know, at home.

HEG.   Well, name your figure !

ERG.   Done ! unless I get
180 A better offer, and on such conditions
As better suit my partners and myself.
As I am selling you my whole estate,
It's only fair that I should make my terms.

HEG.   I fear that this estate you're selling me
Has got a bottomless abyss within't !
But if you come, come early.

ERG.   Now, if you like !

HEG.   Go hunt a hare ; you've only caught a weasel.
The path my guest must tread is full of stones.

ERG.   You won't dissuade me, Hegio ; don't think it !
I'll get my teeth well shod before I come.

HEG.   My table's really coarse.

ERG.   Do you eat brambles ?
HEG.   My dinner's from the soil.
ERG.   So is good pork.
HEG.   Plenty of cabbage !
ERG.   Food for invalids !   190
What more ?
HEG.   Be there in time.
ERG.   I'll not forget.

> [*Exit Ergasilus to the market-place.*]

HEG.   Now I'll go in and look up my accounts,
To see what I have lying at my banker's ;
Then to my brother's, as I said just now.

> [*Exit Hegio into the house.*]

OVERSEER.   PHILOCRATES.   TYNDARUS.

[*Enter Overseers, Philocrates and Tyndarus, each in the other's clothes, and other slaves.*]

OVER.   Since Heaven has willed it should be so,
        That you must drink this cup of woe,
        Why, bear it with a patient mind,
        And so your pain you'll lighter find.
        At home, I dare say, you were free ;
        Now that your lot is slavery,
        Just take it as a thing of course,
        Instead of making matters worse ;
        Behave yourselves and don't be queasy
        About your lord's commands ; 'tis easy.   200
PRISONERS.   Oh, oh !
OVER.   No need for howls and cries !
        I see your sorrow in your eyes.
        Be brave in your adversities.
TYN.   But we're ashamed to wear these chains.
OVER.   My lord would suffer far worse pains,

Should he leave you to range at large out of his custody,
Or set you at liberty whom he bought yesterday.

TYN.   Oh, he needn't fear that he'll lose his gains ;
Should he release us, we know what's our duty, sir.

OVER.   Yes, you'll run off; I know *that.*   You're a
beauty, sir !

TYN.   Run off? run off where?

OVER.   To the land of your birth.

TYN.   Nay, truly, it never would answer
To imitate runaway slaves.

OVER.   Well, by Jove !
I'd advise you, if you get a chance, sir.

TYN.   One thing I beg of you.

210   OVER.   What's your petition, sir?

TYN.   Give us a chance of exchanging a word,
Where there's no fear that we'll be overheard.

OVER.   Granted ! Go, leave them. We'll take our position there.
See that your talk doesn't last too long !

TYN.   Oh, that's my intention. [*To Phil.*] So, now,
come along !

OVER.   Go, leave them alone.

TYN.   We ever shall own
We're in your debt for the kindness you've shown to us ;
You have the power, and you've proved yourself bounteous.
[*The other prisoners withdraw to one side, the Overseer and his
attendants to the other.*]

PHIL.   Come away farther, as far as we can from them ;
We must contrive to conceal our fine plan from them,
220 Never disclose any trace of our trickery,
Else we shall find all our dodges a mockery.
             Once they get wind of it,
             There'll be an end of it ;

For if you are my master brave,
And I pretend to be your slave,
Then we must watch with greatest care;
Of eavesdroppers we must beware.

With caution and skill keep your senses all waking;
There's no time to sleep; it's a big undertaking.

TYN.   So I'm to be master?

PHIL.   Yes, that is the notion.

TYN.   And so for your head (I would pray you remark it),
You want me to carry my own head to market !   230

PHIL.   I know.

TYN.   Well, when you've gained your wish, remember my devotion.

This is the way that you'll find most men treating you ;

                    Until they have
                    The boon they crave,

They're kind as can be ; but success makes the knave !
When they have got it, they set to work cheating you.
Now I have told you the treatment you owe to me.
You I regard as a father, you know, to me.

PHIL.   Nay, let us say,—no conventions shall hinder us,—
Next to my own, you're my father, dear Tyndarus.

TYN.   That will do !

PHIL.   Now then, I warn you always to remember
                    this ;   240

I no longer am your master but your slave ;   don't be
   remiss.

Since kind Heav'n has shown us plainly that the way ourselves to save

Is for me, who was your master, now to turn into your slave,
Where before I gave you orders, now I beg of you in prayer,
By the changes in our fortune, by my father's kindly care,
By the common fetters fastened on us by the enemy,

Think of who you were and are, and pay no more respect to
    me

Than I used to pay to you, when you were slave and I was
    free.

  TYN.   Well, I know that I am you and you are me!

  PHIL.   Yes, stick to that!

Then I hope that by your shrewdness we shall gain what we
250   are at.

HEGIO. PHILOCRATES. TYNDARUS.

[Enter Hegio from his house.]

  HEG. [*addressing someone inside*].   I'll be back again
    directly when I've looked into the case :

Where are those whom I directed at the door to take their
    place ?

  PHIL.   O by Pollux! you've been careful that we shouldn't
    be to seek ;

Thus by bonds and guards surrounded we have had no
    chance to sneak !

  HEG.   Howsoever careful, none can be as careful as he
    ought ;

When he thinks he's been most careful, oft your careful man
    is caught.

Don't you think that I've just cause to keep a careful watch
    on you,

When I've had to pay so large a sum of money for the two ?

  PHIL.   Truly we've no right to blame you, that you watch
    and guard us thus ;

And if we should get a chance and run away, you can't
260   blame *us.*

  HEG.   Just like you, my son is held in slavery by your
    countrymen.

PHIL.   Was he taken prisoner ?

HEG.   Yes.

PHIL.   We weren't the only cowards then.

HEG.   Come aside here ; there is something I would ask
of you alone ;

And I hope you'll not deceive me.

PHIL.   Everything I know I'll own ;

If in aught I'm ignorant, I'll tell you so, upon my life.

> [*Hegio and Philocrates go aside ; Tyndarus standing
> where he can hear their conversation.*]

TYN. [*aside*].   Now the old man's at the barber's ; see my
master whets his knife !

Why, he hasn't even put an apron on to shield his clothes !

Will he shave him close or only cut his hair ?   Well, goodness knows !

But if he has any sense, he'll crop the old man properly !

HEG.   Come now, tell me, would you rather be a slave or
get set free ?   270

PHIL.   What I want is that which brings me most of good
and least of ill.

Though I must confess my slavery wasn't very terrible ;

Little difference was made between me and my master's son.

TYN. [*aside*].   Bravo !   I'd not give a cent for Thales, the
Milesian ! [1]

For, compared with this man's cunning, he is but a trifling
knave.

Mark how cleverly he talks, as if he'd always been a slave !

HEG.   Tell me to what family Philocrates belongs?

PHIL.   The Goldings ;

That's a family most wealthy both in honours and in hold-
ings.

---

[1] The proverbial wise man.   Bacch. 122.

HEG.   Is your master there respected?

PHIL.   Highly, by our foremost men.

HEG.   If his influence amongst them is as great as you
280   maintain,

Are his riches fat?

PHIL.   I guess so! fat as suet, one might say.

HEG.   Is his father living?

PHIL.   Well, he *was*, sir, when we came away;

Whether he still lives or not, you'll have to go to hell to see.

TYN. [*aside*].   Saved again! for now he's adding to his
    lies philosophy!

HEG.   What's his name, I pray?

PHIL.   Thensaurocrœsonicochrysides.[1]

HEG.   I suppose a sort of nickname given to show how
    rich he is.

PHIL.   Nay, by Pollux! it was given him for his avarice and
    greed.

Truth to tell you, Theodoromedes is his name indeed.

HEG.   What is this?   His father's grasping?

PHIL.   Grasping?   Ay, most covetous!
290 Just to show you, when he sacrifices to his Genius,

All the vessels that he uses are of Samian crockery,[2]

Lest the Genius should steal them!   There's his character,
    you see.

HEG.   Come with me then.   [*Taking Philocrates away.*]
                Now I'll ask the other what I want to know.

[*To Tyn.*]   Now, Philocrates, your slave has acted as a
    man should do,

For from him I've learnt your birth; the whole he has con-
    fessed to me.

---

[1] Lit. " The son of gold that exceeds the treasures of Crœsus."
[2] Instead of gold and silver plate.

If you will admit the same, it shall to your advantage be ;
For your slave has told me all.

TYN.   It was his duty so to do.
All is true that he's confessed ; although I must admit to
    you,
'Twas my wish to hide from you my birth, and wealth, and
    family ;
But now, Hegio, that I've lost my fatherland and liberty,   300
Naturally he should stand in awe of you much more than
    me,
Since by force of arms our fortunes stand on an equality.
I remember when he durst not speak a word to do me ill ;
He may strike me now ; so fortune plays with mortals as
    she will.
I, once free, am made a slave and brought from high to low
    degree,
And instead of giving orders must obey submissively.
But if I should have a master, such as *I* was when at home,
I've no fear that his commands will prove unjust or burden-
    some.
Hegio, will you bear from me a word of warning ?

HEG.   Yes, say on.

TYN.   Once I was as free and happy as your own beloved
    son.   310
But the force of hostile arms has robbed him of his freedom,
    too ;
He's a slave amongst our people, just as I am here with you.
Certainly there is a God who watches us where'er we be ;
He will treat your son exactly as He finds that you treat me.
Virtue sure will be rewarded, vice will e'er bring sorrow on—
I've a father misses me, as much as you your absent son.

HEG.   Yes, I know.   Do you admit, then, what your slave
    confessed to me ?

Tyn.   I admit, sir, that my father is a man of property,
And that I'm of noble birth.   But I beseech you, Hegio,
320 Do not let my ample riches cause your avarice to grow,
Lest my father think it better, though I am his only son,
That I should continue serving you and keep your livery on,
Rather than come home a beggar to my infinite disgrace.

  Heg.   Thanks to Heav'n and my forefathers, I've been
  wealthy all my days ;
Nor is wealth, in my opinion, always useful to obtain—
Many a man I've known degraded to a beast by too much
  gain ;
There are times when loss is better far than gain, in every
  way.
Gold ! I hate it ! Oh, how many people has it led astray !
Now, attend to me, and I my purpose plainly will declare :
330 There in Elis, with your people, is my son a prisoner.
If you'll bring him back to me, you shall not pay a single
  cent :
I'll release you and your slave too ; otherwise I'll not relent.

  Tyn.   That's the noblest, kindest offer !   All the world
  can't find your mate !
But is he in slavery to a private man or to the State ?

  Heg.   To Menarchus, a physician.

  Tyn.   Ah ! my client ! all is plain ;
Everything will be as easy as the falling of the rain.

  Heg.   Bring him home as soon as may be.

  Tyn.   Certainly ; but, Hegio—

  Heg.   What's your wish ?   For I'll do aught in reason.

  Tyn.   Listen ; you shall know.
I don't ask that I should be sent back until your son has come.
Name the price you'll take for yonder slave, to let me send
340   him home,
That he may redeem your son.

HEG.   Nay, someone else I should prefer,
Whom I'll send when truce is made to go and meet your
    father there.
He can take your father any message that you like to send.
    TYN.   It's no use to send a stranger; all your toil in
        smoke would end.
Send my slave, he'll do the business just as soon as he gets
    there;
You won't hit on anybody you can send who's trustier,
Or more faithful; he's a man who does his work with all his
    heart.
Boldly trust your son to him; and he will truly play his part.
Don't you fear! at my own peril I'll make trial of his truth;   350
For he knows my kindness to him; I can safely trust the
    youth.
    HEG.   Well, I'll send him at your risk, if you consent.
    TYN.   Oh, I agree.
    HEG.   Let him start as soon as may be.
    TYN.   That will suit me perfectly.
    HEG.   Well, then, if he doesn't come back here, you'll pay
        me fifty pounds;
Are you willing?
    TYN.   Certainly.
    HEG.   [*To his slaves.*]   Then go and loose him from his
        bonds;
And the other too.

            [*The slaves loose Philocrates and Tyndarus.*]

    TYN.   May Heaven ever treat you graciously!
Since you've shown me so much kindness, and from fetters
    set me free.
Ah, my neck's more comfortable, now I've cast that iron
    ruff!

HEG. Gifts when given to good people win their gratitude ! Enough !
Now, if you are going to send him, teach and tell him what
to say,
When he gets home to your father.   Shall I call him ?
360   TYN.   Do so, pray !   .

HEGIO. PHILOCRATES. TYNDARUS.

[*Hegio crosses the stage to Philocrates and addresses him.*]
HEG. Heav'n bless this project to my son and me,
And you as well ! I, your new lord, desire
That you should give your true and faithful service
To your old master.   I have lent you to him,
And set a price of fifty pounds upon you.
He says he wants to send you to his father
That he may ransom my dear son and make
An interchange between us of our sons.
PHIL. Well, I'm prepared to serve either one or t'other ;
I'm like a wheel, just twist me as you please !
370 I'll turn this way or that, as you command.
HEG. I'll see that you don't lose by your compliance ;
Since you are acting as a good slave should.
Come on.   [*He takes Phil. across to Tyn.*]
                     Now, here's your man.
TYN.   I thank you, sir,
For giving me this opportunity
Of sending him to bring my father word
About my welfare and my purposes ;
All which he'll tell my father as I bid him.
Now, Tyndarus, we've come to an agreement,
That you should go to Elis to my father ;
380 And should you not come back, I've undertaken
To pay the sum of fifty pounds for you.

PHIL.   A fair agreement : for your father looks
For me or for some other messenger
To come from hence to him.

TYN.   Then, pray attend,
And I will tell you what to tell my father.

PHIL. · I have always tried to serve you hitherto, Philocrates,
As you wished me, to the utmost of my poor abilities.
That I'll ever seek and aim at, heart and soul and strength
alway.

TYN.   That is right : you know your duty.   Listen now
to what I say.
First of all, convey a greeting to my parents dear from me,
And to other relatives and friends, if any you should see.   390
Say I'm well, and held in bondage by this worthy gentleman,
Who has shown and ever shows me all the honour that he
can.

PHIL.   Oh, you needn't tell me that, it's rooted in my
memory.

TYN.   If I didn't see my keeper, I should think that I was
free.
Tell my father of the bargain I have made with Hegio,
For the ransom of his son.

PHIL.   Don't stay to tell me that.   I know.

TYN.   He must purchase and restore him, then we both
shall be set free.

PHIL.   Good !

HEG.   Bid him be quick, for your sake and for mine
in like degree.

PHIL.   You don't long to see your son more ardently
than he does his !

HEG.   Why, each loves his own.

PHIL,   Well, have you any other messages ?   400

Tyn. Yes; don't hesitate to say I'm well and happy,
    Tyndarus;
That no shade of disagreement ever separated us;
That you've never once deceived me nor opposed your
    master's will,
And have stuck to me like wax in spite of all this flood of
    ill.
By my side you've stood and helped me in my sore ad-
    versities,
True and faithful to me ever.   When my father hears of this,
Tyndarus, and knows your noble conduct towards himself
    and me,
He will never be so mean as to refuse to set you free;
When I'm back I'll spare no effort that it may be brought
410   about.
To your toil, and skill, and courage, and your wisdom,
    there's no doubt
That I owe my chance of getting to my father's home again:
For 'twas you confessed my birth and riches to this best of
    men;
So you set your master free from fetters by your ready wit.
    Phil. Yes, I did, sir, as you say; I'm glad that you
    remember it.
But indeed, you've well deserved it at my hands, Philocrates;
For if I should try to utter all your many kindnesses,
Night would fall before I'd finished; you have done as much
    for me
As if you had been my slave.
    Heg.   Good heavens, what nobility
Shines in both their dispositions!   I can scarce refrain from
420   tears
When I see their true affection, and the way the slave reveres
And commends his master.

TYN.   Truly he has not commended me
Even a hundredth part as much as he himself deserves to be.
  HEG.   Well, as you've behaved so nobly, now you have a
    splendid chance
Here to crown your services by doubly faithful vigilance.
  PHIL.   As I wish the thing accomplished, so I shall do all
    I know ;
To assure you of it, I call Jove to witness, Hegio !
That I never will betray Philocrates, I'll take my oath !
  HEG.   Honest fellow !
  PHIL.   I will treat him as myself, upon my troth !
  TYN.   From these loving protestations, mind you never
    never swerve.   430
And if I've said less about you than your faithful deeds de-
    serve,
Pray you, don't be angry with me on account of what I've said ;
But remember you are going with a price upon your head ;
And that both my life and honour I have staked on your re-
    turn ;
When you've left my sight, I pray you, don't forget what you
    have sworn,
Or when you have left me here in slavery instead of you,
Think that you are free, and so neglect what you are pledged
    to do,
And forget your solemn promise to redeem this good man's son.
Fifty pounds, remember, is the price that we've agreed upon.
Faithful to your faithful master, do not let your faith be
    bought ;
And I'm well assured my father will do everything he ought.   440
Keep me as your friend for ever, and this good old man as
    well.
Take my hand in yours, I pray you, swear an oath unbreak-
    able,

That you'll always be as faithful as I've ever been to you.
Mind, you're now my master, ay protector, and my father
    too !
I commit to you my hopes and happiness.

    PHIL.   O that'll do !

Are you satisfied if I can carry this commission through ?

    TYN.   Yes.

    PHIL.   Then I'll return in such a manner as shall
    please you both.

Is that all, sir ?

    HEG.   Come back quickly.

    PHIL.   So I will, upon my troth.

    HEG.   Come along then to my banker's ; I'll provide you
    for the way.

Also I will get a passport from the praetor.

450   TYN.   Passport, eh ?

    HEG.   Yes, to get him through the army so that they may
    let him go. ·

Step inside.

    TYN.   A pleasant journey !

    PHIL.   Fare-you-well !

    HEG.   By Pollux, though,

What a blessing that I bought these men from the Commis-
    sioners !
So, please Heav'n, I've saved my son from bondage to those
    foreigners.
Dear ! How long I hesitated whether I should buy or not !
[*To the Overseers.*] Please to take him in, good slaves, and do
    not let him leave the spot,
When there is no keeper with him ; I shall soon be home
    again.

                [*Exeunt Tyndarus and slaves into the house.*]

Now I'll run down to my brother's and inspect my other men.

I'll inquire if any of them is acquainted with this youth.

[*To Philocrates.*] Come along and I'll despatch you.   That
   must be done first, in sooth.   460

     [*Exeunt Hegio and Philocrates to the market-place.*]

ERGASILUS.

     [*Enter Ergasilus returning from the market-place.*]

ERG.   Wretched he who seeks his dinner, and with trouble
   gets a haul ;
Wretcheder who seeks with trouble, and can't find a meal at
   all ;
Wretchedest who dies for food, and can't get any anyway.
If I could, I'd like to scratch the eyes out of this cursed day !
For it's filled all men with meanness towards me.   Oh, I
   never saw
Day so hungry ; why, it's stuffed with famine in its greedy maw.
Never day pursued its purpose in so vacuous a way ;
For my gullet and my stomach have to keep a holiday.
Out upon the parasite's profession : it's all gone to pot !
For us impecunious wits the gilded youth don't care a jot.   470
They no longer want us Spartans,[1] owners of a single chair, [2]
Sons of Smacked-Face, whose whole stock-in-trade is words,
   whose board is bare.
Those that they invite are fellows who can ask them back in
   turn.
Then they cater for themselves [3] and us poor parasites they
   spurn ;

---

[1] So called because of the blows and insults they endured without flinch-
ing.   Everyone knows the story of the Spartan boy and the fox.

[2] Whose furniture is limited to one chair, and who, therefore, can never
ask any one to dine with them.

[3] To cater for rich young fellows was one of the services the parasites
rendered in order to get invited to their dinners.

You will see them shopping in the market with as little shame
As when, sitting on the bench, the culprit's sentence they pro-
  claim.
For us wits they don't care twopence ; keep entirely to their
  set.
When I went just now to market, there a group of them I
  met ;
"Hail !" says I ; "where shall we go," says I, "to lunch ?"
  They all were mum.
"Who speaks first ? who volunteers ?" says I.   And still the
480 chaps were dumb.
Not a smile ! "Where shall we dine together ? Answer."
  Not a word !
Then I flashed a jest upon them from my very choicest hoard,
One that meant a month of dinners in the old days, I declare.
No one smiled ; and then I saw the whole was a got-up affair.
Why, they wouldn't even do as much as any angry cur ;
If they couldn't smile, they might at least have shown their
  teeth, I swear !
Well, I left the rascals when I saw that they were making
  game ;
Went to others ; and to others ; and to others—still the
  same !
They had formed a ring together, just like those who deal
  in oil
490 I' the Velabrum.[1] So I left them when I saw they mocked
  my toil.
In the Forum vainly prowling other parasites I saw.
I've resolved that I must try to get my rights by Roman law.[2]

---

[1] The Velabrum was the market for table delicacies at Rome.   It lay
to the north-west of the Circus Maximus.   The oil-dealers were evidently
in the habit of making agreements to keep up the price of oil.

[2] Lit., *barbaric* law ; the point of view being Greek.

As they've formed a plot to rob us of our life and victuals too,
I shall summon them and fine them, as a magistrate would
     do.
They shall give me ten good dinners, at a time when food is
     dear!
So I'll do; now to the harbour; there I may to dinner steer;
If that fails me, I'll return and try this old man's wretched
     cheer.   [*Exit Ergasilus to the harbour.*]

HEGIO. [ARISTOPHONTES.]
[*Enter Hegio from his brother's with Aristophontes.*]
HEG.   How pleasant it is when you've managed affairs
For the good of the public, as yesterday I did,   500
When I bought those two fellows.   Why, everyone stares
And congratulates me on the way I decided.
To tell the plain truth, I am worried with standing,
     And weary with waiting;
From the flood of their words I could scarce get a landing,
And even at the prætor's it showed no abating.
     I asked for a passport; and when it had come,
     I gave it to Tyndarus; *he* set off home.
When he had departed, for home off I started;
Then went to my brother's, to question the others,
Whether any among them Philocrates knew.
Then one of them cries, " He's my friend, good and true."   510
     I told him I'd bought him;
He begged he might see him; and so I have brought him.
     I bade them loose him from his chains,
     And came away. [*To Aristophontes.*] Pray follow me;
     Your earnest suit success obtains,
     Your dear old friend you soon shall see.
          [*Exeunt Hegio and Aristophontes into the house;
             Tyndarus immediately rushes out.*]

TYN. Alas! the day has come on which I wish I never had been born.

My hopes, resources, stratagems, have fled and left me all forlorn.

On this sad day no hope remains of saving my poor life, 'tis clear;

No help or hope remains to me to drive away my anxious fear.

520 No cloak I anywhere can find to cover up my crafty lies,

No cloak, I say, comes in my way to hide my tricks and rogueries.

There is no pardon for my fibs, and no escape for my misdeeds;

My cheek can't find the shelter, nor my craft the hiding-place it needs.

All that I hid has come to light; my plans lie open to the day;

The whole thing's out, and in this scrape I fail to see a single ray

Of hope to shun the doom which I must suffer for my master's sake.

This Aristophontes, who's just come, will surely bring me to the stake;

He knows me, and he is the friend and kinsman of Philocrates.

Salvation couldn't save me, if she would; there is no way but this,

To plan some new and smarter trickeries.

530 Hang it, *what?* What shall I do? I *am* just up a lofty tree,

If I can't contrive some new and quite preposterous foolery.

HEGIO. TYNDARUS. ARISTOPHONTES.

[*Enter from the house Hegio and Aristophontes.*]

HEG. Where's the fellow gone whom we saw rushing headlong from the house?

TYN. [*aside*].   Now the day of doom has come ; the foe's
  upon thee, Tyndarus !
O, what story shall I tell them ?   What deny and what
  confess ?
My purposes are all at sea ; O, ain't I in a pretty mess ?
O would that Heaven had blasted you before you left your
  native land,
You wretch, Aristophontes, who have ruined all that I had
  planned.
The game is up if I can't light on some atrocious villainy !
  HEG.   Ah, there's your man ; go speak to him.
  TYN. [*aside*].   What man is wretcheder than I ?   540
  AR.   How is this that you avoid my eyes and shun me,
    Tyndarus ?
Why, you might have never known me, fellow, that you treat
  me thus !
I'm a slave as much as you, although in Elis I was free,
Whilst you from your earliest boyhood were enthralled in
  slavery.
  HEG.   Well, by Jove ! I'm not surprised that he should
    shun you, when he sees
That you call him Tyndarus, not, as you should, Philocrates.
  TYN.   Hegio, this man in Elis was considered raving
    mad.
Take no note of anything he tells you either good or bad.
Why, he once attacked his father and his mother with a
  spear ;
And the epilepsy takes him in a form that's most severe.   550
Don't go near him !
  HEG. [*to Aristo.*]   Keep your distance !
  AR.   Rascal !   Did I rightly hear,
That you say I'm mad, and once attacked my father with a
  spear ?

And that I have got the sickness for which men are wont
    to spit ? [1]

HEG.   Never mind ! for many men besides yourself have
    suffered it,

And the spitting was a means of healing them, and they were
    glad.

AR.   What, do you believe the wretch ?

HEG.   In what respect ?

AR.   That I am mad !

TYN.   Do you see him glaring at you ?   Better leave him !
    O beware !

Hegio, the fit is on him ; he'll be raving soon !   Take
    care !

HEG.   Well, I thought he was a madman when he called
    you Tyndarus.

TYN.   Why, he sometimes doesn't know his *own* name.
560   Oh, he's often thus.

HEG.   But he said you were his comrade.

TYN.   Ah, no doubt ! precisely so !

And Alcmæon, and Orestes, and Lycurgus,[2] don't you know,
Are my comrades quite as much as he is !

AR.   Oh, you gallows bird,
Dare you slander me ?   What, don't I know you ?

HEG.   Come, don't be absurd.

You don't know him, for you called him Tyndarus : that's
    very clear.

You don't know the man you see ; you name the man who
    isn't here.

AR.   Nay, he says he is the man he isn't, not the man he is.

---

[1] Spitting was used as a kind of charm in many diseases ; especially
in the case of epilepsy.

[2] Typical madmen.   The first two slew their mothers and were driven
mad by the Furies.

TYN.   O yes! Doubtless you know better whether I'm
    Philocrates
Than Philocrates himself does!

AR.   You'd prove truth itself a liar,
As it strikes me.   But, I pray you, look at me!

TYN.   As you desire!   570

AR.   Aren't you Tyndarus?

TYN.   I'm not.

AR.   You say you are Philocrates?

TYN.   Certainly.

AR. [*to Heg.*]   Do you believe him?

HEG.   Yes, and shall do, if I please.
For the other, who you say he is, went home from here
    to-day
To the father of this captive.

AR.   Father?   He's a slave.[1]

TYN.   And, pray!
Are you not a slave, though you were free once, as I hope
    to be,
When I have restored good Hegio's son to home and liberty?

AR.   What's that, gaol-bird?   Do you tell me that you
    were a freeman born?

TYN.   No! Philocrates, not Freeman,[2] is my name.

AR.   Pray, mark his scorn!
Hegio, I tell you, you're being mocked and swindled by this
    knave;
Why, he never had a slave except himself; for *he's* a slave. 580

TYN.   Ah, because you're poor yourself, and have no
    means of livelihood,

---

[1] A slave has no father legally.

[2] The pun in the original lies between the two words, *liber*, free, and
Liber, a name of the god Bacchus.

T

You'd wish everybody else to be like you. I know your
    mood ;

All poor men like you are spiteful, envy those who're better off.

    AR.   Hegio, don't believe this fellow ; for he's doing
    naught but scoff ;

Sure I am, he'll play some scurvy trick on you before he's
    done ;

I don't like this tale of his about the ransom of your son.

    TYN.   You don't like it, I dare say ; but I'll accomplish it,
    you see !

I'll restore him to his father ; he in turn releases me.

That's why I've sent Tyndarus to see my father.

    AR.   Come, that's lame !

You are Tyndarus yourself, the only slave who bears that
590   name !

    TYN.   Why reproach me with my bondage ? I was cap-
    tured in the fray.

    AR.   Oh, I can't restrain my fury !

    TYN. [*to Hegio*].   Don't you hear him ? Run away !

He'll be hurling stones at us just now, if you don't have him
    bound.

    AR.   Oh, damnation !

    TYN.   How he glares at us ! I hope your ropes
    are sound.

See, his body's covered over with bright spots of monstrous
    size !

It's the black bile that afflicts him.

    AR.   Pollux ! if this old man's wise,

You will find black pitch afflict you, when it blazes round
    your breast.[1]

---

[1] Alluding to the punishment of slaves by covering them with pitch,
and then burning them alive.

TYN.   Ah, he's wandering now, poor fellow! by foul spirits
he's possessed! .

HEG. [*to Tyn.*]   What do you think?   Would it be best
to have him bound?

TYN.   Yes, so I said.

AR.   Oh, perdition take it!   Would I had a stone to
smash his head,   600

This whipped cur, who says I'm mad!   By Jove, sir, I will
make you smart!

TYN.   Hear him calling out for stones!

AR. [*to Hegio*].   Pray, might we have a word apart,
Hegio?

HEG.   Yes, but keep your distance; there's no need
to come so close!

TYN.   If, by Pollux, you go any nearer, he'll bite off your
nose.

AR.   Hegio, I beg and pray you, don't believe that I am
mad,

Or that I have epilepsy as this shameless fellow said.

But if you're afraid of me, then have me bound; I won't say
no,

If you'll bind that rascal too.

TYN.   O no, indeed, good Hegio!
Bind the man who wishes it!

AR.   Be quiet, you!   The case stands thus;
I shall prove Philocrates the false to be true Tyndarus.   610
What are you winking for? [1]

TYN.   I wasn't.

AR.   He winks before your very face! [2]

---

[1] Tyndarus makes violent signs to stop Aristophontes (his master's
friend) from making further revelations.

[2] I think these words would be better given with the MSS. to Tyndarus,
though the editors after Lessing assign them to Aristophontes.   Tyn-

HEG.   What, if I approached this madman?

TYN.   It would be a wild-goose chase.

He'll keep chattering, till you can't make either head or tail
of it.

Had they dressed him for the part, you'd say 'twas Ajax [1] in
his fit.

HEG.   Never mind, I *will* approach him.

TYN. [*aside*].   Things are looking very blue.

I'm between the knife and altar, and I don't know what to
do.

HEG.   I attend, Aristophontes, if you've anything to say.

AR.   You shall hear that that is true which you've been
thinking false to-day.

620 First I wish to clear myself of all suspicion that I rave,

Or that I am subject to disease—except that I'm a slave.

So may He who's king of gods and men restore me home
again :

He's no more Philocrates than you or I.

HEG.   But tell me then,

Who he is.

AR.   The same that I have told you from the very first.

If you find it otherwise, I pray that I may be accursed,

And may suffer forfeiture of fatherland and freedom sweet.

HEG. [*to Tyn.*]   What say *you* ?

TYN.   That I'm your slave, and you're my master.

HEG.   That's not it.

Were you free ?

TYN.   I was.

AR.   He wasn't.   He's just lying worse
and worse.

---

darus may mean, "He makes false accusations against me in your very
presence; what length would he go if you were away?"

[1] The madness of Ajax was a favourite subject with the Greeks.

Tyn.   How do *you* know? perhaps it happened that you
were my mother's nurse,
That you dare to speak so boldly!
   Ar.   Why, I saw you when a lad.   630
   Tyn.   Well, I see you when a man to-day! So we are
    quits, by gad!
Did I meddle with your business? Just let mine alone then,
    please.
   Heg.   Was his father called Thensaurocrœsonicochry-
    sides?
   Ar.   No, he wasn't, and I never heard the name before to-
    day.
Theodoromedes was his master's father.
   Tyn. [*aside*].   Deuce to pay!
O be quiet, or go straight and hang yourself, my beating
    heart!
You are dancing there, whilst I can hardly stand to play my
    part.
   Heg.   He in Elis was a slave then, if you are not telling
    lies,
And is not Philocrates?
   Ar.   You'll never find it otherwise.
   Heg.   So I've been chopped into fragments and dissected,
    goodness knows,   640
By the dodges of this scoundrel, who has led me by the nose.
Are you sure there's no mistake though?
   Ar.   Yes, I speak of what I know.
   Heg.   Is it certain?
   Ar.   Certain? nothing could be more entirely so.
Why, Philocrates has been my friend from when he was a
    boy;
But where is he now?
   Heg.   Ah, that's what vexes me, but gives *him* joy.

Tell me though, what sort of looking man is this Philocrates?

AR.   Thin i' the face, a sharpish nose, a fair complexion, coal-black eyes,

Reddish, crisp, and curly hair.

HEG.   Yes, that's the fellow to a T.

650   TYN. [*aside*].   Curse upon it, everything has gone all wrong to-day with me.

Woe unto those wretched rods that on my back to-day must die!

HEG.   So I see that I've been cheated.

TYN. [*aside.*]   Come on, fetters, don't be shy!

Run to me and clasp my legs and I'll take care of you, no fear!

HEG.   Well, I've been sufficiently bamboozled by these villains here.

T'other said he was a slave, while this pretended to be free;

So I've gone and lost the kernel, and the husk is left to me.

Yes, they've corked my nose [1] most finely!   Don't I make a foolish show?

But this fellow here sha'n't mock me!   Colaphus, Corax, Cordalio,

Come out here and bring your thongs.

                                        [*Enter Overseers.*]

OVERSEER.   To bind up faggots?   Here's a go!

HEGIO. TYNDARUS. ARISTOPHONTES.

HEG.   Come, bind your heaviest shackles on this wretch.

TYN.   Why, what's the matter? what's my crime?

660   HEG.   Your crime!

You've sowed and scattered ill, now you shall reap it.

TYN.   Hadn't you better say I harrowed too?

For farmers always harrow first, then sow.

---

[1] See Aulul. 668.

HEG.   How boldly does he flout me to my face !

TYN.   A harmless, guiltless man, although a slave,
Should boldly face his master, of all men.

HEG.   Tie up his hands as tightly as you can.

TYN.   You'd better cut them off; for I am yours.
But what's the matter ? why are you so angry ?

HEG.   Because my plans, as far as in you lay,   670
By your thrice-villainous and lying tricks
You've torn asunder, mangled limb from limb,
And ruined all my hopes and purposes.
Philocrates escaped me through your guile ;
I thought he was the slave, and you the free ;
For so you said, and interchanged your names
Between yourselves.

TYN.   Yes, I admit all that.
'Tis just as you have said, and cunningly
He's got away by means of my smart work ;
But I beseech you, are you wroth at that ?   680

HEG.   You've brought the worst of torments on yourself.

TYN.   If not for sin I perish, I don't care !
But though I perish, and he breaks his word,
And doesn't come back here, my joy is this :
My deed will be remembered when I'm dead,
How I redeemed my lord from slavery,
And rescued him and saved him from his foes,
To see once more his father and his home ;
And how I rather chose to risk my life,
Than let my master perish in his bonds.

HEG.   The only fame you'll get will be in hell.

TYN.   Nay, he who dies for virtue doesn't perish.   690

HEG.   When I've expended all my torments on you,
And given you up to death for your deceits,
People may call it death or perishing

Just as they like ; so long as you are dead,
I don't mind if they say that you're alive.
  Tyn. By Pollux ! if you do so, you'll repent,
When he comes back as I am sure he will.
  Ar. O Heavens ! I see it now ! and understand
What it all means. My friend Philocrates
Is free at home, and in his native land.
700 I'm glad of that ; nothing could please me more.
But I am grieved I've got *him* into trouble,
Who stands here bound because of what I said.
  Heg. Did I forbid you to speak falsely to me ?
  Tyn. You did, sir.
  Heg.   Then how durst you tell me lies ?
  Tyn. Because to tell the truth would have done hurt
To him I served ; he profits by my lie.
  Heg. But *you* shall smart for it !
  Tyn.   O that's all right !
I've saved my master and am glad of that,
For I've been his companion from a boy ;
His father, my old master, gave me to him.
D'you now think this a crime ?
  Heg.   A very vile one.
710 Tyn. *I* say it's right ; I don't agree with you.
Consider, if a slave had done as much
For your own son, how grateful you would be !
Wouldn't you give that slave his liberty ?
Wouldn't that slave stand highest in your favour ?
Answer !
  Heg. Well, yes.
  Tyn.   Then why be wroth with *me* ?
  Heg. Because you were more faithful to your master
Than e'er to me.
  Tyn.   What else could you expect ?

Do you suppose that in one night and day
You could so train a man just taken captive,
A fresh newcomer, as to serve you better
Than him with whom he'd lived from earliest childhood?   720

    HEG.   Then let him pay you for it.   Take him off,
And fit him with the heaviest, thickest chains ;
Thence to the quarries you shall go right on.
And whilst the rest are hewing eight stones each,
You shall each day do half as much again,
Or else be nicknamed the Six-hundred-striper.

    AR.   By gods and men, I pray you, Hegio,
Do not destroy him.

    HEG.   I'll take care of him !
For in the stocks all night he shall be kept,
And quarry stones all day from out the ground.   730
O, I'll prolong his torments day by day.

    AR.   Is this your purpose ?

    HEG.   Death is not so sure.
Go take him to Hippolytus the smith ;
Tell him to rivet heavy fetters on him.
Then cause him to be led out of the city
To Cordalus, my freedman at the quarries,
And tell him that I wish him to be treated
With greater harshness than the worst slave there.

    TYN.   Why should I plead with you when you're resolved ?
The peril of my life is your's as well.   740
When I am dead I have no ill to fear ;
And if I live to an extreme old age,
My time of suffering will be but short.
Farewell ! though you deserve a different wish.
Aristophontes, as you've done to me,
So may you prosper ; for it is through you
That this has come upon me.

HEG.   Take him off.

TYN.   But if Philocrates returns to you,
Give me a chance of seeing him, I pray.

    HEG.   Come, take him from my sight or I'll destroy you !
                        [*The Overseers seize and drag him off.*]

750   TYN.   Nay, this is sheer assault and battery !
             [*Exeunt Overseers and Tyndarus to the quarries.*]

    HEG.   There, he has gone to prison as he merits.
I'll give my other prisoners an example,
That none of them may dare repeat his crime.
Had it not been for him, who laid it bare,
The rascals would have led me in a string.
Never again will I put trust in man.
Once cheated is enough.   Alas ! I hoped
That I had saved my son from slavery.
My hope has perished.   One of my sons I lost,
760 Stolen by a slave when he was four years old ;
Nor have I ever found the slave or him.
The elder's now a captive.   What's my crime,
That I beget my children but to lose them ?
Follow me, you !   I'll take you where you were.
Since no one pities me, I'll pity none.

    AR.   Under good auspices I left my chain ;
But I must take the auspices again.
       [*Exeunt Aristophontes and Hegio to Hegio's brother's.*]

ERGASILUS.

[*Enter Ergasilus from the harbour.*]

    ERG.   Jove supreme, thou dost protect me and increase
      my scanty store,
Blessings lordly and magnific thou bestowest more and more ;
Both thanks and gain, and sport and jest, festivity and
770   holidays,

Processions plenty, lots of drink and heaps of meat and end-
    less praise.

Ne'er again I'll play the beggar, everything I want I've got;

I'm able now to bless my friends, and send my enemies to
    pot.

With such joyful joyfulness this joyful day has loaded me!

Though it hasn't been bequeathed me, I've come into pro-
    perty!

So now I'll run and find the old man Hegio. O what a store

Of good I bring to him, as much as ever he could ask, and
    more.

I am resolved I'll do just what the slaves do in a comedy; [1]

I'll throw my cloak around my neck,[2] that he may hear it
    first from me.

For this good news I hope to get my board in perpetuity.   780

HEGIO. ERGASILUS.

[Enter Hegio from his brother's.]

HEG. How sad the regrets in my heart that are kindled,
    As I think over all that has happened to me.

O isn't it shameful the way I've been swindled,
        And yet couldn't see!

As soon as it's known, how they'll laugh in the city!

When I come to the market they'll show me no pity,
    But chaffing say, "Wily old man up a tree!"

    But is this Ergasilus coming? Bless me!

    His cloak's o'er his shoulder. Why, what can it be?

ERG. Come, Ergasilus, act, and act vigorously!   790

[3]Hereby I denounce and threaten all who shall obstruct my
    way;

---

[1] Cf. Amphitryon III. 4.

[2] As a sign of haste.

[3] Here trochaics begin.

Any man who dares to do so will have seen his life's last day.
I will stand him on his head.

HEG.   'Fore me the man begins to spar!

ERG.   I shall do it.   Wherefore let all passers-by stand off
afar ;

Let none dare to stand conversing in this street, till I've
passed by ;

For my fist's my catapult, my arm is my artillery,

And my shoulder is my ram; who meets my knee, to earth
he goes.

Folk will have to pick their teeth up, if with me they come
to blows.

HEG.   What's he mean by all this threatening ?   I confess
I'm puzzled quite.

ERG.   I'll take care they don't forget this day, this place,
800   my mickle might.

He who stops me in my course, will find he's stopped his
life as well.

HEG.   What he's after with these threats and menaces,
I cannot tell.

ERG.   I proclaim it first, that none may suffer inadver-
tently ;

Stay at home, good people all, and then you won't get hurt
by me.

HEG.   Oh, depend on't, it's a dinner that has stirred his
valorous bile.

Woe to that poor wretch whose food has given him this lordly
style !

ERG.   First, for those pig-breeding millers,[1] with their fat
and bran-fed sows,

---

[1] These local allusions would, no doubt, be appreciated by the
audience.

Stinking so that one is hardly able to get past the house ;
If in any public place I catch their pigs outside their pen,
With my fists I'll hammer out the bran from those same
    filthy—men !   810

    HEG. Here's pot-valour with a vengeance ! He's as full
      as man could wish !

    ERG. Then those fishmongers, who offer to the public
      stinking fish,

Riding to the market on a jumping, jolting, joggling cob,
Whose foul smell drives to the Forum every loafer in the
    mob ;[1]
With their fish baskets I'll deal them on their face a few smart
    blows,
/ Just to let them feel the nuisance that they cause the public
    nose.

    HEG. Listen to his proclamations ! What a royal style
      they keep !

    ERG. Then the butchers, who arrange to steal the
      youngsters from the sheep,

Undertake to kill a lamb, but send you home right tough old
    mutton ;
Nickname ancient ram as yearling, sweet enough for any
    glutton ;   820
If in any public street or square that ram comes in my view,
I will make them sorry persons—ancient ram and butcher,
    too !

    HEG. Bravo ! he makes rules as if he were a mayor and
      corporation.[2]

Surely he's been made the master of the market to our nation.

---

[1] Lit., all who are under the porches of the Basilica, where it would
appear these fishmongers had their stalls.

[2] Lit., "like an Ædile." The Ædiles at Rome had charge of the
markets.

ERG. I'm no more a parasite, but kinglier than a king of
   kings.
Such a stock of belly-timber from the port my message brings.
Let me haste to heap on Hegio this good news of jollity.
Certainly there's no man living who's more fortunate than he.
   HEG. What's this news of gladness which he gladly hastes
      on me to pour?
   ERG. [*knocking at Hegio's door*]. Ho! where are you?
      Who is there? Will someone open me this door?
830   HEG. Ah! the fellow's come to dinner.
   ERG.   Open me the door, I say;
Or I'll smash it into matchwood, if there's any more delay.
   HEG. ¹I'll speak to him. Ergasilus!
   ERG.   Who calls my name so lustily?
   HEG. Pray, look my way!
   ERG.   You bid me do what Fortune never did to me!
Who is it?
   HEG. Why, just look at me. It's Hegio!
   ERG.   Ye gods! It's he.
Thou best of men, in nick of time we have each other greeted.
   HEG. You've got a dinner at the port; *that* makes you
      so conceited.
   ERG. Give me your hand.
840   HEG.   My hand?
   ERG.   Your hand, I say, at once!
   HEG.   I give it. There!
                  [*Gives Ergasilus his hand.*]
   ERG. Now rejoice!
   HEG.   Rejoice! but why?
   ERG.   'Tis my command. Begone dull care!
   HEG. Nay, the sorrows of my household hinder me from
      feeling joy.

---

¹ This and the next four lines are iambic.

ERG.   Ah, but I will wash you clean from every speck
that can annoy.

Venture to rejoice !

HEG.   All right, though I've no reason to be glad.

ERG.   That's the way.   Now order—

HEG.   What ?

ERG.   To have a mighty fire made.

HEG.   What, a mighty fire ?

ERG.   I said so ; have it big enough.

HEG.   What next ?

Do you think I'll burn my house down at your asking ?

ERG.   Don't be vexed !

Have the pots and pans got ready.   Is it to be done or not ?
Put the ham and bacon in the oven, have it piping hot.
Send a man to buy the fish—

HEG.   His eyes are open, but he dreams !

ERG.   And another to buy pork, and lamb, and chickens—·

HEG.   Well, it seems
You could dine well, if you'd money.

ERG.   —Perch and lamprey, if you please,   850
Pickled mackerel and sting-ray, then an eel and nice soft
    cheese.

HEG.   Naming's easy, but for eating you won't find facilities
At my house, Ergasilus.

ERG.   Why, do you think I'm ordering this
For myself ?

HEG.   Don't be deceived ; for you'll eat neither
    much, nor little,
If you've brought no appetite for just your ordinary victual.

ERG.   Nay, I'll make you eager for a feast though I
    should urge you not.

HEG.   Me ?

ERG.   Yes, you.

HEG.   Then you shall be my lord.

ERG.   A kind one too, I wot !

Come, am I to make you happy ?

HEG.   Well, I'm not in love with woe.

ERG.   Where's your hand ?

HEG.   There, take it.

ERG.   Heaven's your friend !

HEG.   But I don't mark it, though.

ERG.   You're not in the *market*, that's why you don't
860   *mark it:* come now, bid

That pure vessels be got ready for the offering, and a kid,

Fat and flourishing, be brought.

HEG.   What for?

ERG.   To make a sacrifice.

HEG.   Why, to whom ?

ERG.   To me, of course !—I'm Jupiter in human
     guise !

Yes, to you I am Salvation, Fortune, Light, Delight, and
     Joy.

It's your business to placate my deity with food, dear boy !

HEG.   Hunger seems to be your trouble.

ERG.   Well, my hunger isn't yours.

HEG.   As you say; so I can bear it.

ERG.   Lifelong habit that ensures !

HEG.   Jupiter and all the gods confound you !

ERG.   Nothing of the sort !

Thanks I merit for re*porting* such good tidings from the
     port.

Now I'll get a meal to suit me !

HEG.   Idiot, go ! you've come too
870   late.

ERG.   'If I'd come before I did, your words would come
     with greater weight.

Now receive the joyful news I bring you. I have seen
    your son
Philopolemus in harbour safe ; and he'll be here anon.
He was on a public vessel; with him was that Elian youth
And your slave Stalagmus, he who ran away—it's naught
    but truth—
He who stole your little boy when four years old so cruelly.

HEG.   Curse you, cease youɪ mocking !

ERG.   So may holy Fulness smile on me,
Hegio, and make me ever worthy of her sacred name,
As I saw him.

HEG.   Saw my son ?

ERG.   Your son, my patron : they're the same.

HEG.   And the prisoner from Elis ?

ERG.   *Oui, parbleu !* [1]

HEG.   And that vile thief,   880
Him who stole my younger son, Stalagmus ?

ERG.   *Oui, monsieur, par Crieff !* [2]

HEG.   What, just now ?

ERG.   *Par Killiecrankie !*

HEG.   Has he come ?

ERG.   *Oui, par Dundee !*

HEG.   Are you sure ?

ERG.   *Par Auchtermuchtie !*

HEG.   Certain ?

ERG.   *Oui, par Kirkcudbright !*

HEG.   Why by these barbarian cities do you swear ?

ERG.   Because they're rude,
As you said your dinner was.

---

[1] As before, I translate the Greek by French.

[2] In the original these are the names of obscure Italian towns ; speaking as a Greek, Hegio calls them barbarian. I have tried to get the same effect by using the names of Scotch towns.

U

HEG.   That's just like your ingratitude !

ERG.   Ah, I see you won't believe me though it's simple
truth I say.

But what countryman was this Stalagmus, when he went
away ?

HEG.   A Sicilian.

ERG.   Well, but he belongs to *Colorado* now ;
For he's married to a *collar*,[1] and she squeezes him, I vow !

HEG.   Tell me, is your story true ?

ERG.   It's really true—the very truth.

HEG.   O good Heav'ns ! if you're not mocking, I've indeed
890   renewed my youth.

ERG.   What ? Will you continue doubting when I've
pledged my sacred troth ?

As a last resource then, Hegio, if you can't believe my oath,
Go and see.

HEG.   Of course I will ; go in, prepare the feast at once ;
Everything's at your disposal ; you're my steward for the
nonce.

ERG.   If my oracle's a false one, with a cudgel comb my
hide !

HEG.   You shall have your board for ever, if you've truly
prophesied.

ERG.   Who will pay ?

HEG.   My son and I.

ERG.   You promise that ?

HEG.   I do indeed.

ERG.   Then I promise you your son has really come in
very deed.

HEG.   Take the best of everything !

---

[1] Lit., he's a Boian, for he is married to a *boia*, *i.e.*, a sort of heavy
collar fixed round a slave's neck by way of punishment.

Erg.   May no delay your path impede ! 900
                        [*Exit Hegio to the harbour.*]

ERGASILUS.

Erg.   He has gone ; and put his kitchen absolutely in my
   hands !
Heav'ns ! how necks and trunks will be dissevered at my
   stern commands !
What a ban will fall on bacon, and what harm on humble
   ham !
O what labour on the lard, and what calamity on lamb !
Butchers and pork dealers, you shall find a deal to do to-
   day !
But to tell of all who deal in food would cause too long
   delay.
Now, in virtue of my office,[1] I'll give sentence on the lard,
Help those gammons, hung though uncondemned—a fate for
   them too hard.
                        [*Exit Ergasilus into the house.*]

A BOY.

[*Enter a boy from the house of Hegio.*[2]]

Boy.   May Jupiter and all the gods, Ergasilus, confound
   you quite,
And all who ask you out to dine, and every other parasite.   910
Destruction, ruin, dire distress, have come upon our family.
I feared that, like a hungry wolf, he'd make a fierce attack
   on me.
I cast an anxious look at him, he licked his lips and glared
   around ;

---

[1] *Pro praefectura mea* (Ambrosian palimpsest).
[2] An interval must be supposed to have taken place between this scene
and the last, during which Ergasilus runs riot in Hegio's kitchen.

I shook with dread, by Hercules! he gnashed his teeth with
fearsome sound.

When he'd got in, he made a raid upon the meat-safe and
the meats ;

He seized a knife—from three fat sows he cut away the dainty
teats.

Save those which held at least a peck, he shattered every pan
and pot :

Then issued orders to the cook to get the copper boiling hot.

He broke the cupboard doors and searched the secrets of the
storeroom's hoard.

So kindly watch him if you can, good slaves, whilst I go seek
my lord.

920 I'll tell him to lay in fresh stores, if he wants any for himself,

For as this fellow's carrying on, there'll soon be nothing on
the shelf.

[*Exit boy to the harbour.*]

HEGIO.   PHILOPOLEMUS.   PHILOCRATES.
STALAGMUS.

[*Enter from the harbour Hegio, Philopolemus, Philocrates,
and Stalagmus.*]

HEG.   All praise and thanksgiving to Jove I would render
For bringing you back to your father again ;
For proving my staunch and successful defender,
When, robbed of my son, I was tortured with pain ;
For restoring my runaway slave to my hands ;
For Philocrates' honour ; unsullied it stands.

PHILOP.   Grieved I have enough already, I don't want to
grow still thinner,

And you've told me all your sorrows at the harbour, pending
dinner.

Now to business !

PHILOC.   Tell me, Hegio, have I kept my promises, 930
And restored your son to freedom ?

HEG.   Yes, you have, Philocrates.
I can never, never thank you for the services you've done,
As you merit for the way you've dealt with me and with my son.

PHILOP. Yes, you can, dear father, and the gods will give
     us both a chance,
Worthily to recompense the source of my deliverance.
And I'm sure, my dearest father, it will be a pleasing task.

HEG. Say no more. I have no tongue that can deny you
     aught you ask.

PHILOC. Then restore to me the slave whom, as a pledge,
     I left behind.
He has always served me better than himself, with heart and
     mind.
To reward him for his kindness now shall be my earnest care. 940

HEG. For your goodness he shall be restored to you ; 'tis
     only fair.
That and aught beside you ask for, you shall have. But
     don't, I pray,
Be enraged with me because in wrath I've punished him
     to-day.

PHILOC. Ah, what have you done ?

HEG.   I sent him to the quarries bound with chains,
When I found how I'd been cheated.

PHILOC.   Woe is me ! he bears these pains,
Dear good fellow, for my sake, because he gained me my
     release.

HEG. And on that account you shall not pay for him a
     penny piece.
I will set him free for nothing.

PHILOC.   Well, by Pollux ! Hegio,
That is kind. But send and fetch him quickly, will you ?

HEG.   Be it so.

[*To a slave.*]   Ho, where are you?   Run and quickly bid
950   young Tyndarus return.

Now, go in ; for from this slave,[1] this whipping-block, I fain
      would learn

What has happened to my younger son, and if he's living still.
Meanwhile you can take a bath.

PHILOP.   Come in, Philocrates.

PHILOC.   I will.

[*Exeunt Philopolemus and Philocrates into the house.*]

HEGIO.   STALAGMUS.

HEG.   Now stand forth, my worthy sir, my slave so
      handsome, good, and wise !

ST.   What can you expect from *me*, when such a man as
      you tells lies ?

For I never was nor shall be fine or handsome, good or true;
If you're building on my goodness, it will be the worse for
      you.

HEG.   Well, it isn't hard for you to see which way your
      interest lies ;

If you tell the truth, 'twill save you from the harshest
      penalties.

Speak out, straight and true ; although you've not done right
960   and true, I guess.

ST.   Oh, you needn't think I blush to hear you say what I
      confess.

HEG.   I will make you blush, you villain ; for a bath of
      blood prepare !

ST.   That will be no novelty ! you threaten one who's oft
      been there !

---

[1] *i.e.*, Stalagmus.

But no more of that ; just tell me what you want to ask of
me.

Perhaps you'll get it.

HEG.   You're too fluent ; kindly speak with brevity.

ST. As you please.

HEG.   Ah, from a boy he was a supple, flattering
knave.

But to business ! Pray attend to me, and tell me what I
crave.

If you speak the truth, you'll find your interest 'twill best
subserve.

ST. Don't tell me ! D'you think that I don't know full
well what I deserve ?

HEG. But you may escape a part if not the whole of your
desert.   970

ST. Oh, it's little I'll escape ! and much will happen to
my hurt :

For I ran away and stole your son from you, and him I sold.

HEG. O, to whom ?

ST.   To Theodoromedes of the house of Gold
For ten pounds.

HEG. Good Heav'ns ! Why, that's the father of Philocrates.

ST. Yes, I know that quite as well as you do—better, if
you please.

HEG. Jupiter in Heaven, save me, and preserve my darling
son !

On your soul, Philocrates, come out ! I want you. Make
haste, run !

PHILOCRATES. HEGIO. STALAGMUS.

[*Enter Philocrates from the house.*]

PHIL. Hegio, I am at your service.

HEG.   This man says he sold my son
To your father there in Elis for ten pounds.
PHIL.   When was this done?
ST. Twenty years ago.
980   PHIL.   O, nonsense!   Hegio, he's telling lies.
ST. Either you or I am lying; for when you were little
    boys,
He was given you by your father to be trained along with
    you.
PHIL. Well, then, tell me what his name was, if this tale
    of yours is true.
ST. Pægnium at first; in after time you called him
    Tyndarus.
PHIL. How is it that I don't know you?
ST.   Men are oft oblivious,
And forget the names of those from whom they've nothing
    to expect.
PHIL. Then this child you sold my father, if your story is
    correct,
Was bestowed on me as valet.   Who was he?
ST.   My master's son.
HEG. Is he living, fellow?
ST.   Nay, I got the money; then I'd done.
HEG. [*To Phil.*] What say *you?*
PHIL.   That Tyndarus is your lost son!   I
990   give you joy!
So at least this fellow's statements make me think; for he's
    the boy
Who received his education with myself all through our
    youth.
HEG. Well, I'm fortunate and wretched all at once, if you
    speak truth;
Wretched that I treated him so cruelly, if he's my son;

Oh, alas! I did both more and less[1] than what I should have
   done !

How I'm vexed that I chastised him ! Would that I could
   alter it !

See, he comes ! and in a fashion that is anything but fit.

TYNDARUS.   HEGIO.   PHILOCRATES.   STALAGMUS.

[Enter Tyndarus from the quarries.]

TYN.   Well, I've often seen in pictures all the torments of
   the damned ;

But I'm certain that you couldn't find a hell that's stuffed and
   crammed

With such tortures as those quarries.   There they've got a
   perfect cure   1000

For all weariness ; you simply drive it off by working more.

When I got there, just as wealthy fathers oft will give their boys

Starlings, goslings, quails to play with in the place of other
   toys,

So when I got there, a *crow* [2] was given me as plaything pretty !

Ah, my lord is at the door ; and my old lord from Elis city

Has returned !

HEG.   O hail, my long lost son !

TYN.   What means this talk of " sons "?

Oh, I see why you pretend to be my father ; yes, for once

You have acted like a parent, for you've brought me to the light.[3]

PHIL.   Hail, good Tyndarus !

TYN.   All hail ! for you I'm in this pretty plight.   1010

PHIL.   Ah ! but now you shall be free and wealthy ; for
   you must be told,

Hegio's your father.   That slave stole you hence when four
   years old ;

---

[1] More evil and less good.   [2] *i.e.*, A crowbar.   [3] *i.e.*, Out of the quarries.

And then sold you to my father for ten pounds, who gave you
   me,
When we both were little fellows, that my valet you might be.
This man whom we brought from Elis has most certain proofs
   supplied.

TYN.   What, am I his son?

PHIL.   You are ; your brother too you'll find inside.

TYN.   Then you have brought back with you his son who
   was a prisoner?

PHIL.   Yes, and he is in the house.

TYN.   You've done right well and nobly, sir.

PHIL.   Now you have a father ; here's the thief who stole
   you when a boy.

TYN.   Now that I'm grown up, he'll find that theft will
   bring him little joy.

PHIL.   He deserves your vengeance.

1020   TYN.   Oh, I'll have him paid for what he's done.
   [*To Hegio.*]   Tell me though, are you my father really?

HEG.   Yes, I am, my son.

TYN.   Now at length it dawns upon me, and I seem,
   when I reflect,
Yes, I seem to call to mind and somewhat vaguely re-
   collect,
As if looking through a mist, my father's name was Hegio.

HEG.   I am he!

PHIL.   Then strike the fetters off your son and let him go !
And attach them to this villain.

HEG.   Certainly, it shall be so.
Let's go in, and let the smith be summoned to strike off your
   chains,
And to put them on this fellow.

ST.   Right ! For they're my only gains.

The Company.

Epilogue.

Gentlemen, this play's been written on the lines of modesty;
Here are found no wiles of women, no gay lovers' gallantry;
Here are no affiliations, and no tricks for getting gold ;   1030
No young lover buys his mistress whilst his father is cajoled.
It's not often nowadays that plays are written of this kind,
In which good folk are made better.   Now then, if it be your
  mind,
And we've pleased you and not bored you, kindly undertake
  our cause,
And to modesty award the prize with heartiest applause.

THE END.

Printed by Cowan & Co., Limited, Perth.